The Padnell Prowler

All rights reserved. No part of this publication may be reproduced, transmitted, or stored in a retrieval system, in any form or by any means, without written permission from Terry Wheeler

ISBN: 978–1–4092–4911–5

Copyright © Terry Wheeler 2008

For more information about Terry Wheeler and his books see
www.terrywheeler.net

The Padnell Prowler

Terry Wheeler

Children find body in Padnell Woods

This is the season of the school holidays and it's the time when children go out to play. But beware, in the words of Henry Hall's famous record, *'If you go down to the woods today, you're sure of a big surprise ...'*

'Ten' Thomas, the leader of The Bramble Gang, agrees. *'I was riding up the track on my bike,'* Ten told us, *'and I was doing okay. But then my front wheel hit a fallen branch, and when my bike twisted I came off.'*

And we can picture Ten, like that daring young man on the flying trapeze, flying through the air with the greatest of ease. But what broke Ten's fall? And why wasn't Ten hurt? That is the 'big surprise' because the leader of The Bramble Gang landed on a dead body.

Inspector Johnson has informed us that the police have not as yet been able to identify the corpse but there can be no doubt that the man was murdered.

'He seems to have lost a great deal of blood from the wound on his head,' the Inspector said, *'and the post mortem confirmed that this blow to his head was clearly not accidental and led to the man's untimely death.'*

Even as we write, the police are checking finger print records to see if the man had a criminal record.

The Inspector went on to say, *'This is a murder enquiry and we are treating it as a matter of the greatest urgency. If anyone has any information that can assist us in our enquiries we ask them to contact us without delay.'*

Chapter 1

The summer of 1958 was hot and dry. I was twelve and I had just survived my first year at the local grammar school. I lived in the village of Cowplain which was in Hampshire, about ten miles north of Portsmouth, in a house in Padnell Road with my Mum and Dad and my goofy big sister, Cath.

Most people describe Cowplain as a blot on the landscape, and it's true that there isn't much to look at. Anyone passing through along the main road from Portsmouth towards London would see a string of houses with a few shops and nothing more. There isn't a village centre with an ancient church, and even the village pub, The Spotted Cow, isn't in the middle of the village.

Cath says it's a dump but Mum says it's not as bad as Gosport because they ate the Christian missionary there, and at least we're not heathen savages. Dad says that the worst place in Hampshire is Hayling Island because that was what God did with all the bits he'd got left over when he made the world. I tried to tell Cath that there was plenty to do in Cowplain, and I was about to tell her about our den in the woods, but she just said that there was nothing for *intelligent* people to do in Cowplain. That's the snotty sort of thing Cath always said when she wanted to make me feel small.

The summer holiday had just started and stretched invitingly in front of me. At first I had enjoyed not having to get up early and go to school, but now the novelty was beginning to wear off and I was casting around, looking for something to do.

One of Dad's favourite sayings is 'the grass is always greener on the other side of the fence'. I always thought that it was silly, and I once asked him if it would still be true if you jumped over the fence. He just looked at me, thought for a moment, and then said 'I think the fence would be too tall for you to jump over.' It was very difficult trying to catch Dad out.

But now, trying to think of something to do, I was beginning to understand what he meant. It's one of life's quirks that when you can't have something, it seems so attractive that you'd do almost anything to get it and yet finally, when you can have it, you don't think it's so much fun any more. It's a bit like that with holidays. All the time you're in school you dream of the things you could do if you weren't in school but, as soon as the holidays begin, you can't think of anything that you particularly want to do.

And that's just how it was on this Monday morning. Mum was indoors, up to her elbows in soap suds doing the washing and I was staying out of her way in case she press–ganged me into turning the mangle or helping her peg the washing on the line. I contemplated cleaning my bike but it didn't look dirty enough to need cleaning. At least, not yet anyway, and I could see no point in wasting all that effort unless I had to. The shed needed clearing out but that would take all day. What I wanted was fun, not hard labour. After all, I was on holiday.

I wandered down the garden to see if any of my friends were playing football out the back on the field by the council houses but it was deserted. I sat under the apple tree for a while and contemplated doing some more digging. I'd been working on a huge hole behind the bonfire and it was progressing nicely, but I'd have to move some of the earth I'd already dug out before I could carry on, and it was already too hot to do that.

I was at the point of going round to Pud's house when he rode in and propped his bike against the shed.

'Hey, Ten,' he said. 'What's on?'

I should have told you that we lived at number 10 which explains how I got my nickname. Pud's proper name was John Proust, but owing to his size he was usually called Pud – although he rather fancied being called JP, probably because of PeeDee. I'll tell you more about PeeDee in a minute. Pud, as I've just hinted, was not thin. No doubt because of his shape he was always pulling up his shorts which, despite his braces, always seemed to be working their way down. Today, like most days, he was dressed in grey – a grey shirt, grey shorts and grey socks. In fact the only bits of him that weren't grey were his hair, which was greasy brown, his braces which were a dull brown and his sandals which, like mine, were scuffed Clark's brown. Even the white crepe soles of his sandals had turned a dirty dull grey.

'Nothing much,' I said, trying not to sound too bored.

'Try the woods?'

'Could do.'

The woods were where we went if we couldn't think of anything else to do. In fact, it was the place where we spent most of our time. We'd ride up the road and just beyond the church, where the made–up road surface stopped, we would dodge the ruts and the loose stones and ride our bikes past the houses that fronted the track and ride on into the woods. There was a farm at the far end of the track called Padnell Farm. Apart from the lorry which came to collect the milk, very little traffic went that way and the woods were a great place to hang out. Within a minute of leaving our houses we were in a different world. Civilisation ended at the last house and then we were alone. There was no one to tell us what to do. We were free and when the days were hot and airless the woods were always cool and shady.

The grass out the back by the council estate was fine for some things, but it was always mown short and you could see right across it. That was good for us if we were playing football or cricket, but our parents could always see us and that wasn't always convenient. The woods, on the other hand, were a secret place. In the summer, bracken grew thick and high, laced with brambles, and you couldn't even see over the ditch at the road edge let alone into the trees and beyond. Who could say what we might find? We always hoped for an adventure but, so far, we had never found anything unusual. There were paths leading into the trees, but we always ignored those. The only way in for us was over the ditch and along the dirt–track.

When the weather was hot it was like riding a switchback – the clay would bake dry and the challenge was to see how fast you could bounce over the track. Of course, there were two ways to do it. The first was the quickest and the most challenging – if you took it too fast you'd part company from your bike as you came over the second hump, which was really vicious, but on the other hand if you took it too slowly you'd never make it to the top of the rise. The second route avoided the notorious second hump and was safer, but it took you round the trees. It was called the 'girlie' route and it was a point of honour never to ride into the woods that way – I'd rather have been roasted over a hot fire or been boiled alive by cannibals than be seen going that way.

When the weather was wet everything changed. For a start you had to ride through the water in the ditch. There was no chance of putting your foot down to steady yourself, and if you misjudged it you got very wet. And then as soon as you hit the clay, it was like an ice rink. Only the most daring and skilful made it to the top of the second hump. I came off many times before I mastered the technique – and when you fell off you slid right back down to the mud at the bottom.

'Where have you been?' Mum would ask when I got in.

'Nowhere,' I'd answer, 'just out for a ride.'

'You've been in the woods again, haven't you?'

I guess the combination of ditch water and sticky yellow clay was a serious give away as to where I'd been.

'Make sure you're with someone,' was all Mum said. 'I don't want to have to come out looking for you if you fall off your bike and break your neck.'

I tried suggesting that if I fell off my bike and broke my neck she needn't bother coming looking for me, but all that did was to get me a clip round the ear for being cheeky.

So there Pud and I were on the first Monday morning of August with the holiday just three days old. We had all the time in the world to do something, but we couldn't decide what. I guess it was inevitable that we'd go to the woods, and in the end we cycled up the road and attacked the dirt track with enthusiasm. As I crested the second hump, I could hear voices further in, up by the pond. We ploughed on to the end of the track and pulled up in front of the pond.

A long time ago someone had tied a rope on to one of the branches of the huge oak tree on the bank of the pond. We often used to come and spend time here. The dare was to swing from one side of the pond to the other without getting wet. It had taken me several attempts to achieve this, but now I nearly always landed safely on the far side. You had to throw caution to the wind, grab the rope, hang on tight until you saw the bank on the far side, and then you had to let go and leap as far up the bank as you could manage. If it was wet and the bank was slippery you usually slid back into the water.

As we came to the pond we could see PeeDee and his lot swinging over the water. PeeDee was the leader of his gang – The Flag Boys – and was a tall kid with ginger hair. He'd only been called 'Ginger' once and it had taken Beaky nearly a year to grow a new tooth in place of the one PeeDee knocked out. After that everyone called him by his initials so Peter David Harris became PeeDee.

We nearly always used our nicknames. Beaky had a prominent nose, a bit hooked like a beak, and he was always sniffing. He was posh – he didn't use his wrist like the rest of us – he used a hanky. And he had the disgusting habit of blowing his beak noisily. That wouldn't have been so bad but he always opened up the handkerchief afterwards to look at his snot. That was disgusting, particularly if he found something interesting and tried to show us.

PeeDee and Beaky were both on the rope, swinging over the pond. Goat – his father kept goats (well you can't always be imaginative, but I bet Goat was glad his Dad didn't keep chickens) – was on one side and Chris was on the far side of the pond. They were trying to stop PeeDee and Beaky from landing on the banks.

As everyone knows, if the rope loses its swing and ends up over the water you just have to let go and fall in. We sat on our bikes and watched for a bit. Incidentally, Chris was really called Christopher but his nickname had nothing to do with that. It came from the tragic fact that he was born on Christmas Day.

'You wanna try?' PeeDee yelled over when he saw us.

We had been going to ride on up to the farm to see if the pigs were out. When it was hot and the sows were in the field, it was fun to watch them wallowing in the mud. And if they'd baked in the sun and gone to sleep you could aim a clod of mud at them and they'd grunt. If you were really lucky they'd stagger to their feet and lumber towards you. They never got past the fence and they'd stand there with their snouts down, swinging their heads from side to side, squinting evilly at you as if they'd like to kill you.

It didn't take us long to decide that we'd have more fun here, so Pud and I joined in with PeeDee's gang. PeeDee and Beaky were working together and had got the rope swinging. With a bit of luck they'd manage to get it far enough over the bank to jump. They'd have done it, too, if Beaky hadn't let his foot slip off the knot and fallen in.

'He's fallen in the water!' Pud remarked – like most of us, he was a Goon Show fanatic.

The rope started to spin and PeeDee followed Beaky into the water, unable to control the rope on his own. They scrambled out, covered in mud and slime. They wrung their shirts out and spread them on the brambles to dry.

'Who's next?' PeeDee asked.

It had to be me. If PeeDee had done it, as leader of my lot I had no choice. Pud looked apprehensive.

'We'll do it in one,' I said. 'We'll attack it fast and jump as soon as we're near enough.'

With Pud's extra weight I thought we might just have enough inertia to carry us a bit further than normal. It worked and we let go the instant we were near the far bank. It was nearly a disaster but I grabbed Pud as he began to slip back and we made it without getting wet. We were triumphant and PeeDee was gutted.

'Goat and Chris next,' Pud said. 'It's only fair.'

The one thing that mattered more than anything else was that games had to be fair. That didn't mean we couldn't cheat and, of course, we did – knowing that if we were caught out we'd have to pay a forfeit. After all, it was only fair – it was all part of the game. Once, PeeDee had taken my shoes and I had to walk all the way home with bare feet. Another time we'd challenged PeeDee to cartwheel all the way round the pond. He nearly made it but as he stood up after his last one he slipped and fell into the water. I think he was feeling dizzy because Goat had to jump in and help him out.

Pud went to the far side and we tried to slow them down. Pud missed them but they weren't ready to jump and they swung back. I grabbed at the rope and we nearly had them but somehow they managed to swing back and drop at the very edge of the water. They scrambled up triumphantly.

'One in and one over,' PeeDee said. 'You'll have to go again otherwise it's not fair.'

We were spared in the nick of time because Merlin and Oz, both members of my gang, arrived. Merlin's name was Arthur and he was seriously considering changing his name by Deed Poll. Arthur, apparently, was a family name – his father and his grandfather were also called Arthur. His mum thought it was a huge joke when they were all together to call out 'Come on Arthur,' and they'd all have to go and see what she wanted. Oz, or to give him his whole handle, Austin, wasn't happy with his name, either. We'd thought about calling him Morris Minor to keep his name in with cars and on account of his having an older brother, but he'd come up with Oz which he thought was much cooler.

Merlin and Oz were only too eager to prove the superiority of our gang and leapt off on the rope without a moment's hesitation. And they made it, too. They executed a triumphant war–dance on the far side of the pond because our gang had won the right to choose what to do next. We plumped for fox and hounds with Merlin as the fox. He was off like a shot while we counted to a hundred and then we set off on his trail.

Chapter 2

It rained on and off for most of Tuesday so I couldn't go out. Merlin came round and we hung out in the shed, shooting our catapults from the doorway at a tin that we set up on the handle of the roller by the vegetable plot.

Later, just as I was thinking that the holiday was going to be dead boring we had a break-in. Not at our house but in the village. Mum saw a police car pulled up on to the pavement outside the wireless shop when she went down the road on Wednesday morning and Mr Patterson told her that sometime the previous night Mr Tumber's shop had been broken into. They had taken the new wireless he had just got in and all sorts of other electrical bits and pieces.

'It looks as if it was all stuff that whoever did it could sell quickly,' I heard Mum telling Cath. 'It must have been an amateur because he left finger prints all over the place.'

A real robbery! And in our village! This was great news and I rushed off up the woods to see if any of the others knew about it. None of my lot was around but PeeDee was in his den.

'What d' you want?' he asked rather crossly.

'You heard about the break in?' I asked.

'Where?'

'Tumber's.'

'When?'

'Last night.'

'Nope.'

For a moment I thought the conversation was going to end there. If PeeDee didn't want to talk I knew I'd be wasting my time, so I turned to go.

'Did they take much?' I heard him ask.

'Don't know. Mostly small stuff Mum said.'

'Easier to fence,' PeeDee said knowingly. 'Bet Plod'll be round our place tonight asking where Dad was last night.'

'He didn't do it, did he?'

'He don't do things like that. Just 'cause he's got a bit of a reputation for drinking, every time something's on Plod comes nosing round our place.'

'If they've got finger prints they'll know it wasn't your Dad,' I suggested.

'That won't stop 'em. They do it just to let him know they're watching him!'

'D'you want to walk up and see if they're still there?'

PeeDee looked at me as if I'd gone barmy. Then I suppose he worked out that there wasn't anything better to do.

'If we don't go now it'll be too late this afternoon,' I said. 'It's early closing day.'

'S'pose so,' he said. 'Might be worth a gander.'

If any of the rest of our gangs had seen us they'd have wondered what we were up to. Normally, seeing as how we were sworn enemies, we wouldn't even walk on the same side of the road. But today was different, I told myself. It was research for a new game so it was all right to be seen out with PeeDee.

Quite what we expected to find I hadn't worked out, but it was a wasted walk because there was nothing to see. Literally, because Tumber's shop was shut and the blind in the window was pulled down so we couldn't even see in. The barber's shop was set back along side Tumber's and he was open for business.

'You could go into the barber's,' I suggested. 'He might know what happened.'

'I ain't got enough hair to have another cut,' PeeDee said.

It was true. He'd just had a short back and sides and there was no way he could have it cut again so soon.

'I'll go into Patterson's and see if he knows anything,' I said.

'Have you got any money?' PeeDee asked. 'You could always try the sweet shop!'

'Don't be daft. I'll say Mum wanted to know if anything more had happened. She was here earlier. He won't mind. If he's not busy he likes a gossip!'

But Mr Patterson didn't know anything more and so we went back up to Padnell Road. We stopped at the corner of Padnell Avenue.

'What are you going to do?' I asked PeeDee. 'We could have a meeting this afternoon. One of the others might know something.'

'S'pose so. See you!'

PeeDee turned down Padnell Avenue and I went on up to our house. It was a bit early for dinner so I went down to the shed. Dad and I shared the shed. He used it for his garden tools and I used it as a place to hang out when I didn't want to be indoors. The trouble with being inside was that my bedroom was too small to be comfortable on a hot day, and Cath was always moping about downstairs. Mum would be finishing the ironing and so Cath would be getting dinner and if I went in she'd try and press–gang me into helping.

The idea of the break–in fascinated me. I'd read a few detective stories and I knew about finger prints. I was trying to work out how we could turn it into a game. Most holidays we mucked about up in the woods but we also had what we called 'big' games when both our gangs came together and had a major challenge. I liked the idea of a cops and robbers game, but the trouble was the break–in was too simple for a real detective game.

After dinner I rode up to the woods and met the rest of my gang. We had a pow–wow, but none of the others even knew there'd been a break–in so they were no help at all. We ended up riding the dirt track because PeeDee and his lot didn't appear.

'Perhaps the police went round PeeDee's' Merlin said, 'and found the stuff.'

'And took them all into custody,' Oz said with relish. 'They'll be thrown into jail and we'll never see him again!'

'Does that mean we can take over his den?' Pud asked.

'Perhaps we'd better wait,' I suggested.

I knew PeeDee would be back but I didn't want to disappoint Merlin and Oz who were quite sold on the idea of PeeDee going to jail.

The day had started so well but the afternoon began to drag so we had a race up the track towards Horndean. Oz won. Pud came off his bike and he couldn't ride back because the chain came off. I walked back with him. It was quite late when I got in and since Wednesday night was choir practice night, I had to stay home to tidy up.

Just as the church services didn't stop for the holidays, so choir practice went on right through the year. Singing in the church choir was one of the few things that we could do in the village. There was a scout troop in Waterlooville and some of the boys in the village went down to it, but it wasn't for me. The choir was more fun and we earned half a crown if we sang at a wedding. There were other advantages too, like the choir outing in the summer and the choir party at Christmas. We had a couple of men who came and sang with us from time to time and a few ladies who sang with us on Sundays, but it was us kids who came to choir practice and who seemed to do all the work.

Usually choir practice began with hedging. The church was a rather ugly red brick building, not an old one built of stone with a tower or a spire – all it had was one bell hanging in a niche over the main door. There was a patch of rough grass between the church and the road. The vestry was on that side too, and we hung about there waiting for the organist to open up for choir practice. There were a number of scruffy macrocarpa trees growing along the road edge and we would lie in wait and see how many of the younger kids we could push through the hedge. It was like going through a turnstile because the branches were thick and bushy right down to the ground but where they met you could just about force your way through. It was best when there was one of us each side of the trees and then we could push the kids through and back again and there was nothing they could do except keep going backwards and forwards.

When I first joined the choir it was nearly always me they shoved through and I used to try and arrive on time so that they didn't have much chance. Now, because I'd been there a while, I began to join in with the bigger boys, helping to push the smaller kids through and I started going early because it was fun shoving them through. Needless to say, we were nearly always in a mess when Mr Norman, the organist, arrived and we had to go through the vestry and comb the muck out of our hair before he would let us take our places in the choir stalls.

One of the best things about being a chorister was that from time to time you got to pump the organ. If the electricity went off, and it did quite often, two of us had to pump the bellows. It was best when the power went off in the middle of a hymn because then the organ died with a terrible wailing sound and if it was at evensong in the winter we had to light candles.

We took turns at pumping. There was a huge wooden lever, a bit like an arm, sticking out of the back of the organ and you had to keep it going up and down steadily. It wasn't hard, but it got tiring after a whole hymn – that's why we took turns. The trick was to see just how slowly you could pump without the organ wailing. If you went too slowly and let the organ make terrible noises the Vicar would come in and change you for another chorister so you had to judge it just right. Sometimes, if we did a good job, the organist gave us sixpence each for our efforts.

In the winter, choir practice was a bit like punishment because they didn't put the heaters on and the church was like an ice box. We could see our breath so Mr Norman knew if we weren't singing. If there was snow on the ground we went into the church hall which was behind the church, but the piano was rubbish. Some of the notes stuck and it was not only out of tune, but also two notes down from the organ. You wouldn't think it would make such a difference, but if the men were there, they complained that they couldn't reach their notes. In the summer the church was fine – except that the sun came through the windows and those of us on our side had to squint. Bunny, named because of his bouncing walk, brought a pair of sun glasses once but Mr Norman told him off and Bunny never tried it again.

Swede was on holiday; Lars had gone to visit his grandparents in Sweden – you can guess how we arrived at his nickname – and wasn't even going to be back in time for the outing. Roller, Billy Hooper, was away for the week visiting his granny and so there weren't many of us left for the first practice of the holidays. We guessed something was up when we saw the Vicar waiting for us outside the vestry door.

'Go straight in,' he said when we came up the path.

We would have protested but the Vicar looked a bit straight so we went in without arguing. We sat in the choir stalls and chatted. We didn't have long to wait until Bunny came in. He was the head chorister and was supposed to keep us in order, but he was the worst one of us, always getting up to some prank or other. He was only head chorister because he was the oldest. Mr Norman was the last to arrive and he came in with the Vicar.

'Before we say our prayer,' the Vicar said, 'I want to warn you about something that has given us cause for concern.' He cleared his throat and looked down at the floor. 'It has come to our notice that there is a man prowling round the village and I want to warn you that you should be careful when you go home. Make sure you're not on your own. Stay together until you reach your houses, stick to the road and don't take short cuts.'

'Is he dangerous?' Bunny asked.

'I don't know, but he's been seen skulking about at dusk. I don't think you should take chances. If you don't meet him then he won't be any danger to you.'

'What's he done?' Chris asked.

'I don't think we need to talk about this any more,' the Vicar said. 'Remember what I've said – just be careful when you go home.'

Chris was about to ask another question but the Vicar cut him off.

'Let us pray,' he said.

Well, of course, we didn't do much at choir practice that night. Mr Norman tried to keep us in order and kept telling us to concentrate but we were too busy constructing fantasies about the Prowler. Chris suggested that the Prowler had a long knife and was cutting people up into little bits and posting their body parts through people's letter boxes. He always did have a vivid imagination! Bunny suggested that we ought to form a vigilante squad and track him down. On the way home we stopped and looked over everybody's hedges, but we didn't see anyone at all.

'It's still too light,' Chris said. 'If you were going to do somebody in you'd wait until it was dark.'

All the same, it did seem to make the evening a bit more exciting. We split up and walked right round the council estate and back over the recreation ground, meeting up again at the church, although we met behind the hedge so that the Vicar couldn't see us. None of us had seen anything unusual, although Bunny said old Mr Sparshott had come out when he saw Bunny looking over his hedge.

'He asked me what the hell I was doing,' Bunny said. 'I told him I'd lost my dog.'

'D' you think he's the Prowler?' Chris asked.

'Shouldn't think so,' Bunny said, scornfully. 'I bet he's had his cocoa and is tucked up in bed before it gets dark.'

We would have done another round of the village but it was getting dark and we'd have had too much difficulty explaining why we were so late getting back, so we called it off until the next day and agreed to meet in PeeDee's den at eleven. I went to bed thinking it was all a fuss about nothing – although I didn't ask Mum or Dad about the Prowler in case they wouldn't let me go out tomorrow.

Next morning we were hanging about by PeeDee's den waiting for him to come.

'I bet the Prowler doesn't even exist,' Chris said. 'I bet you it was just the Vicar trying to spoil our fun.'

'Perhaps the Prowler did the break-in,' Pud suggested.

I hadn't thought of that. Word had gone out about the Prowler and even Merlin, who wasn't in the choir – his parents were heathens, they went to the chapel – had heard about him.

'My Dad said he'd heard Mr Gibson talking about him, so he must exist.'

'Does Monkey know anything?' Oz asked.

'Don't know. Beaky's going to bring him along so you can ask him yourself.'

It all seemed to be a bit of an anti-climax after last night's excitement and we were beginning to think that we were wasting our time. Even PeeDee hadn't bothered to turn up. That was a sure sign, we agreed, that there wasn't going to be anything in the rumour.

Oz was on his bike, ready to go, when we heard PeeDee and his crowd coming through the woods. We were on the alert at once because usually you came as quietly as you could. I mean, if someone was raiding your den you would want to catch them at it so you wouldn't make a heap of noise, you'd creep up as quietly as you could. We'd had a fantastic fight, once, when we caught PeeDee's lot in our den and we knocked the hell out of them before we let them go.

It stood to reason, therefore, that if PeeDee was making a noise he wanted us to know he was coming. We waited with baited breath.

'Perhaps he's caught the Prowler,' Oz said, getting off his bike.

'Well, he ain't in jail,' Merlin said, trying not to sound too disappointed.

PeeDee and Beaky came through the bracken and we saw they'd got Monkey in tow. We called David Gibson 'Monkey' because he even looked like a Gibbon monkey – his arms were long and his legs were short and his hair was black. We didn't have time to make our usual monkey greetings though because PeeDee launched straight into his story as soon as he saw us.

'He nearly got my sister last night,' he said proudly.

I think he expected us to be impressed, but Oz wasn't going to make it easy.

'I'd have thought you'd have been only too pleased to get rid of her,' he said.

PeeDee gave him a look that would have done the Prowler credit.

'I ain't joking,' he said. 'She only got away because my Dad was in the garden.'

'Your Mum chucked him out again?' Oz asked.

'Don't be daft, that's all done and dusted, now.'

There had been a time, not so long ago, when PeeDee's Dad had been brought home roaring drunk by the police and PeeDee's Mum had refused to have him in the house. The police had to take him back and bang him up for the night in the cells.

'He was having a quick fag,' PeeDee said, 'when he heard Sandy kicking up a fuss. He looked over the gate and saw her running up the road followed by a man in a dark suit. He got her in and she said that this guy had jumped out at her as she came round the corner and then chased her.'

We digested this in awed silence. We all knew that PeeDee's sister, Sandy, was a bit of a goer but she didn't usually run away from men, quite the opposite. This just wasn't her style so we knew it must be the real thing. PeeDee called a war meeting and we all piled into his den.

PeeDee's den was a posh affair. They'd built it from old doors and rubbish they'd taken from the dump and it even had a window. Mind you, it was small inside and some of my lot had to listen from the doorway. We posted Roller as the sentry and turned our attention on Monkey.

Monkey's Dad was the landlord of the village pub, The Spotted Cow, and he knew all the gossip. Monkey told us that he'd heard his Dad talking to PC Norris.

'Plod said that there is a Prowler,' he said. 'And he's not the guy who did the break–in. That was some bloke from Leigh Park. They matched his finger prints and caught him at his place with all the stuff. He hadn't even had time to get rid of it!'

We digested the news in awed silence.

'The police have been put on the alert and they've got to do the rounds at night to see if they can catch the Prowler before he hurts someone. Plod's furious. He said he'd got better things to do than walk round the village on a wild goose chase.'

So it was true, the Prowler really existed.

'My Dad said that he'd heard that the Misses March had seen him in their garden,' Goat said, 'and they'd been so scared they sat up all night expecting him to break down the door at any moment.'

The sisters, Barbara and Eileen March were over seventy and went everywhere together. If you saw Barbara in the baker's, then Eileen would be waiting outside. If Eileen was in the chemist's, then Barbara would be standing guard in the doorway. They sat next to each other in church, caught the bus into Waterlooville together and the rumour was that they'd even had a twin coffin made ready for when they passed on. Quite what they'd do if they didn't manage to die at the same time we didn't know, but we reckoned that the one who was left would be interred alive because she wouldn't want to leave her sister.

We passed a unanimous vote that we'd keep a watch out for the sisters. It wouldn't do to have them murdered in their beds – it would ruin our fun if they actually died together. PeeDee brought us back to the matter in hand.

'My Dad says he'll kill the bastard if he gets his hands on him. He went back outside after Sandy had told him, but the Prowler had gone.'

Knowing PeeDee's father, and his temper, none of us doubted him.

'I vote we try and catch him first,' Oz said. 'We'll give him the once over and then we can dump him in PeeDee's front garden and Sandy can have a go.'

That was the second unanimous vote of the morning. I can't remember another time when we'd actually agreed on more than one thing.

Chapter 3

We left PeeDee's den to have our own council of war, and made our way back to our den. We took a roundabout route just in case PeeDee had set us up and had sent someone to spy on us. Our den wasn't as posh as PeeDee's but it was more difficult to find. PeeDee's was instantly visible because it had been made from real wooden doors, boards and sheets of old tin. They'd even tried to paint it but they didn't have enough paint so it was all sorts of colours. But it did have a flag pole and when they were in the den it was Goat's job to raise the flag as a warning to others to keep out.

We had made our den almost by accident. We were playing war, chucking hand grenades that Oz had made by cutting up a fence post in his Dad's shed. If you were hit by a clod of mud or a stone you could always say that it had been there before and you hadn't been hit, so he'd painted them yellow so that we couldn't argue. If you were near a yellow grenade you were deemed to have been blown up and had to sit out for a count of three hundred. It was a pretty good game because you could crawl through the bracken and ambush the other lot. Once, we were in the middle of a major battle when we lost a grenade in a clump of brambles. The brambles were too thick to reach over and too scratchy to wade through so Merlin tried tunnelling under to see if he could reach it. Pud and I lifted the edge and Merlin started to slither through, just like a Marine on combat duty. His feet had almost disappeared when he called out –

'Hey, there's a big hollow under here.'

'Hollow to you, too,' Oz called back.

He thought he was a bit of a wit but Merlin wasn't amused.

'Bugger off, Oz. I mean there's room under here to make a secret den. It'll be better than PeeDee's if we clear it out a bit'

'Nobody 'd know it was there,' Oz said, serious now.

We all followed Merlin in, and were amazed at the space under the brambles. It took us a while to clear away all the dead stuff and to get rid of all the old brambles, but when we'd done it there was a large, domed space. The only problem was that when it rained the ground got a bit wet so we had to get boards to make a floor. We scrounged some wooden boards from the dump and rolled some logs in to set them on. When PeeDee made fun of our den we boasted that at least it had a proper floor even if it didn't have a roof, not just mud and dirt. We didn't have a flag pole but we had a secret stone and when one of us was in we turned it over. We thought it was better than the flag because it was a real secret sign. In fact, knowing the secret of the stone was one of the things that made you a member of The Bramble Gang. You had to swear never to reveal the secret on pain of being beaten with stinging nettles on your bare bum. There were five of us in our gang, although we were only four at the moment on account of Swede being away, and none of us had ever given the secret away.

When we reached our den I flipped the stone over and we crawled in through the entrance. I asked if anyone had any sweets. Pud had got Black Jacks, so we all had one to get us in the right frame of mind.

'It won't be any fun if we go all soft on PeeDee's lot,' Oz said. 'I vote we only call a truce for this morning, just to see how it goes.'

It was true – half the fun of being in the woods was that you always had to be on the lookout for PeeDee's lot. You never quite knew when you might be ambushed or when you might be able to take one of them prisoner.

'But it's serious if there's someone out there who wants to do us in,' Pud said.

I think he was a bit nervous because, owing to his size, he couldn't run as fast as the rest of us.

'The thing is,' I said, trying to sound wise, 'if it's a man then he'll be at work during the day. So we don't really have to bother until it gets past tea time.'

'He might not have got a job,' Merlin pointed out.

We hadn't thought of that. Trust Merlin to put a spanner in the works. But I suppose he would have thought of that because his Dad had been out of work last year. All the time he was hanging out around the house it had cramped Merlin's style because he kept asking Merlin where he was going and what he was going to do. I made the best of it that I could.

'Plod said he'd been seen at night and the cops had to do their rounds after dark,' I pointed out. 'He didn't say anything about during the day.'

'What about the sisters?' Oz asked.

'I'll do them,' I said. 'They're only just up the road from me so I can pop in and out and see if they want anything. I could offer to do their shopping.'

We decided that this was a good idea, particularly if the sisters gave me sweets for doing it. I agreed that if they did, I'd bring the sweets to the den and share them since I was only doing the job on behalf of the gang. We discussed the rest of our business and then made our way back to PeeDee's den to let them know what we'd decided. PeeDee was going to keep watch up his end of the council estate and Chris was going to do the other part. Goat was going to do his road and I told them that I was going to keep my eye on the sisters. They suggested that I should do the rest of our road and watch the church, too.

'You never know,' Beaky said, 'he might be using it as a hideaway. It's always open and he could slip in and nobody would notice. They'd just think he'd gone in to pray.'

'I don't mind watching the church,' I said. 'I could go in and pretend to tidy the choir stalls and then I could see if anyone else was in there.'

We set out to do a search through the woods. My lot took the side by the farm and PeeDee's lot did the side nearest the houses. We cut sticks just in case we met the Prowler and set off.

'Rendezvous at mid–day,' PeeDee said.

Needless to say, we didn't find the Prowler, but we had a good time. The pigs were out and we chucked mud at them, but they were too lazy to notice so we went and spooked the cows instead. They came to the fence when we got there and then Merlin flapped his arms and they stampeded off up the field. We didn't stay there too long because we thought that the farmer, Mr Byrne, might hear the cows and come to see what was bothering them. He'd caught us once before and threatened to tell our Dads – so now it was more of a dare to spook the cows and not get caught.

We thrashed the edges of the path nearly into Horndean and then made our way back to PeeDee's den. They hadn't had any luck, either, so we agreed to do a road patrol after lunch.

Unfortunately Mum had other ideas for what I was going to do after lunch and so I didn't get to check up on the sisters or do our road. I spent the afternoon dragging round endless shops. Mum had got the stupid idea into her head that if she bought next term's school uniform now, there would be more choice. I mean, what's there to choose between? This white shirt or that white shirt? These socks or those socks? That's adults for you!

Next morning I went round to the Misses March, all sweetness and smiles, and knocked on their front door. They had a huge knocker in the shape of a fish and when I banged it the sound echoed through the whole house. When Miss Eileen opened the front door I offered to do their shopping. Eileen was a cunning old girl.

'What are you after?' was the first thing she asked. She didn't even bother to wish me a good morning.

'Nothing,' I replied, desperately trying to keep my stupid smile in place. 'I thought that you might like some help.' I let my smile go. I couldn't speak properly with my mouth all contorted like that. 'We thought, my friends and me, that with undesirable men on the prowl,' I thought that bit was very good, 'you might like some help with your chores.'

I fixed the smile back on and waited. She fell for it!

'Come in then, and I'll see if I can find some money for the bread. That's all we need today.'

I stepped inside. It was like walking into a museum. The walls in the hall were papered with the most hideous flowery wall paper and there were faded pictures everywhere. There was a stuffed animal head fixed above one of the doors and a set of deer antlers over another. The stairs went up just inside the front door and looked incredibly steep. It was quite dark in the hall but I could see a hallstand just inside the door. It was bristling with walking sticks and umbrellas but my eyes were drawn to a huge knobbly club. Miss Eileen saw me looking at it.

'It was my father's,' she said. Then she grinned. She looked quite evil, I thought for such a sweet old lady. 'We got it out for Mister Hitler but he never came so now it's waiting for the Padnell Prowler. We heard all about him at the chemist's yesterday.'

I found it hard to imagine the two of them sitting up all night in fear of their lives. It was much more likely, I thought, that they were sitting there licking their lips in anticipation! I didn't give the Prowler much chance if he tried to break into their house. On reflection I decided not to tell the gang about this development, it would be more fun if they thought the old dears were helpless and frightened. Miss Barbara came back and gave me the money so I didn't hang around. When I came back a bit later with their bread, Miss Barbara opened the door. She invited me in.

'We've got a little something for you,' she said and took me through to the kitchen. There was a huge iced cake on the kitchen table and she cut me a slice. So much for sweets for the gang. What could I do? I ate it!

'If you come back tomorrow we might have something else for you,' Miss Eileen said.

'I can do anything,' I offered, 'or I can bring a friend if you need something big doing.'

I walked up to the church but it was empty so when I came out I stopped and patted the horse's head. There was a field opposite the church where an old horse lived. It was a plot that hadn't got a house on it and had stayed as a field. The horse had been there so long that there was no grass left and his field was all mud and stones. The mud had baked hard in the sun and his hooves slipped as he moved. He'd got some fresh hay and was munching his way through it, but he looked pleased to see me and came up to the fence. He lowered his muzzle and I scratched his head between his ears. I pulled some handfuls of fresh grass from the verge and he seemed to like them as well. I think he was lonely and bored, but I couldn't spend more time with him, I needed to get to our den to report back to the gang about the sisters.

Merlin was already there when I arrived and Oz came soon after with Pud. None of us had seen anything unusual and it all looked as if it was a load of fuss about nothing.

'What about the sisters?' Oz asked. 'Did they give you anything?'

'No,' I said. They looked at me, sensing that I hadn't told them everything. 'Not anything that I could bring,' I added. 'They gave me a slice of cake and I had to eat it. It was on a posh plate.'

'Jammy!' Oz said.

'I checked the church, too,' I said, 'but it was empty. And I gave Joey a couple of handfuls of grass.'

'Better go and let PeeDee know,' Merlin said.

We traipsed over to PeeDee's den. They'd drawn a blank, too.

'My Dad wouldn't let me out after dark last night,' PeeDee said. 'And he went and collected Sandy from the bus stop. Denis was cross 'cause he couldn't make out with her before he went home.'

Denis was Sandy's boyfriend and they'd been to the pictures in Portsmouth. He usually walked her home and then caught the next bus back. That gave him half an hour to snog her. We'd watched, once, but it was too disgusting so we didn't do it again. I bet he was furious, seeing Sandy's Dad at the bus stop. PeeDee said Denis didn't even bother to get off the bus.

PeeDee's lot went off to play football on the green so we went back to our den. But the morning had gone sour. Without PeeDee's lot to plague and without any developments on the 'Padnell Prowler' there didn't seem to be much worth doing. Merlin had brought his catapult and we set up a tin and took turns to see how far away we could get and still hit it. We fired acorns at it, but even that palled after a while.

We went over to the pond to see if we could catch frogs. Because PeeDee's den had a door we used to collect frogs and let them loose in his den. The first time we did it PeeDee's lot had been really spooked, but now they kind of expected it so it wasn't so funny any more. It was too hot and we didn't find any frogs, so that put paid to that idea as well. We swung on the rope and Oz fell in. We desperately needed something new and exciting to do but none of us had any ideas. Pud suggested that we go back to his place and play chess, but that got the thumbs down before he'd even finished suggesting it. Anyway, I was the only other one who could play. In the end, out of desperation, we decided to go to Monkey's place and see if his Dad had heard anything more about the Prowler.

The Spotted Cow was set back from the road and had a large space in front of it. Monkey and his family lived upstairs, over the pub. They had their own entrance round the back, up an iron staircase which gave on to an open space in front of their rooms. It was covered in tarmac and was really the roof over the toilets down below. It had railings and you could stand up there and look down on all the junk in the yard below. Their front door – I could never understand why they called it their front door because it was at the back and next to their backdoor – led into a long hall and they had a kitchen to one side of it and the sitting room on the other. The bedrooms were along the front of the house. The place stank of stale beer and there were crates and all sorts of other rubbish stacked up in the yard at the back. Monkey's parents were downstairs in the pub so he was pleased to see us.

'Did Plod come in last night?' Merlin asked.

'Don't know,' Monkey said.

'Well, did your Dad say anything more about the Prowler?' Pud asked.

'It was a bit noisy last night,' Monkey said. 'PeeDee's Dad was in. He went early to meet Sandy off the bus so he had to drink up quickly. Dad said it was just as well he went early or he'd have had to throw him out.'

No wonder Sandy's boyfriend didn't get off the bus, we thought. One look at her father in that state and he'd have known it wasn't worth his while walking her home.

'Where's PeeDee?' Monkey asked.

'Football, on the green.'

'Oh.'

Monkey seemed a bit spaced out.

'What're you up to, then?' Merlin asked.

'Come and see,' Monkey said, leading us into his bedroom.

The place reeked of glue. Monkey was in the middle of making an Airfix.

'Open a window,' Pud said. 'Stinks in here.'

'I didn't!' Monkey said indignantly.

'Glue!' Pud said.

I opened the window. The fumes were getting to me and I already felt dizzy. I picked up the Airfix instructions. It was a Lancaster bomber and said the model would have a 17" wingspan when it was finished. There were hundreds of tiny pieces to sort out and glue together. Someone was bashing out a tune on the piano in the bar downstairs.

'How do you sleep with that racket?' I asked Monkey.

'What noise?' he asked, looking at me as if I was stupid.

'The piano,' I said.

'Oh, I don't hear that. But it can get noisy on Fridays and Saturdays. Dad says the noisier it gets the more money he takes so it's all right. I just go to sleep.'

Merlin was sorting through the bits on the table. He was a model freak, and I guessed he'd stay there until they'd finished it. Pud and I left them to it and I ended up back at his place playing chess.

Pud and I went back to our den after lunch but Merlin didn't show up so we guessed he was still doing the model with Monkey. Oz didn't show, either.

'I bet he got a wigging from his Mum for getting wet,' Pud said.

'If she's anything like mine,' I said, 'she'll have done the house ready for the weekend and if he went in still dripping ...'

I made the sign of having my throat cut. Oz's Mum was a bit strict. We checked the church on our way back but it was still empty. The sisters' house looked like it always did, all shut up, and there was no one in sight.

'Perhaps they've been done in,' Pud said hopefully. 'Should we check?'

I think Pud was more interested in the cake than the sisters.

'I don't think after lunch is what she meant,' I said. 'She told me I could come back tomorrow.'

Pud looked disappointed.

'You can come with me tomorrow if you like.'

He brightened up at my suggestion. I could almost see 'cake' written in his eyes. We drifted on down the road and when we got to my gate I went in. Pud hung about for a bit but I didn't ask him in. It was more than my life was worth to risk him mucking the house up. Mum would have done the vacuuming and would be sitting down with her magazine. She wouldn't even like me taking him down the garden. I could just hear her 'I've been working all day while you were out. All I want is a bit of peace and quiet and a chance to put my feet up ...' she always made a fuss if I brought anyone back on a Friday afternoon. In any case, I had things to do. Being the leader of The Bramble Gang was an onerous duty and I had to write up the log book of the week's activities.

Chapter 4

Pud didn't come the next morning so I ran some errands for the sisters on my own – and had another slice of cake! I checked out the church but it was full of people doing flowers and sweeping the floor. There was going to be a wedding in the afternoon, which was good news for me since they wanted the choir, but it meant that I wouldn't be able to see the rest of the gang until Monday. I couldn't do anything too mucky that morning since I had to look tidy for the wedding and so I went back home.

I was always arguing with Mum about my clothes. Okay, I had to wear uniform for school but when I was home I didn't see why I couldn't wear what I wanted. It took a while but in the end she let me choose some clothes from the catalogue. She didn't approve of my choice but she gave in gracefully so long as I looked tidy for Sundays and when she took me out. Personally, I thought my stuff was dead smart, but I knew I'd never convince her.

The wedding was a really posh affair, and the bride was nearly fifteen minutes late. We stood around in the porch waiting for her and counted the number of times that Mr Norman played the same piece. He kept looking down the church, and the Vicar kept shrugging his shoulders. In the end Mr Norman gave up and started on a new piece but, of course, that was the moment when the bride arrived, so he kept her waiting until he couldn't ignore the Vicar clearing his throat any more. As soon as the first notes of 'Here comes the Bride' sounded I set off up the aisle.

We had to sing an anthem while they signed the register and Bunny had to sing the solo bits. He didn't do badly but I could have done it better. I think he knew it, too, because when he'd got to the end of his bit he stuck his tongue out at me. As soon as the bride and groom had gone back down the aisle we snuck off into the vestry and the Vicar paid us our half-crowns. I thought we should have got more since we'd been kept waiting for so long but I didn't dare to say so. The Vicar was a bit straight about money and he'd have launched into his bit about avarice and ended up by suggesting that we should give our money to charity. We'd heard it all before. Our voices were a free gift from God, to be used in his glory and not for our personal gain. I had no argument with that but it was our time we were being paid for, just like he was paid for being the Vicar!

Bunny was standing by the hedge watching them take pictures of the bride and groom so I pushed him through the hedge while he was busy gawping, and ran down the road to the sweet shop. Mum let me spend sixpence after a wedding but I had to put the rest in my money box. Because the wedding was late, and the bride even later, I didn't get out again on Saturday so instead of sharing the sweets with my gang I ate them in my bedroom. Saturday was bath day, too, so I had to have a bath before tea and then Mum wouldn't let me out again, not even in the garden, because I was all clean so I ended up reading a book.

Sunday was always a weird day. It started with Dad bringing me a cup of tea in bed. It was always disgustingly strong – he said he made it a bit thick so it didn't slop about so much – but he always put an extra spoonful of sugar in so it wasn't too bad. Then he cooked bacon and eggs and fried bread for breakfast and we ate it round the kitchen table in our pyjamas. Even Cath, my elder sister, who was also at the Grammar School sat with us. Usually, on school days, she caught an earlier bus than me and was out of the house before I had breakfast and she came back late so she had her tea with Dad when he got in. Being older, she had to be in school earlier, and because she was a prefect she had duties to do.

We had to wash our faces after breakfast.

'We don't want egg on your chops,' Mum said every week.

Then we put on our Sunday clothes and she brushed our hair. I pointed out that I was going to wear a robe so nobody would see what I was wearing.

'God will know,' she said.

That used to scare me but I was older now, and I knew she was just trying to be clever and stop me from arguing. Then we'd have to wait until half past ten. As soon as the clock struck we'd walk up to church and they'd watch me as I went to the vestry. I don't know if they thought I'd do a runner. If I wasn't in the choir surely they'd notice, I thought. When I asked her, Mum said she was proud that I sang in the choir and that was why she liked to see me going in.

Since we'd had a wedding yesterday my ruff was all stiff. Mum had starched it and then curled it with the gofering tongs so that it looked just like a pie frill. I hated it because it dug into my chin and rubbed my neck sore but Mum said it made me look like an angel! It was a pity it didn't give me angelic thoughts!

Sunday morning service was always Matins and we had to sing the Venite, the Te Deum and the Benedictus as well as the psalm. It was easy now I knew the pointing and I quite liked it all, but it made the service a bit long. Most of the congregation just mumbled or looked round the church. They sang the hymns with gusto but they left most of the other bits to us.

The sermon was the worst bit. The choir stalls were quite tall and when you sat down you banged your head on the bit where the people behind you put their books. When you knelt down the pew was too far away to rest your bottom on so you had to kneel up straight and the stall we knelt against was too tall to rest your arms on. I was usually too uncomfortable to pray although I usually managed to ask God to make the Vicar hurry up. The seats were shiny, too, and if you didn't keep awake during the sermon you slipped off. I think the ladies who cleaned the church polished our seats on purpose to make sure we didn't doze off.

This week the Vicar went on about unbridled lust. It was one of his favourite topics, and as soon as he read the text I knew what was coming. He got very red in the face and shook his fist a lot. He even knocked his hymn book off the pulpit and Bunny had to go and pick it up for him. I was having trouble staying awake. I'd already counted all the window panes on the other side of the church and I'd even counted the organ pipes as well. Just as I was thinking about reading the Psalter – the sermon was that long – the Vicar said 'Let us pray' and we all dived to our knees.

He went on and on about lost souls and we prayed that they might be gathered in like the lost lambs to the Good Shepherd's fold. I never did understand why the Vicar always spoke so much rubbish, but that's how he was. Then he prayed for our village. That was unusual because we nearly always prayed for Africa, so I started to listen a bit more carefully. He prayed that all lonely people, all aged people and all women and children might be kept safe and protected from the ravages of the Prowler. It was news to me that he'd ravaged anybody but, if the Vicar said so, I guessed it must be right. I made a mental note to ask Mum what the Vicar meant when we got home.

Lunch was always cold on Sundays. We had our roast joint hot on Saturday and then we had cold cuts on Sunday. If there was anything left it was cooked up into something with potatoes on Monday because Mum didn't have much time to cook. Since she always did the washing on Monday morning she was usually exhausted by the afternoon.

As soon as lunch was finished we had a cup of tea, and then Cath and I had to go to Sunday school. It wasn't too bad but we were in the Vicar's class and he even managed to make the good Bible stories sound boring.

Evensong was at half–past six and I usually went on my own, although Mum came sometimes when she had nothing better to do. The evening service was always shorter than the morning one and we were usually out in fifty–five minutes.

I found it quite hard to concentrate this week because I knew the gang would be out doing their evening patrol, looking for the Prowler. Even Chris wasn't there so I was doubly annoyed, thinking of him and PeeDee doing their rounds. We were talking about the Prowler before the service. Bunny said the Prowler wouldn't be out on a Sunday so they'd be wasting their time. I didn't agree.

'If he's really that bad,' I said, 'he'll be out taking advantage of everybody thinking he won't be out.'

Bunny looked at me as if I was speaking double Dutch. We didn't have time to argue because we had to line up ready to process in.

Dad came up to collect me after the service. I felt a right idiot. And worse, I wasn't allowed out afterwards.

'We think you ought to stay in after tea,' Mum said, 'until they catch this man.'

And that was that. The curfew was in place and I had no chance to argue. I ended up finishing the book I was reading. I'd nearly read all the 'Swallows and Amazons' stories now and there was only one more to go.

'At least you can get a new one out of the library now,' Mum said.

We were allowed to stay up a bit later during the holidays but it was Sunday and there was nothing much on the wireless so I didn't really mind when Mum said it was time for bed. It was only when I went into the bathroom to clean my teeth that I remembered that I'd run out of tooth stuff. I used Gibbs Dentifrice because it came in a nice red tin with a tight-fitting lid. As soon as the tin was empty it made an ideal place in which to keep beetles and it fitted into my shorts pocket as well. Once Cath had opened one which I had left on the table and she nearly screamed the place down when she saw the stag beetle I'd got in it.

'Can I borrow your toothpaste?' I called through to Cath.

'What's wrong with yours?' she called back.

'It's run out.'

'Well, go and fetch it back in!'

That's the kind of humour Cath had – pretty useless and not funny at all. But I had to play along.

'Ha! Ha! Can I?'

'Be careful, you'll wonder where the yellow went with Pepsodent,' Cath said.

'Can I?' I repeated, trying not to sound too irritated.

'I suppose so,' she said grudgingly. 'But don't let it touch your toothbrush. I'm particular about what I put in my mouth.'

She was referring to the black jack I'd had after tea, the last of my wedding sweets. But I didn't rise because I knew things that she didn't. One Saturday, about a couple of weeks ago, I'd come up to clean my teeth after she'd finished her bath and hair wash. I always did my hair in the bath but she washed her hair over the basin. Anyway, I was about to spit down the basin when I saw it was all blocked with her hair and there was a gooey, disgusting mess in the plughole. It quite put me off for a moment.

I looked around for something to pick the muck out with, but it was the bathroom and there wasn't anything so I used her toothbrush – well it was her hair – and I found that I could push it down and get a lot of the soap muck off as well. It kind of mashed up the bristles on her brush a bit but I pulled the hair out and put her brush back. She never noticed – that's how particular she was!

It was my secret and there was no way I was going to tell anyone, but when Cath was being mean to me it gave me enormous satisfaction. I checked the basin plug hole. It was clean, so her tooth brush was safe for the moment!

Chapter 5

It was the first Monday of the month, so it was what Mum called the big wash day. There were piles all round the breakfast room, sorted into colours, and all the 'delicates' were in another pile. She and Cath would be there all the morning, with their aprons on and their sleeves rolled up, and they'd work through the lot by lunch time. Cath was in charge of the boiler and Mum did the scrubbing with a big block of Sunlight soap. They'd tried to rope me in not so long ago but I got the piles mixed up and the sheets went blue because I put Mum's best jumper in with them – and her jumper shrunk so much that even I couldn't wear it. I got a telling off and she stopped my pocket money for a week but she made sure I didn't touch the washing again!

I went to the den first thing on Monday morning. I'd seen the sisters walk past our gate earlier on the way to do their shopping, so I knew there was nothing doing at their place. Merlin and Oz would have been at the den on Sunday and Pud might have gone as well so I wanted to get there before they arrived. I flipped the stone over, crawled in and looked around. Everything seemed to be in order so I sat and waited. I didn't have to wait long. Merlin was the first to arrive.

'Where's Oz?' I asked.

They usually came together.

'He's outside,' Merlin said. 'He's got Tod with him. Tod wants to join our lot.'

Tod was a bit younger than most of us. His birthday was in October and so he was in the year below us at school, but he was big – taller than me. He'd be good when we took on PeeDee.

'We'll have to wait and see what Pud thinks,' I said. 'Tell Oz to tie him up.'

When someone wanted to join our gang they had to be voted in unanimously. Swede wasn't here so he couldn't vote, but if everyone else agreed then that would have to be good enough. Oz and Merlin came back.

'We tied him to the tree,' Oz said.

'And I blindfolded him with my hanky,' Merlin added, 'just in case he could hear us talking about him!'

We sat and waited for Pud to arrive. We'd agreed to meet first thing because we needed to know if anyone had seen the Prowler over the weekend. Pud took his time. When he finally came he was all apologies.

'I had to do things for me Mum,' he said. 'I got here as soon as I could. What's Tod doing tied up? Did you catch him snooping?'

Once, a while ago, we'd caught Goat's younger brother hanging around our den so we'd tied him to the tree while we decided what to do with him. In the end we took him up to the pond and then said he could go. We stood around him with sticks and started swishing them at his legs. We weren't going to hurt him, well, not much – just enough to teach him not to come snooping again – but he panicked and ran straight through the pond in his haste to get away. But he slipped over and Merlin had to go in and rescue him. We expected PeeDee's lot to attack but they didn't. All Goat said was he wished he'd been there – he'd have pushed him in for us.

I called our meeting to order.

'Merlin says Tod wants to join us,' I said. 'We could do with someone while Swede's away. Has anyone got anything to say against him?'

I always tried to do things properly and gave everyone the chance to speak.

'He's got a good bike,' Oz said. 'We could borrow it for the dirt track.'

'That's speaking for him,' Merlin said, 'not against him. He's a bit young.'

'He's only four months younger than me,' Pud said, 'and Merlin's seven months older than me. I can't see it makes a lot of difference.'

'But he's not in our year,' Merlin said.

We considered the point in silence.

'Has anyone got anything to say for him – apart from his bike and that we need someone to make up our numbers?'

'He was in the cubs so he'll know about knots,' Oz offered.

'He lives in Durley Avenue,' Merlin said. 'That'd mean we could cover more ground looking for the Prowler.'

'His Mum's in the WI with my Mum,' Pud said.

Merlin flattened Pud and I sat on him.

'Let's vote,' I said.

We all agreed to have Tod in the gang so we sent Oz out to fetch him in. I sat opposite the entrance with Merlin on one side and Pud on the other. Oz pushed Tod down in front of me and then stayed behind him so that Tod couldn't change his mind and get out.

'As leader of The Bramble Gang,' I began, trying to sound really posh, 'it has been brought to our notice,' – I liked that bit, the Queen always said *we* and *our* – 'that you are desirous of joining our numbers. Is this true?'

I think Tod was a bit surprised by how formal it all was. He'd expected to come along and hang out with us. He didn't say anything and he just looked at me as if I was mad. Oz kicked him.

'Ow! Yes,' Tod said.

'Yes, sir,' I said, looking daggers at him.

I waited and Oz kicked him again.

'Yes, sir,' Tod said sullenly.

'Do you swear never to give away our secrets to anyone, no

matter how much they torture you?'

Tod's eyes widened.

'Yes, sir,' he said.

'Before we give you the pass word you have to swear the oath of allegiance. Are you willing to do this?'

'Yes, sir.'

'Repeat after me: I, Tod, swear never to give any of The Bramble Gang's secrets away.'

'I, Tod, swear never to give any of The Bramble Gang's secrets away.'

'And if I crack under torture,'

'And if I crack under torture,'

'I shall be beaten with stinging nettles on my bare bum.'

Tod spluttered and looked at me as if I was mad.

'Ten's our leader,' Merlin said. 'Ten will do the beating.'

'And if you back out now,' Oz added for good measure, 'we'll beat you anyway 'cause you already know the oath.'

Tod looked at me and I stared him straight in the eye. Tod looked down.

'I shall be beaten with stinging nettles on my bare bum,' he mumbled.

'I welcome you as a full member of the Bramble Gang,' I said, leaning forward and shaking Tod by the hand. 'We don't have a pass word but we turn the stone to the left of the door over if we're in the den. Go and show him, Merlin.'

Merlin took Tod out and showed him which stone to turn over.

'The last one out always turns it back down,' I said, when they came back in.

'Now he has to swear the secret oath,' Oz said.

'I thought I'd just done that,' Tod said.

They pushed Tod in front of me and, like before, Oz crouched behind him.

'You do understand that you're bound by your oath of allegiance never to disclose the secret oath?' I said.

Tod nodded. He looked uncomfortable.

'Right,' I said. 'Hold this.'

Merlin produced a stinging nettle stalk. The hairs on it looked vicious and Merlin was holding it very carefully. He handed it to

Tod who took it and immediately dropped it. He blew on his fingers.

'Bare bum,' Oz said, menacingly.

Tod picked it up again.

'I swear to do everything I can to defeat the Flag Boys and to keep the Bramble Gang on top.'

Tod repeated the oath and Merlin gave him a handful of dock leaves for his hand which was covered in white bumps.

'Are you really the best?' he asked, awed.

'Of course *we* are,' I said, emphasising the 'we' just to make sure he understood he was one of us now.

'Has anyone got any news of the Prowler?' Merlin asked.

We looked at each other.

'The Vicar prayed for his soul,' I said. 'And we prayed that he might turn away from his path of wickedness.'

'I hope it don't work,' Oz said. 'It'll ruin our fun if it does.'

'It already has,' I said. 'Mum says I can't go out after tea so if we want to meet in the evening it'll have to be in our shed.'

We found that most of us were under curfew and the Prowler suddenly seemed more threatening.

'What's that?' Oz suddenly asked.

We all listened. Then we heard it, the 'whoo–whoo' of an owl. Tod looked surprised. We hadn't told him about that.

'It's PeeDee's lot,' I said. 'They're waiting outside for a parley.'

'What if it's a trap?' Tod asked.

'Don't be daft,' Merlin said. 'We never use the owl call for a trap. It's a point of honour. If you use the owl call then it means a genuine truce and neither side can take advantage.'

I led my lot outside and, sure enough, PeeDee's lot were partially concealed in the trees but they made no effort to take advantage of us. As soon as I came out PeeDee came forward. He had a newspaper in his hand.

'Have you seen this?' he asked.

'Your ugly face? Too many times,' Oz said, ever ready with something witty.

'Hah, bloody hah!' PeeDee said, ignoring him.

We were all used to Oz's feeble attempts at wit. PeeDee held out the newspaper, a copy of last Friday's Evening News. The rest of my lot gathered round as I read it. The headline on the front read **Daring Bank Raid in Full Daylight**. I skimmed it quickly. It seemed that a gang of bank robbers had walked into a bank in Portsmouth and had held the cashier up at gun point. They'd got away with over £5,000. We pored over the article, trying to imagine all the details.

'Why doesn't anything like that happen here?' Oz asked wistfully.

'You can't have a bank robbery without a bank!' Merlin pointed out.

'We've got a Post Office,' Pud said. 'They've got lots of money.'

My mind was instantly busy. PeeDee and I were much alike, really.

'Thought it might give us something to do,' he said.

'Ain't it enough that we're trying to catch the Prowler without going after a gang of bank robbers?' Oz said.

'Don't be daft,' PeeDee said scornfully. 'They'll be far gone. And anyway, they're in Portsmouth, not here.'

'I only asked,' Oz said grumpily.

'What I thought,' PeeDee said pompously, 'was that we could do a bank robber thing. You know, you could be the bankers and we'd be the robbers.'

'Only if we can do it the other way round,' Merlin said. 'I mean, it's obvious – your hut's better than ours, it'll make a perfect bank.'

'Or *we* could use *your* hut,' Pud said.

PeeDee thought about it. If we used his hut we'd be able to poke about while they were getting ready to raid us. But if we were the robbers then they wouldn't get the chance to chase us. It was a dilemma and I could see he was having difficulties deciding.

'Why don't we raid you,' I suggested. 'Naturally we'd kill you all and you could die agonising deaths. You'd have to count to three hundred while we got away and then you could become the police chasing us.'

I saw his eyes light up. PeeDee was renowned for his dying impression.

'And the best team wins?'

'Every one for themselves,' I said.

He spat on his hand and held it out, I spat on my hand and we shook on it. We sat down and planned it out. We decided to have the raid after dinner because there wasn't enough time to have a good chase now. PeeDee made a list of the rules and we split up to make our plans. The only thing that was fixed was that every one of PeeDee's gang agreed to be killed when they were bankers.

'It don't mean that we can't try to escape, though,' Roller said. He was back from visiting his granny.

'And we'll come after you and kill you,' Oz said.

Before we split up I introduced Tod.

'Tod's become a member of The Bramble Gang,' I said. 'And he enjoys all the privileges and obligations of The Bramble Gang.'

'We'll be in the bank from two o'clock,' PeeDee said, 'and we'll have posted security guards against bank robbers.'

'Armed guards,' Beaky said.

I saw the glint in Beaky's eye and I knew it was going to be one of our better games. PeeDee's lot left and we went back into our den and had a war council. We made our plans and then we broke up.

'Check Durley Avenue for the Prowler,' I told Tod, 'and report back as soon after half–past one as you can.'

Merlin went with Tod to teach him our secret call signs. Well, he couldn't do it in the woods with PeeDee's lot hanging around, could he? Oz agreed to check over our armoury and Pud went off to make some of his special mix.

I dropped in on the sisters on my way home, just to make sure they'd got back safely and hadn't forgotten that I was around. They were touched by my kindness and gave me some Spangles for my effort. I shoved them in my short's pocket – the sweets would come in useful after lunch.

Chapter 6

'We can't take them by surprise 'cause they're expecting us,' I said. 'That means we have to use a diversion.'

'Why don't we just take them by force?' Tod asked.

'That's what they'll be expecting,' Merlin said. 'There's no one more devious than Ten. You've got to be cunning and do what they don't expect. That's why Ten's our leader.'

We talked over some ideas and settled on making Tod the victim.

'I don't think it's fair,' he said. 'I want to do something more than just be an idiot.'

'It's what suits you best,' Oz said, rather unkindly I thought as I kicked him.

'It's perfect,' I said. 'They'd know if it was one of us, but if it's you they won't be expecting it and they're bound to fall for it if you're good enough.' I tried to sound convincing. It's always difficult trying to fool PeeDee's lot, but if Tod could pull it off it'd be a great victory. 'It's all up to you. Think of it like an initiation test – if you can do it then you'll be the hero.'

Tod thought about it and I could see him going through it in his head.

'And you've got the best bike of any of us,' I said, trying to weasel him into doing it. 'They'll think you're so stupid if you can't ride it that they'll come just to laugh at you. If you can fool them we're bound to win.'

'It's always best if you get up and fall over again,' Pud said. 'Makes it look more convincing. If you just lie there they'll think you're a sissy.'

'I ain't no girl,' Tod said.

I looked at him and he coloured.

'We don't mention 'girls' in here,' I said. 'It's another of our rules. We're members of The Bramble Gang.'

'How many more secret rules have you got?'

'Have *we* got,' Oz corrected him.

'Not many,' I said. 'But I'll try and think of some more.'

We talked over our plan again.

'They must have at least one of them in the den,' I said, 'and I bet they'll have two. One will be behind the door when we go in.'

'They'll have one behind the den, too,' Merlin said. 'They always do in case we creep up and try to take out the loose plank. I'll cover him.'

'That leaves two out front,' I said. 'PeeDee will be out there, he always is and he'll be the last to show. I'll look after him. That just leaves one more and if you do your stuff you can probably get him,' I said to Tod. 'Everything depends on you.'

We checked our plan yet again and then we checked our weapons. It was a tradition that PeeDee's lot always filled their pistols with red paint and we always used blue – that way there was never any argument about who'd shot who. Pud had been working on a special mixture with wall paper paste in it so that it didn't come off so quickly. I checked the back pocket of my shorts for my secret weapon.

'Right, before we go,' I said, getting out my Spangles, 'special agent rations.'

We each had one and then piled our fists into a column.

'Let's go and get them,' I said and we left the den.

Tod got on his bike ready to go. Merlin vanished into the bracken. He was the best at Commando crawl so he was going to creep up on the back of their den. It was my guess that they'd not see or hear him until it was too late. Oz and Pud were going to take the bank so that just left me. I was going to watch out for PeeDee – once you've got the leader the gang usually falls to bits. I left to take up my position and told Tod to count up to fifty and then to do his stuff.

And he really did do his stuff very well. I heard him come rattling over the dirt track and yelling like fury. He was making enough noise to raise the dead. He had a cap pistol and was firing away like mad and yelling encouragement to his gang of raiders.

I saw Roller break cover to try and see what was going on and I could see Chris look round from the back of the den. Judging by the look on Roller's face I think he must have thought that Tod had gone barmy. A moment later Tod came into the space in front of PeeDee's den and did an impressive wheelie. He was still yelling and firing his gun. He kept calling to the rest of his gang and I saw Roller and Chris looking around to see if they could spot them.

Then Tod fell off. The bike landed on top of him and he went silent. Then he struggled free, took a step and fell over clutching his ankle.

Then he started crying and pulled his master stroke – he called for Oz to come and help him. He was so convincing that, as his crying started to turn into real yelling, I nearly went to check that he was all right. I could see Roller peering over the bracken.

'Bloody hell,' Tod yelled, 'where are you Oz, I think it's broken!'

It was too much for Roller and he went to see if Tod was really hurt. He had his gun in his hand and was careful. Tod kept yelling and rolling around. I moved round to the side where Roller had come from. If I was right, PeeDee would be on the other side and I needed to have a good view of him.

Roller had reached Tod and was dithering. He still couldn't make up his mind if Tod was hurt or just putting it on.

'Help!' Tod said rather weakly, seeing Roller. 'I think it's broken. I can't stand up! Give us a hand.'

I don't know if it was because Tod was so convincing, or if it was because Roller thought he was a bit young and sissy, but Roller put his gun in his pocket and reached out a hand to help Tod up. Quicker than a blink, Tod put his feet between Roller's ankles and toppled him. In a second Tod was on top of him and, fishing his gun out of his pocket, he drilled a hole through Roller's temples.

This was too much for PeeDee who took his chance to try and shoot Tod who had his back to him. I saw PeeDee creep out of his cover and I shot him straight between the eyes, the paint ran down his nose and dripped on his shirt. I've never seen PeeDee look so surprised.

As soon as PeeDee went down, Oz and Pud came in. Oz went first and pushed the door hard back as Pud went in. Oz stayed against the door while Pud robbed the bank and shot Beaky, who was the banker. Oz let the door go and Pud finished off Goat who was still trapped behind the door. Merlin brought Chris round from behind the den, dripping in blue paint. We'd shot the lot of them and they hadn't even fired! PeeDee looked pretty sick as we rounded them up.

'Right men,' I said. 'They're dead for three hundred. Let's go!'

We left as PeeDee started counting. He went at a fair old pace and so we legged it pretty quick. We'd made our plans and knew what we were going to do. I knew that PeeDee would be pretty cross that we'd out-smarted him and he would be wary this time. He wouldn't take any chances and he'd probably work his lot in twos so that they could watch each other's backs. The problem was where PeeDee was going to be. If he was going to regain his honour he'd be coming after me so I made myself scarce down by the pond.

It was an unwritten rule that we nearly always ended up by the pond, and the losers usually in the pond. PeeDee was sure to be there in the end and I was counting on that. Even if all my lot were taken I could probably still take him out with the element of surprise. All I had to do was be patient and not give myself away, no matter what happened. Even if we lost, so long as we'd taken out PeeDee their victory would be pretty hollow.

On his way to the back of PeeDee's den, Merlin had tied the rope on the nearside of the pond, inviting one of them to take it to get away. I hid myself at the far side, tucking so far down behind the rushes that my feet were nearly in the water. It was the only place where you could stand up quickly without the danger of slipping into the water.

It seemed that I wasn't the only one who was using guile because almost as soon as I was hunkered down I heard someone creeping along through the rushes behind me. I turned very slowly, trying not to move the rushes, and I saw PeeDee creeping along the top of the bank. I knew he'd drop down to where I was 'cause there was nowhere else for him to go. I was glad I hadn't come along the bank so I'd left no footprints. The ground was soft where PeeDee was and he was having trouble not slipping. I counted to five and then stood up like a Jack–in–the–box and shot him.

If he'd been surprised last time, it was nothing compared to the look on his face this time. Of course, he could start counting to three hundred so I went and sat on him, just to make sure he didn't yell out. I took my handcuffs out of my back pocket and clicked them on to one of his wrists. He was about to argue but I told him he was dead and he couldn't move 'till he'd got to three hundred. I clicked the other one on before he had time to think and then I gagged him with my hanky so that he couldn't yell out when he'd got to three hundred.

I was tempted to go and look for the others but my lot knew where I'd be. I couldn't let them down so I sat down beside PeeDee and waited.

'It's all to do with the strategy,' I whispered.

PeeDee looked daggers at me and tried to kick me. I moved and sat on his feet.

Our plan was to break their pairs up and to finish them off, one by one. If possible, my lot were going to stay together.

'After all,' I'd told them, 'if they're in pairs the worst they can do is to take two of you out and our other two can take the two of them so we'll still be even.'

I think Tod had been going to argue but Merlin had said it was the best plan and Tod respected Merlin so he shut up.

We'd made a lot of noise leaving the dead bankers, and I'd certainly gone to the pond, but the other four had circled back so that they could watch where PeeDee's lot went. As I thought, PeeDee's lot had gone off in pairs and so my lot had to split up, just in case PeeDee's lot were setting us a trap. When they got near the pond my lot saw PeeDee branch off and they left him to me.

Beaky and Goat didn't seem to have much of a plan and they circled round our den, trying to see if we'd gone in there. Beaky was quick on his feet and when he heard a branch snap he dived to the ground, rolled over and fired. Oz looked surprised for a moment.

'You rotten swine,' he said in his best Bluebottle imitation, fixing his eye on Beaky, 'you deaded me!' He collapsed on to the ground with a few twitches for good measure.

That was a bad move for us but Beaky was so pleased that he'd taken one of us out that he turned to Goat and gave him a thumbs up. Merlin shot them both and then tied them up.

Chris and Roller split up. They had their bikes and so it was easy to hear where they were but it was more difficult to catch them because it meant that Pud and Tod had to use their bikes as well and it was difficult getting in an accurate shot from a bike at a moving target. I could hear Chris and Roller rattling round and round and I guessed they were acting as decoys so that the rest of PeeDee's lot could shoot us down. Of course, they didn't know that we'd already taken out Beaky and Goat. I was trying to decide whether to go and help when Merlin slithered down the bank beside me. His eyes lit up with delight when he saw I'd got PeeDee handcuffed and gagged.

'Beaky got Oz,' he whispered. 'I got them and they're tied up to the oak. I'm going back to keep watch.'

It was just as well he did go back because Chris had found Beaky and Goat, and was busy untying them. Merlin shot him and sat on him – he'd run out of rope. Chris started counting and as soon as he got to two hundred and ninety–nine Merlin shot him again.

Pud was on the trail of Roller and they were scorching through the bracken. Roller was easily managing to stay out in front and Pud, owing to his size, was beginning to tire. They'd gone back round the road and Roller was on the dirt track. Pud was always slow on the track and Roller would have escaped if it hadn't been for Tod. Just as Roller was coming down the long slope after the second hump, whooping with triumph that he'd stayed on his bike,

Tod rode out of the bushes on to the path in front of him.

Roller slammed on his brakes, lost control and fell off. For the second time Tod proved he could do things his own way. Instead of shooting Roller he produced his lasso and bound Roller up so that he could walk but not escape. Tod left the bikes and he and Pud led Roller back to the pond.

As soon as they got there Pud gave our call sign, a cockerel crowing, and Merlin and Oz brought the others to the pond. The four of them looked sorry for themselves, three tied up and one with more blue paint on him than an ancient Brit covered in woad. I judged it was my moment so I hauled PeeDee to his feet and paraded him out to join the rest.

It was getting late or we might have had another round. One of them might have escaped and we'd have had to round him up. But there wasn't time, so we had a quick council and chose the gangplank. Merlin fetched a log and Oz hauled out the plank from the rushes. Pud and Tod sat on one end and I sentenced each of them in turn to walk the plank. Roller went first then Chris followed by Beaky and Goat. PeeDee went last. Just to prove that there were no hard feelings we all piled into the pond behind them.

It was a great afternoon and it took us ages to dry out. Goat had brought biscuits from home and I had the rest of the Spangles.

'We could do it again, tomorrow,' Goat suggested.

'I can't,' Chris said. 'Got to go out. Blinkin' school uniform!'

It seemed that not only my mum thought buying school uniform early was a good idea.

'Don't forget the Prowler,' I reminded them as we left the woods. 'If you've got news we'll meet in the morning.'

'Make it on the football green,' PeeDee said. 'The olds won't be so suspicious then.'

Chapter 7

When I got home Mum went spare. She made me strip off in the kitchen and she put all my clothes in the washing tub. I guessed she was annoyed because it was Monday and she'd spent all the morning doing the washing.

'When you've washed and put some clean clothes on you can come down and wash these,' she said, pointing to my muddy clothes. 'And don't think you're going out again today,' she yelled at me as I turned to go.

I thought I got off quite lightly since my shorts were stinking of mud so I concocted a fib about how Tod had slipped on his bike and had slid into the water.

'I had to go in after him,' I said, 'I didn't know if he'd hurt himself.'

I knew he'd got a few bruises from his wheelie and I knew that Mum would see his Mum and they'd check up on us. Tod and I had agreed our stories on the way home, so I knew she'd let me off in the end.

Cath was sitting at the kitchen table and she sniggered when Mum said I had to wash my own clothes. I went and looked over Cath's shoulder.

'Get away from me, you stinking little brat!' she yelled.

'I only wanted to see what you were doing,' I said. 'There's sisterly love for you!'

'Cath, watch your language!' Mum said.

Cath pinched her nose.

'It stinks!' she said. 'I think I'm going to be sick!'

I beat it then, there was little more I could do. My feet were filthy and I left marks all over the kitchen floor. The geyser was off and there wasn't any hot water so I had to wash in cold water. I drew a basin full and did the best I could. I could even smell myself, so I splashed on some of Mum's 4711 before I came down – I didn't like the pong but it was better than mud and there was nothing else to hand. It took me nearly an hour to squeeze all the mud out of my shorts.

'I hope that'll teach you to be more careful,' Mum snorted when I'd finished.

I pretended to be contrite but I was still buzzing from our famous victory over PeeDee's gang so it was hard looking miserable. Fortunately Mum was rattling round cooking dinner so she didn't have time to fuss. Usually we had our main meal in the middle of the day but on Mondays, on account of Mum doing the washing, we had a cooked meal in the evening.

A famous victory is all very well but I knew that PeeDee would want to get even. I had to be on my guard and I reckoned the best plan was to go on the offensive. Although we'd won the bank raid it had been PeeDee's idea and it was up to me to come up with the next one. At the moment my mind was a blank. What with the Prowler and the bank raid all the good ideas seemed to have been used up and I was beginning to feel desperate.

Dad had the paper when he came home and I saw the headline was something about a foreign naval ship visiting the dockyard in Portsmouth. Ever since the diver, Lionel Crabbe had vanished nearly two years ago, there was always a piece in the paper when a foreign ship visited. Everyone thought the diver had been on some secret spying mission when he vanished. He might have been working for the secret service, but their spokesman said that he was nothing to do with them. We all thought the Reds had done him in because he was snooping round one of their ships that had been visiting the dockyard at the time. My head was still half full of the Swallows and Amazons book I'd just finished and as I tried to read the paper Dad was holding up it suddenly came to me. The print on the paper was backwards, of course, and I couldn't make much sense of it but it didn't really matter. My idea didn't really have anything to do with Buster Crabbe although I thought we could probably work him in when we got towards the end.

Unfortunately my idea had to wait because Mum and Dad were in a fussy mood and I couldn't go out again after tea. I fretted the time away upstairs in my bedroom. There were two bedrooms and the bathroom upstairs. Cath's bedroom was the best in the whole house. She had a window looking down the back garden, just like me, but she had another window looking out the side of the house over the garage. If you opened the window and leaned out you could see a fair chunk of the road out the front. She had a fitted wardrobe, too, as well as another cupboard. My room was less than half the size of hers and had just the one window looking down the back garden. Because the bedrooms were in the roof the ceilings sloped. Cath's room had the extra space where the hall cut into my room so she had plenty of space to walk around. More of the ceiling was sloping in my room, so I could only stand up by my desk in the window and alongside my bed.

The bathroom was next to my room and there was a gas heater for the water above the bath. I used to wait until Cath was in the bath and then I'd turn the tap on at the kitchen sink downstairs and wait for her to shriek when the geyser lit. It always went with a huge woomf and once I'd managed to singe her hair. Mum and Dad used the front room downstairs as their bedroom. We had a hall and their room was the first on the left as you came in the front door. The living room was the other room on the left and it opened into a conservatory where Dad grew tomatoes. The stairs twisted up on the right behind the front door and there was a big cupboard under them where Mum kept the Electrolux vacuum and all her cleaning junk. The door immediately in front of you when you came through the front door led into what Mum called the breakfast room. I don't know why she called it that because we ate all our meals in there, not just breakfast. It had a huge dresser on one wall where we kept all our china and there was a pantry that ran under the stairs.

The kitchen was tiny and led off the breakfast room. It was just big enough for the sink, the stove and two people if you didn't move around too much. The washing boiler lived in the space under the wooden draining board. The back door out of the breakfast room also led into the conservatory, which also had what we called the 'outside' toilet just inside the door out into the garden. It always froze in winter and the seat was like sitting on ice.

It was stuffy in my bedroom and I had the window wide open but it still didn't let any breeze in. Dad said that this was typical August weather and that it would only get better when we'd had a decent thunder storm. I looked at the sky. It was clear so I guessed we'd not be having a storm tonight. I crawled up on to my desk and hung out the window, trying to get some cool air. The slates on the roof were radiating heat back up at me so I gave that idea up as a bad job. I could hear the wireless on in the lounge – Mum and Dad had the French doors open and the sound was drifting up. I took my secret chest out from under my bed, fished the key out of the sock in the bottom of one of my drawers and unlocked it.

I kept all my treasures in it. I took out the log book for the Bramble Gang and amended the membership list. 'James Carter, known as Tod, was admitted to The Bramble Gang on Monday 6th August 1958,' I wrote. We called James 'Tod' because he was an only child. Then I turned to a new page and wrote the title 'The famous victory of The Bramble Gang.' I added a brief account of how we had beaten the Flag Boys not only when they were bankers but also when they were the police. Then I found a blank page in the back of one of last year's exercise books and started to plan my new idea.

I heard Cath come upstairs and go into the bathroom. I didn't know what the time was but I guessed it was getting late because the shadow of the apple tree on the lawn had nearly reached the pond and it was getting difficult to see what I was writing. It must be close on half past nine if Cath had come up so I was on borrowed time. Any minute now I expected to hear Dad yell up that it was time I got ready for bed.

I don't know what I dreamt about but the next morning I had the plan for our next challenge all worked out in my head. It wasn't so much a competition as a combined operation and I reckoned it would keep us busy for the best part of a week. I lay in bed watching the sun move the shadow of the window along the wall, the patch of sunlight creeping ever nearer the foot of my bed. Because my room was quite small it got hot very quickly in the summer and I knew I'd have to get out of bed and open the window soon.

In the winter my room was freezing and most mornings the window would be frosted over. I used to blow on it until I'd got a round hole big enough to see through, but by the time I'd got back into bed it had usually frozen over again. Last winter I'd written 'Cath stinks' in the frost. I had to keep licking my finger to keep it warm enough to melt the ice and I'd had to write it out on paper a couple of times so that I could be sure the letters were the wrong way round so that it read properly from the garden. The weird thing was nobody noticed. It was too cold for Cath or Mum to go out so all my hard work was wasted. By the time Pud came the ice had melted and it had gone although I could still see the marks on the window from inside. It was quite good in the evening because the writing reappeared as the window misted up. Mum saw it and I had to clean all the windows in the house as a punishment.

As soon as the sun touched the end of my bed I got up and dressed. I stopped outside Cath's door and sang 'Green door, what's the secret you're keeping?' Her bedroom door wasn't green, it was painted a dull cream, but it was the only song I knew about doors. She moaned something I couldn't catch so I left her to it and went down to breakfast. I don't know why Mum let her sleep so late. Once, when I pointed out that Cath could have been doing some of my chores Mum, just said that because Cath helped with the washing on Mondays she deserved a sleep in on Tuesdays. It didn't make much sense to me but I didn't argue the point. I think that Mum wanted some time on her own having had to put up with Cath all day Monday. Anyway, it meant that I didn't have to worry about Cath poking her nose into what I was doing.

I was still singing when I went through to Mum and she looked up from the newspaper – she liked reading the gossip in The Daily Sketch. If Monday was washday, Tuesday was ironing day and I suppose it gave her something to think about while she was working. In the winter when it was too cold to go outside I helped her by sprinkling the washing. She had a medicine bottle and Dad had added a sprinkler top so I used to damp down the clothes before she ironed them.

'What are you so cheerful about?' she asked.

'Nothing,' I said.

She hated most of the songs I liked and I think she was beginning to get irritated so I stopped. I didn't want her coming on all heavy and stopping me from going out. I whistled the beginning of 'Que sera, sera,' – I knew that she liked Doris Day.

'Have you done your practice?' Mum asked.

'Sure,' I said. And then, because I couldn't resist it I sang 'There's an old piano and they play it hot behind the green door!'

'Just go,' Mum said, clearly irritated but in a nice sort of way.

'But don't be late for lunch. I may need you to go down the shops this afternoon.'

I went out. There was no point in tempting fate.

Chapter 8

PeeDee and Merlin were already on the green by the time I got there. PeeDee was very quiet and not at all his usual boisterous self and I asked Merlin if he was all right.

'Bad night,' he said. 'His Dad went off on one!'

We all knew that PeeDee's father liked to drink. He was a tall, burly man. He worked for a local builder and was as strong as an ox. When he'd been drinking it was a good idea to stay out of his way because, like PeeDee, he had ginger coloured hair and the same short temper. When he was sober he could be fun and he'd often played football with us on the recreation field. But when he'd had a bit too much to drink he became aggressive and violent. I suppose the business of Sandy being chased by the Prowler had upset him. There wasn't anything he could do and he felt powerless. PeeDee's Dad was old–fashioned and he liked to be the boss in his own home, he liked to sort things out his own way.

Tod was the last to arrive and the first thing PeeDee did was to split everybody up into pairs, one of his lot and one of mine. Because Chris was missing – he was out shopping with his mother for the dreaded school uniform – Merlin was left on his own. He looked at me and raised his eyebrows in a question.

'It's the sensible thing to do,' I said. 'If we join together neither PeeDee's lot nor ours will have the honour of catching him.'

Merlin shrugged then PeeDee sent them off to do the rounds of the village.

'I want to be sure there's nobody hanging about,' he said. 'This Prowler bloke's getting in the way.'

My lot didn't argue and Pud went off with Roller.

'We'll wait here and you can report back,' PeeDee said.

That was enough to get me really worried about him. Normally he would be out and about, bossing everyone and leading the search.

'You all right?' I asked PeeDee when the others had gone.

He looked at me a bit strangely.

'What do you care?' he said.

'We're enemies,' I said. 'But if you aren't up to it, how can we have a fair fight?'

'It's only me Dad,' he muttered.

'Did he hit you again?'

PeeDee nodded. He looked really shaken. He sniffed and wiped his nose. He looked as if he was going to blub, but PeeDee was made of sterner stuff. This was serious and I didn't know what to say. I fished in my pocket and found the gobstopper I'd been working on. It was about half its original size and had turned a delicate shade of pale green. I offered it to PeeDee.

'You can work on it for a bit,' I said. 'I got it after the wedding on Saturday. It was red at first and then it went pale mauve.'

'Thanks,' he said, popping it into his mouth. 'It's all right, though,' he went on, his cheek bulging with the gobstopper, 'he only got me once. Mum stopped him before he'd really got into his stride.'

'What happened?'

'He told Sandy that she couldn't go out and she gave him a lot of lip and went out anyway. Then he went down the pub and he was a bit merry when he got back. Sandy was still out so he decided to wait for her out the front.' He paused. 'It was my own fault, I wasn't thinking. I asked him what he'd do if he caught the Prowler and he took it the wrong way. I could see he was going to give me a clout so I ducked and bumped into the sideboard. I knocked a vase off and it broke. He grabbed me. He took his belt off and ...' he paused again. 'Well, Mum stopped him so it wasn't so bad. He didn't mean to hurt me. It wasn't his fault – it was the drink and the Prowler.'

If my Dad had hit me like that I don't think I would have been so calm about it. PeeDee might be bossy but he was fair and he didn't hold grudges.

'So,' I said, changing the subject, 'after your lot's abject humiliation as bankers and policemen, what are you going to lose at next?'

He grinned.

'Just because you've got one puny victory it doesn't mean you've won the war!'

'It wasn't puny, it was magnificent. We totally obliterated you.'

'Okay, you were lucky.'

'Not lucky, just better than you!'

'Don't you ever give up?'

'Not when I'm winning!'

PeeDee was beginning to sound more cheerful so I dropped in my latest idea for a new game. I suggested that we could try our hand at building rafts and have a sea battle.

'We could be pirates and go up to the big pond,' PeeDee said, suddenly enthusiastic. 'It could work. But would your Mum let you?'

'If she didn't know,' I suggested, 'then she wouldn't need to stop me.'

'We'll get wet, she'll find out. They always win in the end.'

'Who?'

'Parents!'

There was a touch of bitterness in his voice and I sympathised. Mine weren't too bad. Mum nagged me and Dad came on a bit heavy at times but they never hit me. The worst they had done was to keep me at home during the evenings because of the Prowler. I felt sorry for PeeDee — he had so much more to put up with.

'We could wait until we've caught the Prowler,' I suggested. 'We could start building the rafts in your den.'

'You seem very sure we're going to catch him.'

'I am. So far he hasn't actually hurt anyone so he's probably quite harmless. If we keep watch he's bound to make a mistake sooner or later and then we'll have him.'

'I hope my Dad's drunk when we find him,' PeeDee said darkly. 'He won't prowl round here after that!'

Tod and Goat were the first ones back. They'd been along the main road and up as far as the fish and chip shop.

'The place is deserted,' Tod said.

'Like a ghost town,' Goat added. 'Even the chip shop's shut.'

'He don't open until just on lunch,' PeeDee said.

'Did you check the back of the pub?' I asked.

'Not worth it. Monkey said he'd keep his eyes open and he hasn't said anything so it must be all right,' Goat said.

The others were in sight. Merlin had gone off over the

recreation field and had come back down Padnell Road. He'd run all the way and was puffed out. His face was bright red and you could almost see steam coming out of his clothes. He flung himself down on the grass, panting.

'All clear,' he said in between his breaths. 'I checked the church, too. Nothing.'

Oz and Beaky followed. They'd been round the other way, along Winscombe Avenue and up Park Lane. They must have followed Tod and Goat along the road.

'We looked in the cop shop,' Oz said, 'but it looked all shut up like it always does.'

We were just waiting for Pud and Roller who'd been doing the long route up the side roads because they had their bikes.

'We started at Hart Plain Avenue,' Roller said, when they finally returned, 'and then Pud did Silvester Road while I did Kings Road.'

'We did the same with Mission Lane and Durley Avenue,' Pud added. 'We thought it'd save time if we did alternate roads.'

'We stopped at Longwood Road, though,' Roller said. 'We didn't think he would be on our patch if he was up Lovedean Lane.'

'So there's no sign of anybody strange,' PeeDee said.

'But he might just be an ordinary guy,' Merlin said. 'You know, he might be someone we all know and not a stranger at all.'

'The only other thing we know,' I said, 'is that PeeDee's Dad said he was wearing a dark suit so that suggests he's a bit posh. He's probably not a tramp at all so there's no point in looking for one.'

'My Dad's still got his demob suit,' Goat said, 'and he's not posh. He says lots of men still have their old demob suits so it could be almost anyone.'

We were beginning to go round in circles so I thought it was time we stopped and did something else. We were sitting on the grass outside the prefabs. There was a long line of them snaking round the edge of the green. There must have been about ten or even more on the other side of the road and there were as many on our side. The grass was wider outside the prefabs on our side of the road and whereas the patch of grass on the other side was long and thin over here it was more rectangular so this was where we played football or cricket.

Mum called the prefabs tin boxes and Cath said that the people who lived in them were packed in like sardines, but the prefabs all had back and front gardens. They weren't bad. I'd been in Ray's and it was small and compact but it had everything they needed.

'Look, it's no use sitting here. He's not going to walk up to us in broad daylight on the green is he?' I said.

'Check the dens?' Beaky suggested.

None of us had a better idea so we drifted off down the road towards the recreation ground. Goat was right, there was nobody around – not even the little kids were playing outside the council houses. We jogged across the rec. and turned up Padnell Road towards the woods. PeeDee's lot peeled off towards their den and we went on to ours. After the heat of the sun, the leafy shade in the woods struck us as almost being cold.

The morning was rapidly turning out to be a waste of time. After the excitement of yesterday's bank raid everything felt a bit flat. We needed something to happen, and the problem with the Prowler was that we hadn't found him and nor were we likely to during the day.

'We need to start something,' I told the members of my gang. 'It's no good sitting around thinking we're going to catch the Prowler.'

'I thought you said it was only a matter of time,' Tod said.

'So it is,' I said, somewhat irritably. It wasn't nice being reminded of what I'd said so glibly. 'But it will take time and we're not likely to catch him during the day. That's why we need something else to do.'

'Ten's right,' Merlin said.

How good that sounded after Tod's remark!

'I vote we stage a raid on PeeDee's lot.'

'Why?' Tod asked.

Merlin looked at him as if he was mad.

'Because he's PeeDee and they're the Flag Boys. They're our enemies. We don't need any other reason!' he said scornfully.

'I bet they're thinking up some dirty little scheme while we're sitting here,' Oz said, picking up Merlin's idea.

'I've got some rope at home,' Tod suddenly said. 'We could lash it round their den and then they wouldn't be able to get out.'

'We could lob in a hand grenade and that'd be the end of them,' Oz said.

'Only problem is,' Pud said, 'by the time you've gone and got the rope and come back they'll probably all be gone.'

'We could keep the rope here and use it another time,' Merlin said. 'It's worth a try.'

Tod went off on Pud's bike to get the rope and we went out and played marbles. Oz nearly always had some in his pockets so we had target practice using his big red one as the target which he threw some distance away. We took turns to see if we could hit it using the smaller cat's–eye ones. Oz was ace and he always won. I was useless which is why I never played marbles.

Tod was gone ages and PeeDee's lot drifted over before he got back. Seeing what we were doing they offered to join in.

'Only as a practice,' Oz said. 'You ain't getting my marbles.'

Chapter 9

Mum was just finishing the ironing when I got in. Cath was getting dinner and so I decided to stay out of the way.

'Where are you going?' Mum called after me as I went out. 'It's nearly dinner. It wouldn't hurt you to lay the table.'

'In a minute,' I called back, slowing enough not to look too rude. 'I'm just going down the garden for a mo.'

I knew if I stayed in the kitchen Cath would have me stirring something or mashing potatoes, not one of my favourite activities. I climbed the apple tree and sat up in the fork of the trunk. I could see over the hedge and into the gardens of the prefabs that had been built along the edge of the green on our side of the road.

Ray's mother was hanging washing out on the line. Because their kitchens were so small most of the people in the prefabs did their washing over one or two days. A bit further along, Mrs Peters was hanging out nappies on her line. She had a new baby and most days she flew a line of nappies like the flags on a battleship.

I climbed a bit higher so that I could see over the gardens to the house where the Misses March lived. It was all shut up and looked deserted – perhaps they'd gone out. Cath was yelling at me. Dinner was ready so I made a mental note to check them out later on my way up to the woods.

The best laid schemes o' men an' mice, gang aft agley – that's from Robbie Burns' poem about a mouse. It was one of Dad's favourite sayings. He wasn't Scottish but he used to say it with what he thought was a thick Scottish accent and when I was little it used to make me laugh. Nowadays he only got as far as 'The best laid plans ...' before we shut him up. All the same, it turned out to be true that afternoon.

First of all I had to do the washing up.

'It's only fair,' Cath said. 'You've been out all the morning having fun doing goodness knows what while we've been here doing all the work.'

I didn't even argue. I knew I wouldn't win and the best way to upset Cath was to look meek and do what she wanted.

No sooner had I finished the washing up – I even dried the things and put them away – than Mum asked me to go up the shops. I took my bike because she wanted me to go to the butcher's as well as the green grocer's and they were at opposite ends of the village.

'If you've got your bike,' Mum said, 'could you pick up another ball of wool and a magazine from the news agent's?'

That was about an hour's worth of errands so I guessed I wouldn't be up the woods after all. Tying up PeeDee's lot in their den would have to wait until tomorrow.

The sun had gone in by the time I got back. It had been a glorious morning, hot and sunny, but now it had become muggy and I was sweating like a pig. Mum gave me a glass of orange squash and said I ought to have a rest. I was about to argue when it started to rain. Not the gentle stuff but huge drops that hit the windows with a ping. I ran out into the garden and put my bike in the back of the garage. Cath had been sewing under one of the trees. She was gathering up her embroidery silks and trying to keep them dry. I gave her a hand and we dashed back in just as lightning flashed. She went pale. Cath didn't like thunder.

I stayed in the conservatory, watching. I liked thunder and lightning. It was so powerful and noisy, and best of all, if it was overhead it made the glass in the windows rattle. Cath was hiding nervously in the kitchen with Mum. It wasn't so bad during the day but if we had a storm at night Cath would hide under her bedclothes and cry until it was over. The storm passed as quickly as it had arrived and soon the road out the front was steaming as the sun burnt down again.

'Can I go out now,' I asked Mum.

'What's the hurry?' she said. 'Everything's still wet.'

'I know. That's the point. The dirt track will be ace!'

She looked at me. I tried to put on my most angelic face. She shook her head.

'I don't know where I went wrong,' she said. 'Why can't you be more like Cath?'

What a question! Cath was my lunatic sister! I was tempted to suggest that Cath was where she'd gone wrong, but I wanted to go out before the track had dried off too much so I bit my tongue and stayed quiet.

'I thought that Cath's nerves would be upset after the storm and if I wasn't here to bug her she'd get better more quickly!'

'You've always got an answer, haven't you?'

I smiled and stayed silent – twice in as many minutes! I began to wonder how long I could keep this up.

'Go on then, and don't get too dirty!'

'Thanks Mum. I did wash my clothes yesterday!'

I escaped before she changed her mind. They were all at the track by the time I arrived, even Chris who had come back from shopping with his Mum.

'What kept you?' PeeDee asked.

'Cath threw a wobbly over the thunder,' I said. 'It took time to get away.'

Judging by the look of PeeDee the track was dead slippery. He was smeared in yellow clay and had even painted streaks on his cheeks.

'I like your war paint,' I said to him as Chris set off.

Chris was going far too quickly and I knew he'd come off. He did! And the words he used were definitely not ones that he'd heard in church. Oz was next. He was skilful and took no chances. Judging by his whooping, he must have made it. Chris came back covered in mud and with a bleeding elbow where he'd scraped it. PeeDee rubbed some clay into it.

'It'll stop the bleeding and keep it clean!' he said, picking bits of grass out of it.

Goat went next and, like Oz, he took it carefully. He made it, too. Pud set off but I knew he'd be back because he took it much too slowly. He never even made it through the ditch and came back with both his feet squelching. Beaky made it and so did Tod and Roller. Then it was my turn. I nearly came off but I just managed to put a foot down and keep going as I came up the second hump.

Merlin was grinning like an idiot as I wheeled round alongside him. We waited for PeeDee who came roaring up like a lion. He made it this time although I could see that he was still moving awkwardly. I guessed he was still a bit tender and didn't find the saddle too comfortable.

We pushed on into the woods towards what we called the 'lookout' tree. This was on one of the highest points in the woods and if you climbed up you could see right over the woods. One of the other trees here had grown almost horizontally. I got Pud to give me a bunk up and I climbed up until I couldn't see them on the ground below. We used to call it the 'Aeroplane' tree because once you were in it the ground vanished and all you could see was the sky above. PeeDee climbed up and joined me. We stayed there, the two gang leaders, and no one could hear what we were saying.

'You better?' I asked.

'Yeah, no sweat,' PeeDee said, trying to look as if nothing had happened. 'When're we going to tell them about the rafts?'

'Tomorrow. It's too late to do anything today.'

'I'm off,' Merlin called up. 'Got some bottles to take back to the pub.'

'See if Monkey's got any news,' PeeDee called down. 'And don't eat all the sweets!'

Usually when Merlin did a 'bottle trip' he either bought chips from the chip shop opposite or, if it was shut, he came up to the Bon Bon and bought sweets. Since the chip shop was shut it was a safe bet that he'd buy sweets.

'I'm off, too,' Pud said. 'My feet are wet.'

'Your lot are bunking off,' PeeDee said. 'You want to go too?'

'No. I'm fine here. It's like the rest of the world don't count for anything.'

I liked the quietness of the woods and the privacy its shaded paths gave, but sitting up here was even better. We could hear Goat calling over from the look out tree.

'You coming up?'

'In a mo,' Beaky replied.

'Seems like they've forgotten us,' PeeDee said.

'Ow, you bugger. Shove off!'

Chris was yelling. I guessed he was fighting with Oz. They usually did when they had nothing better to do.

'Flippin' heck,' Oz complained, 'you didn't have to do that!'

'Want to join in?' I asked PeeDee.

'No. Let them get on with it.'

He fished in his trouser pocket and produced the rear half of a sugar mouse.

'I thought you might like it,' he said, holding it up by its tail. 'In return for the gobstopper.'

The afternoon was getting more and more freaky. PeeDee and I were supposed to be sworn enemies and here we were, sitting up a tree together and getting on. It just didn't feel right.

'We ought to do something,' I said as soon as I'd finished the mouse.

'They've all gone now,' PeeDee said.

It was quiet. Eerily quiet. The sun was beginning to slant through the trees and I guessed it must be getting near tea time. I had no idea how long we'd been sitting up there. All I knew was that it was quite late before I came out after the storm.

'It looks quite late,' I said. 'Perhaps I'd better get going.'

I began climbing down and stopped on the bottom branch.

'You coming?' I called up to PeeDee.

'Might as well,' he said noncommittally.

I sat on the branch and wriggled myself round until I was able to slide off and hang by my hands. It wasn't far to the ground but I waited for PeeDee who was scrambling about coming down from where we'd been sitting.

'Damn!'

'What's up?'

'Caught my shorts,' PeeDee said. 'Ripped the blinkin' things!'

I let go of the branch, dropped to the ground and rolled out of the way. I could see PeeDee's feet – he always wore black shoes with studs in the soles. He looked a bit like Plug from the Bash Street Kids in the Beano, except that he didn't wear socks and his legs were quite skinny. He dropped to the ground beside me and started to feel his backside.

'Turn round,' I ordered.

He'd caught the back pocket of his shorts on the dead stub of a branch and it had nearly ripped the pocket off. It was hanging by a few threads and the hole was enormous. I could see his pants through the hole.

'You're going to get into trouble,' I said.

PeeDee looked at me and I swear he looked frightened.

'I could get my Ma to mend it,' I suggested. 'I think it will stitch back and you'll scarcely be able to see it. At least until your Mum does the washing.'

PeeDee's face lit up.

'Would she?'

'Don't see why not. Come on, we can only ask.'

Since my clothes were still clean I thought we had a fair chance.

'You'd better wash your face, though. You've still got clay on it.'

PeeDee was all for going back by the dirt track but I thought that, since I was still clean, it would be tempting fate.

'Let's get you mended first,' I said.

Mum mended PeeDee's shorts but she made him wince when she called him 'my little friend'. If only she had known he was my sworn enemy! And he hadn't been too happy when she told him he'd have to take them off! She told me to lend him my dressing gown while she mended them.

Cathy was a bit snotty about it and when PeeDee'd gone she couldn't resist baiting me.

'How many more poor waifs and strays are you going to bring here?' she asked.

'He's had enough trouble for one day,' I said. 'He needed a break.'

'Pity he couldn't have made do with just a tear,' Cath said, thinking she was so witty.

He wasn't the only one who needed a break, I thought.

'Next time,' Mum said, sensing that she needed to come between us before we came to blows, 'you can do the mending.'

'Me and a needle?' I said. 'You must be joking! Anyway, Cath's much better than me, she's always sewing.'

'I wouldn't touch his dirty clothes for all the tea in China,' she said with a shudder.

'He's all right,' I heard myself saying. 'He's just been going through some trouble at home. His Dad's a bit worried about Sandy.'

'About time somebody was,' Cath said and flounced out of the kitchen.

But she'd got over it by tea time and we played catch with a tennis ball out in the garden after tea. For someone who was so unsporting, I could never understand how she managed to catch the ball. No matter where I threw it she seemed to be able to get to it. I was soon on both my knees with one hand behind my back. I think she took pity on me and I managed to get back up on my feet but she still won in the end. When she went in I went round the front and bounced the ball against the front wall of the house. Because the porch had a concrete floor I could bounce the ball on the ground as well as against the wall which made it a bit more interesting.

It was getting dark but I didn't want to go in. All of a sudden I felt that someone was watching me. I carried on bouncing the ball and looked over my shoulder. I could just see a man moving away quickly. The gate was closed so I couldn't see him clearly but I'm sure he was watching me. I ran up the drive and hung over the gate but he was nowhere to be seen. For a moment I felt quite odd. Was it the Prowler? I went in but I didn't say anything to Mum or Dad.

Chapter 10

Beaky came round first thing next morning. I'd only just finished my chores.

'PeeDee's calling a meeting,' he said. 'About the Prowler.'

He was out of breath from running.

'Where?'

'On the green. Out the back. As soon as you can.'

I wondered why PeeDee had chosen the green and not his den but I didn't ask. Beaky was only the messenger so he probably wouldn't know and I thought it would make me look stupid if I didn't know. As leader of The Bramble Gang I was supposed to know everything, so I sent Beaky on his way.

'I'll be there in five minutes if I can spare the time.'

Beaky was too dozy to notice that I wasn't doing anything and he left in a hurry to go and find Monkey.

'Don't forget Tod,' I called after him.

I called to Mum through the back door.

'I'm just going down the green to play football. Give me a shout if you want anything.'

I hot–footed it down the garden before Mum had time to say anything and pushed my way through the hedge at the bottom. We didn't really have a way out down there but if I jumped into the ditch I could scramble up on to our neighbour's garden and they did have an opening on to the road. I was waiting on the green when PeeDee and his lot came up from the council houses.

'What kept you?' I asked. 'I thought this was an urgent meeting.'

Pee Dee kicked the football over to me. He kicked it deliberately wide but I'd seen where he was looking so I made a spectacular dive and caught it. He looked daggers at me but I just grinned and sat on the ball.

'So, what's this all about?' I asked as they came up.

'Better wait until Beaky gets back,' he said. 'Don't want to have to keep repeating everything.'

Merlin took off his shirt and dropped it down to make a goal post and PeeDee did the same to make the other. I threw the ball out to Oz and he started dribbling it round Goat who tried to tackle him but Oz was too quick. They spread out and started passing the ball, teasing Goat who was nearly as bad at football as I was. It was about fifteen minutes before the rest arrived. Beaky and Monkey were the last to come, Beaky riding on the crossbar of Monkey's bike. It was just as well PC Norris wasn't about or he'd have told them both off – it was one of his favourite complaints. His bark was worse than his bite though, because we all did it.

PeeDee nodded to me and we abandoned the game.

'It's the flippin' Prowler again,' he said. 'Late last night someone saw him in the passageway by Mrs Bates' house.'

'What time?' I asked. 'Only, I think I might have seen him as well. I think he was watching me over our front gate.'

PeeDee wasn't sure but he said it was just as it was getting dark. On the council estate some of the houses, like PeeDee's, were semi–detached but others were built in blocks of four. The upstairs was continuous but there was a passage way between the second and third houses at ground level. There were gates at the end of the passage way so that the people living there had access to their back doors and their gardens.

'Who saw him?' Merlin asked.

'Did they see his face?' Tod asked.

'Don't know,' PeeDee replied. 'It's only what I heard. Mrs Bates was over at Mrs Williams' house and she told my Mum that when she looked out the front window she saw this man lurking in the shadows by the passageway.'

'Bet she was scared?' Tod said. 'What did she do?'

'She got Mr Williams to go back with her.'

'And what did he do?' Oz asked

'When they came out they saw the man run down through the passage. They think he must have gone over the fence at the bottom of Mrs Bates' garden 'cause they couldn't find anyone there.'

We considered this development for a moment. After the excitement of the bank raid game and after we'd drawn a blank yesterday morning, we'd forgotten about the Prowler. Now, here he was right back at the top of our menu. Oz suggested that we go and look for clues in Mrs Bates' garden but PeeDee said he didn't think Mrs Bates would like us trampling all over her vegetables so we abandoned that idea. Chris said we could go and look at the field behind her garden.

'What do you think you'll find?' Goat asked him.

'He might have caught his clothes on the fence,' Chris said. 'Then we'd have a piece of cotton to identify him by.'

'Sure,' PeeDee said scornfully. 'Are you suggesting we go around looking at every man's trousers to see if they've got a rip in them and then we try and match to fabric? Plod will have us in for a caution quicker than you can say knife.'

I didn't mention the rip in PeeDee's shorts yesterday but he was still wearing them so I guessed his mother hadn't spotted the mend.

'We've got to do something,' I said. 'The only two sightings we're sure about have been up your end, PeeDee.'

And then I had a brainwave.

'Did Sandy say anything? Was she out last night?' I asked PeeDee. 'Only if she was, she might know something. Ask her when she gets home. She might have vital clues.'

'Are you saying she knows something?' PeeDee asked indignantly. 'Are you saying she's involved?' he demanded, even more aggressively. He was very protective of his sister.

'No, 'course not. But if she was out it might be that this bloke was keeping his eye on her and she might have seen something. We don't want her getting hurt, do we?'

'Or him!' Oz muttered under his breath.

But not quietly enough. PeeDee heard him and instantly leapt on him.

'Take it back!' he demanded. He drew his fist back for extra persuasion.

'Give him a break,' Merlin said.

'Bugger off,' PeeDee retorted angrily.

'Everybody knows your sister's not backwards in coming forwards,' Merlin said.

I felt it was my duty to defend Oz because he was one of my gang.

'No offence, PeeDee, but if she does know something it might help us. The sooner this is cleared up the sooner the olds will lift the curfew.'

PeeDee relaxed and Oz pushed him off.

'I think you should redouble your watch at dusk,' I suggested to PeeDee. 'Tell your Mum you're just going to pop round to see Chris and then hide and watch what's going on. And I'll keep watch at my place. You never know, he might come again.'

'You mean we could be like private detectives?' PeeDee suggested. 'And Chris and Merlin can do the same – that way we could cover quite a large area.'

He seemed quite taken with the idea and all of a sudden we were back on the trail of the Prowler.

'If we solve it before Plod, he'll be dead miffed,' Pud said.

We were united in the hope that we could get one over PC Norris. It wasn't that we had any particular reason but he represented 'authority' and we were the rebels. It was our bounden duty to beat him at his own game.

PeeDee's news had fired us all up and we wanted to do something. For a moment the gangs were forgotten and PeeDee took Chris, Beaky and Merlin off to see where they could keep watch. Tod and Monkey rode off on their bikes, and Oz and Goat set off up the shops. That left Pud, Roller and me. We looked at each other, not quite sure what to do. Roller said he couldn't really spare the time because his mother was dead ratty and hadn't liked him coming out in the first place. I think it was an excuse because he didn't like the idea of being stuck with me and Pud.

'Why don't you go back home,' I said, 'and see if your Mum's caught up with the gossip? She might have heard something that we don't know about.'

Roller looked relieved and set off.

'See you, Ten,' Pud said as he rode off after Roller leaving me on my own.

I made my way home, the long way round. As I walked up the road my head was buzzing with new ideas. It looked as if the hunt for the Prowler might just turn into the best thing that had happened all the holiday. I mean, he was a live person and we were going to catch him. It wasn't like a game where we were pretending to be bank robbers or policemen – this was the real thing. I didn't think the Prowler could be really dangerous because he'd been seen twice now and nobody had been hurt. I stopped for a moment, trying to remember what the Vicar had said on Sunday. I grinned as the words came back to me. We'd prayed that 'all women and children might be kept safe and protected from the ravages of the Prowler.' I still wasn't quite sure what 'the ravages' meant but I knew that the Vikings had ravaged the English women so I supposed it was quite serious. On the other hand, if he was into ravaging women he wouldn't worry about us kids.

As I turned the corner I saw the Misses March walking back from the shops. Blast! I'd missed out today. All the same, I ran to catch them up and offered to carry their bags for them.

'We haven't got any cake today,' Miss Eileen said.

'I'm not worried about cake,' I said, trying not to sound disappointed. 'I like helping you. They still haven't caught the Prowler yet. It doesn't hurt to be careful.'

'I don't think the Prowler, whoever he is, will be very interested in two old ladies,' Miss Barbara said.

'I'll come, all the same,' I said.

Miss Eileen handed me her bag but Miss Barbara, who was

much more independent, kept hold of hers. As we passed my house I looked in down the drive but there was no sign of activity. I wondered if Cath had got up yet. It must be quite late by now because my stomach was beginning to rumble. When we reached the house where the Misses March lived I was ready to go, but Miss Eileen asked me to come in.

'Mr Hardcastle's coming to cut the grass this afternoon,' she said. 'Perhaps you could unlock the shed ready for him. It will save us having to go down the garden.'

'Don't be so feeble, Eileen,' Miss Barbara said. 'We're not in our dotage yet!'

'But you are always saying the padlock's difficult to undo.' She turned to me. 'It's a bit rusty and the key sticks. Last time Barbara cut her finger trying to take the key out.'

'I'll put some oil on it,' I said. 'That usually helps. The bolts on our garage door get rusty and that's what Dad does.'

When I'd put Miss Eileen's bag on the kitchen table they gave me the shed key. Miss Eileen told me to be careful not to hurt myself. I went down and, sure enough, the padlock was rusty and the key was stiff but it turned without too much trouble. Once I was in the shed I had a good look around. It was like an Aladdin's cave, full of interesting things. It was very neat and tidy, quite unlike our shed. The garden tools were hung along one side and there was an old push mower at the far end. It looked in good condition so I redoubled my efforts to find some oil. I opened the door of the cupboard next to the mower and found all sorts of cans and tins. I couldn't see any oil but there was a tin of grease so I pushed the key into it and then worked the key in and out of the padlock. By the time I'd finished it was working much more easily so I took it back up with me to the kitchen. They were impressed.

'We'll know who to ask next time we need a job doing,' Miss Eileen said.

'I'm sorry we haven't got any cake today,' Miss Barbara said, 'but we can offer you a glass of orange squash.'

I thanked them and said it was late, anyway, and I ought to be getting back home. Mum had done hard–boiled eggs for dinner and we had a salad. She'd got a lettuce from Mr Looker who lived next door. Gardening was his passion and he had two big greenhouses where he grew tomatoes. His real interest was in growing show dahlias and he had rows and rows of them in his garden. He started them off in his greenhouses in the winter and then when he'd planted them out he grew tomatoes in their place. It wasn't all he grew because he had rows of runner beans as well, which he said were to keep the wind from damaging his dahlias. I didn't take much notice of him, but it did mean that we had a good supply of vegetables throughout the summer and sometimes he let me pick the tomatoes and beans.

Mum was a bit odd after lunch. I wondered if Cath had been getting to her, and she wasn't keen on my going out.

'You've got choir practice tonight,' she said. 'I don't want you running wild again and coming back filthy. I thought we might take the bus down to Waterlooville. There's some things I want from Gauntlet's dairy.'

I made a face but when she spoke in that tone of voice I knew there was no chance of my escaping. At least I'd see Chris at choir and Bunny might have some more news.

Chapter 11

I woke up Thursday morning with the feeling that this was going to be the day we'd catch the Prowler. After yesterday I was sure that PeeDee and his lot would have news about him. I'd asked Bunny last night at choir practice but he said he hadn't heard anything more. Mr Norman wasn't prepared to talk about the Prowler, either. He just told us to take care when we went home and stay together. But we were approaching the halfway point in the holidays and we needed to do something to put some real excitement back in our lives. It was down to me and I wanted to get started on the rafts.

But putting excitement into my life had to wait until after lunch because Mum had decided that we'd all go shopping this morning. She announced this when she came into my room to get me up for breakfast.

'And Cath's coming, too,' she said. 'I saw some nice things in Wadham's yesterday that will be just right for her.'

'Do I have to come?' I asked.

'Of course,' she said as if amazed that I didn't want to go. 'We might find something for you, too.'

'I don't need anything,' I protested.

'Well I think you do. You need something more suitable for you now you're getting older. You can't run around like an urchin for the rest of your life.'

She went to get Cath up, pulling the door to after her. The rest of my life, I thought – I'd be happy to remain an urchin for the next few weeks. There were times, I thought, when she was really so un–cool!

The morning was wasted and I sulked round the shops. I managed to escape for a bit while I went to the bookshop. They ran a private library and you could take books out for 1d a week. And, to add insult to injury, we missed the bus and Mum decided that it would be nice to walk home.

'It's such a lovely day,' she said, 'and we've got nothing else to do.'

It was all right for her, I thought. She might have nothing else to do but I had plenty I wanted to get on with. The only good thing about walking home was that Cath had to walk as well and she was dead narked about it.

'Why don't we walk on to the next stop,' she said, 'and then we could catch the bus from there?'

'What's the point? If we're going to walk let's just enjoy it!'

Mum might have enjoyed herself, but the only reason I enjoyed the walk home was that Cath hated it. Every step of the way! I kept pointing out things for her to look at and she had to be polite because Mum was clearly in a good mood. We stopped outside Foden's Garage because Cath had got a stone in her shoe. When I was little I was always frightened of Foden's because it looked so big and seemed so dark when you looked in.

Once, a long time ago, we had been walking past when the siren went off. The siren had been used in the war to warn people to take cover in their shelters because of an air raid but after the war it was only used to summon the firemen for a callout. As soon as they heard the siren they stopped what they were doing and came, on foot, by bicycle or any other way they could. The noise of the siren was deafening and it had scared me so much that I cried and hid my face in Mum's coat.

'Just think,' Mum said, 'if the trams were still running we could have caught one at the end of our road.'

They used to keep the trams that ran between Horndean and Portsmouth in Fodens's Garage. That's why it was so big and tall. But the trams had stopped and now Foden's garage housed the fire engine and was used to work on agricultural vehicles. I'd seen a traction engine in there not so long ago. It was getting up steam and its chimney was belching black smoke.

'We caught the bus at the end of our road,' Cath said pointedly, 'and we could have caught one back again!'

'Is it true they stored torpedoes here during the war?' I asked.

'They certainly did,' Mum said. 'And the Canadians stored more stuff in the Queen's Inclosure. They say there's still some left. That's why it's closed to the public because they still don't know where it all is.'

'Perhaps you could go and do some exploring,' Cath said to me.

'I'm sure if anyone could find a bomb you could!'

'Don't you dare,' Mum said.

Clearly she thought I might! The woods they called the Queen's Inclosure were too dark and menacing. I knew some of the older kids went in there to have a smoke but anyway, the woods at the end of Padnell Road were my stamping ground. We resumed our walk in silence. Cath's dark mood was beginning to depress me and I didn't want to make a fuss in the village where I might see people I knew. It would be too un–cool to be seen bickering with Cath in public.

I went in search of my lot after lunch. I could see PeeDee playing football on the green out the back. I didn't really want to go and crash his game and anyway, I was rubbish at football. Cath was sitting in the back garden doing embroidery – that gives you some idea how bored she was.

Sometimes, when I looked at her, I found it hard to believe she was my sister. Take today, for instance. She was sitting in the shade of the apple tree wearing a gingham dress with a smocking panel at the front. All her friends were with it and wore jeans but Cath always dressed like a little old lady. And her hair! I ask you, instead of having a bob she had it long and pulled back into a pony tail. It might have looked better if she hadn't got it tied with a matching gingham ribbon.

I contemplated going indoors and practising my scales, that's how fed up I was. I didn't mind piano lessons but I'd never heard any proper pianist playing scales so I didn't see the point in them. All I wanted to be able to do was to bash out tunes like the bloke in Monkey's pub. I'd already managed the beginning of Rock around the Clock but I couldn't work out the bass. It was a pity Cath was outside or I would have had a go at the piano. It always annoyed her. She was into Elvis, her only concession to being up to date, but I thought his stuff was soppy. Although I liked the way he wiggled his hips. It had taken me two days to work out how he did it. I showed Mum but she just told me to behave myself. Sometimes I just don't understand her, either. I liked Lonnie Donegan but I couldn't find the right notes for Rock Island Line at all. It never sounded right. I whistled the beginning but Cath didn't rise, it was too hot.

Pud turned up. Not before time, I thought. I tried to be off hand – I didn't want him to think I had nothing better to do than hang out with him.

'It's dead quiet out there,' he said, jerking his head over his shoulder.

'We'd better goof off and liven it up,' I said. 'Hang on and I'll get my bike.'

Cath had a moan as I took it out of the shed.

'I don't think you should do that until Mum gets back,' she said.

'She won't be long. She's only gone round to see Mrs Carter.'

'What difference will that make?'

'She'll be cross if she thinks I let you go out.'

'You're not letting me out,' I said. 'I'm going out because I want to.'

She looked cross. She knew she couldn't stop me.

'I'm going up the dirt–track with Pud,' I told her. 'If Mum wants to know, you can tell her.'

We pushed off before she had time to say anything more. It had turned into another of those sticky afternoons when you could almost feel the air. I guessed we were going to have another thunder storm later but the sky was still clear blue at the moment. We cycled up the middle of the road – it was that deserted. Pud went up on the pavement and then down, back on to the road, weaving a drunken pattern as we came towards the church. I balanced without any hands on the handlebar and then nearly fell off as my front wheel hit a stone.

The road was always stony as you came to the end of the made–up bit. We dodged on to the other side of the ditch and rode along in front of the garden fences. We pulled off the road and went into the recreation ground to see if there was anyone there. It was deserted.

'Where is everyone?' Pud asked.

'Perhaps they've got the plague,' I suggested.

That gave me an idea for a game and I was thinking about how we could have a plague as we came into the woods. PeeDee's lot could mutate into monsters instead of dying. We stopped for a moment and I started to explain my idea to Pud.

'It could be a deadly ray from space,' I suggested. 'It's zapped all the village and people are laying dead in their houses.'

'How did we escape?' Pud asked, ever practical. He had no imagination.

'We're superior beings. The future of the world rests with us,' I told him, warming to my theme. 'And with our superior intelligence we'll discover a secret potion to make us immune.'

I was really getting into it now and the more I talked the more I thought that this could turn into one of our better games – not that it was likely to be better than the bank raid.

'Can't you smell the rotting corpses?' I asked him.

'All I can smell is pigs,' Pud said, rather prosaically.

It was true, the pigs were a bit smelly today. Perhaps it was the heat. When the pigs became too hot they smelled particularly unpleasant. The cows weren't so bad – cow pats dry in the sun but pig manure just goes on smelling worse and worse. Dad said that when the wind was from the east you could smell the farm. There wasn't any wind today so it couldn't have been that, so I guessed that the pig pong must have been caught in the still air and was wafting down the road under the trees.

'We'll go and check them out later, after we've neutralised the space ray.'

Pud looked at me as if I'd gone totally stark raving mad. Like I said, he had no imagination and unless you told him exactly what to do he just stood and stared blankly.

'We've got x–ray zappers on our handlebars,' I told him, ringing my bell to make the point, 'and we can fire them as we ride so that we're not sitting targets.'

I rode off up the road. Pud followed, ringing his bell like a lunatic.

I turned towards the dirt track and nearly came off my bike as I bounced over the ditch but at the last moment I managed to pull the handlebars straight and pushed down hard on the pedals to get over the first hump on the dirt track. I was back in control and everything seemed to be going well as I freewheeled down the other side of the hump, ducking under the low branch of the tree. As the track bottomed out I gathered speed and started to pedal up the second hump. I made it to the top without any problem but I think I must have been a bit too enthusiastic because my wheels left the ground as I crested the rise and I flew off the top.

It's a great feeling, flying on your bicycle, but you know that the difficult bit is staying on when you hit the ground.

If you turn your handlebars, even just a fraction, and your front wheel is a bit askew when you land, it usually means that the whole bike skids and the chances are you'll fall off. I made a perfect landing and was feeling dead chuffed when my front wheel hit a fallen branch, the back of the bike slewed round and I came off. I had the sense to let go of the bike and landed in the bushes. My feet hit the ground just before the rest of me and I fell backwards. The bushes helped and the ground was strangely spongy. How I avoided cracking my head open I'll never know but there I was, slightly dazed and spread-eagled in the bushes.

I lay there a moment wondering if I'd broken anything and then I opened my eyes. As I rolled over I looked straight into a pair of eyes staring at me. I'm not easily scared but I can tell you those eyes put the wind up me and I yelled before I had a chance to get a hold of myself. Pud dumped his bike and came running. The eyes were still staring, unblinking, looking directly at me. For a moment I didn't know if I was awake or unconscious. I think I must have been in shock. Why didn't the man move out of the way when he saw me flying towards him? And why hadn't he said anything when I landed on top of him? Pud was standing on the top of the hump looking at me and I wondered why he didn't offer to help me up. Somehow I managed to turn and get my feet on the ground. I knelt up. I think I must have scraped my knee because it hurt like hell, but I didn't have time to worry about that because the bloke was still staring at me.

It was then that I worked out that he was dead.

My mind was still partly on the game I was planning and for a moment finding a corpse seemed quite natural, even though it had scared the hell out of me. I backed away as I realised this was real, not part of a game. I turned and looked at Pud. He'd gone white as a sheet and looked as if he was going to puke at any moment.

'Is he all right?' he asked nervously.

'Hardly. I think he's dead!'

'Did you hit him that hard?'

For someone who could play chess, Pud was incredibly stupid at times.

'He was already dead,' I said.

I bent and looked at the man. I'd never seen a dead person before. His skin was very pale and his hair was all messed up. I poked him with my toe. He felt hard. He rolled a bit and I could see that he had a gash on the back of his head and where his blood had seeped into the ground there was a red stain on the earth.

'I think he might have been murdered,' I said, backing away.

'Do you think he's the Prowler?' Pud asked. 'Perhaps PeeDee's Dad caught him.'

'I think we should tell someone.'

'Who?'

'I don't know. The police will have to know. You stay here and I'll cycle home and tell Mum. She'll know what to do.'

'I don't want to stay on my own.'

'He won't hurt you. He's dead.'

'Perhaps the bloke who killed him is still here.'

I hadn't thought of that and I looked around. Pud had put his finger on what I felt but hadn't realised – the murderer was probably watching us at this very moment.

'Come on, then, we'll both go.'

Pud didn't need telling again. He was on his bike before I'd picked mine up. And he didn't go back along the dirt track. He was so scared that he went the 'girlie' way. For once I gave in and followed him. We pedalled like mad and we seemed to reach home in record time. I found Mum in the kitchen.

'You've got to call the police,' I said. 'We've found a body in the woods. He's dead. His head's all bashed in.'

She looked at me as if I'd gone mad.

'If this is another one of your silly games,' she began.

'It's true,' Pud said. 'I was there. I saw him, too.'

I was miffed that Mum believed Pud when she didn't seem to believe me.

'Wait here,' she said. 'I'll go and get some money for the telephone. We'll have to call the police.'

She went upstairs and Pud looked at me. He seemed to have got over his shock and he grinned.

'I said it was dead quiet out there today,' he said.

Suddenly I began to feel a bit strange. I think it had only just sunk in that I'd landed on top of a dead body. I went to the cupboard and pinched a lump of sugar.

'I need the energy,' I said when Pud raised his eyebrows. 'It's good for shock. D' you want one?'

Pud took a lump and sucked on it. He heard Mum coming downstairs and popped the sugar lump into his mouth.

'Come on you two,' Mum said. 'We'll have to go down to the call box.'

'Aren't you going to dial 999?' Pud asked. 'You don't need money for that.'

'I know that,' Mum said irritably, 'but I'll have to call Dad's work to let him know what you two have been up to.'

Cath had gone out so Mum locked up and we pushed our bikes down the road with her. It seemed ages before she got through and then she explained that I'd found a dead body in the woods. The police asked to speak to me.

'Are you sure he was dead?' they asked.

'His eyes were open and he didn't close them,' I told the sergeant. 'And his head's been bashed. There's blood on the ground. And his face is white,' I added.

I know my information wasn't very well presented but I wanted to tell him everything I remembered and it all kind of tumbled out. He told us to wait at our house and he would send the constable round. Mum telephoned Dad and then we went back home and waited.

It seemed like hours before PC Norris came.

'If this is one of your jokes,' he said, 'I'll be very cross. Wasting police time is a serious offence.'

Of course, Mum had to come, too. We made a curious procession. I went in front with Pud and PC Norris, we were all wheeling our bikes, and Mum came along behind. PC Norris looked flustered and his face was very red. He must have been suffocating in all his uniform, even his jacket was buttoned right up. As we went further, he dropped back and chatted to Mum.

'Never heard of anything like this,' I heard him say. 'Not in Cowplain. I get the odd bloke who's had a bit too much to drink and we get some petty theft but we've never had anything big like this.'

'I remember when Mr Sylvester blew his brains out,' Mum said. I pricked my ears up. I didn't know anything about that.

'He was a miserable old codger,' PC Norris said. 'Didn't want to live so he did the best thing, I reckon. It was all his doing. No one else was involved.'

We'd reached the end of the houses now.

'He's just up here,' I said. 'Just off the road.'

We began to walk a bit faster and then we turned off the road. Pud and I pushed our bikes over the ditch but PC Norris left his by the edge of the road. Mum looked at the ditch and offered to watch his bike.

'It'll be all right,' he said. 'I think you ought to come. Just as a witness.'

Mum stepped down into the ditch and scrambled up the bank.

'There's an easier way in,' I said as she looked about to slide down. 'Pud'll show you.'

I led PC Norris over the two humps and showed him where I came off.

'My front wheel hit a branch,' I said, 'and I came off here,' I told him proudly. 'And I landed there.' I pointed to where I'd landed. 'He's in there, under the bushes.'

Chapter 12

I dumped my bike on the track. PC Norris and I walked up to the bushes. Pud and Mum had arrived and she was fussing about.

'Do be careful,' she said.

'He's dead,' I said. 'He's not likely to jump up and hit me. Not with that hole in his head!'

Mum gasped and looked away.

'Don't worry Mrs Thomas, I'm here,' PC Norris said.

All the same, he pulled out his truncheon as we walked over to the bushes. I pointed to where I'd landed and he carefully stepped off the path and into the bushes.

The bloke was still there. Well, it wasn't very likely that he'd have moved on account of his being rather dead! There was a cloud of flies on the blood on the ground and some were crawling over his face. PC Norris bent down and put his fingers on the man's neck.

'Just checking for a pulse,' he told me. 'I have to be sure.'

I thought it wasn't very likely that the bloke would be lying there with his eyes wide open and flies crawling all over his face if he was still alive. Still, I made a mental note of what he'd done. This was going to be a game like none other and I wanted to be sure that I knew all the proper police procedures.

PC Norris stepped back on to the path and wrote in his notebook.

'Right,' he said. 'The man's certainly dead and it looks like murder. There's nothing there he could have hit his head on, even if he had slipped. I'll have to report this in to my sergeant.'

'Are you going to leave him there?' Mum squawked.

'He's not likely to move,' PC Norris said.

'I could go and call,' Mum offered. 'I don't like to think that other innocent children might trip over a dead body.'

I liked the bit about 'innocent children' even if it was a strange thing to say. I suppose it was a roundabout compliment. She didn't usually fuss over me and I thought it was funny that she called me innocent.

'That would be very kind of you,' PC Norris said.

He took a page from the back of his book and wrote a name on it and a series of letters and numbers.

'Ask for Sergeant Marks and give him this reference. Tell him I think we need the murder squad out here as soon as possible. He'll know what to do. Tell him I'm guarding the corpse.'

Mum turned to go.

'Come along,' she said to me. 'I think you've done enough for one day.'

I began to protest.

'He'll need me as a witness,' I said.

'We will, indeed,' PC Norris said. 'And I'm sure the sergeant will interview you. He'll probably collect you in the squad car and bring you up here to check the details. Like your Mum says, it might be a good idea if you wait at home.'

'It'll give you time to have a wash and change into something clean,' Mum said.

'It might be best to keep the same clothes on,' PC Norris said. 'Just until after the sergeant's finished. He'll want to see everything just as it was.'

Reluctantly I followed Mum as she made her way back to the road. Pud came, too, and we rode our bikes back to my house. When Mum eventually got back she told us to stay there.

'I'm just going to phone the police,' she said, 'and then I'll be right back. You can have a biscuit if you want.' She turned to go and then turned back. 'Make sure you wash your hands.' She shuddered. 'You've been touching a dead body.'

I don't know what she expected us to catch, particularly since the bloke had died from a hole in his head. All the same, we did wash our hands. It was all beginning to feel a bit creepy now.

'Do you think he's the Prowler?' Pud asked.

'Don't know. If he isn't, the Prowler might have killed him.'

'I hadn't thought of that.' Pud said, spitting biscuit crumbs as he spoke. 'It might really be dangerous out there.'

I began to think and it didn't take me long to work out that Mum wouldn't let me out of her sight now. I might be imprisoned for days, for the rest of the holidays even. This needed some serious planning.

'We've got to let the others know,' I said.

'I can't go 'til we've seen the sergeant,' Pud said. 'He might want to speak to me. I'll have to corroborate your story in case he thinks you killed him.'

'Me?' I squawked.

'They might think you were careless and rode your bike without due care and attention, and in your thoughtless haste you ran him down and he hit his head and died from the wound you maliciously and heartlessly inflicted on him.'

That was a long sentence for Pud and he was clearly proud of it.

'Rubbish!' I said. 'You know he was dead before I landed on top of him.'

'Exactly, my dear Watson. That's why you need me. I'm your alibi!'

My mind was buzzing, now. As well as the murder and the detective work we could have a trial – what a game this would be!

'Remember all the posh phrases,' I said. 'We'll need them for the trial.'

'I don't think they'll take you to court,' Pud said. 'You're too young.'

'For our game, stupid! Anyway, if I'd murdered him I wouldn't have told Mum to call the police, would I, blockhead?'

'I can cycle round and tell the others after we've seen the sergeant.'

'Wait here,' I said. 'I'm going down the garden to see if PeeDee's still playing football.'

I ran down and climbed up the tree in the hedge. The field was empty. Since I had no other plan they'd just have to wait until the police had finished with us and Pud could ride round.

Mum came back and made us sit in the lounge. I could see she was agitated.

'You could at least wash your face,' she said to me.

'I don't think I should,' I said. 'They might want to take pictures. I might even have his blood on me!'

She looked horrified and made me fetch a newspaper to sit on.

'I don't think you realise how serious this is,' she said primly. 'It's not a joke.'

'I'm the one who landed on a dead body,' I said. 'I can't think of anything more serious than that.'

She carried on fussing over Pud. I think she was more worried about him than me. She even gave him another biscuit. He was beginning to enjoy himself and he poked his tongue out at me when she wasn't looking.

'I hope my Mum won't be too upset,' he said with an angelic smile.

My Mum stopped in her tracks. She hadn't thought about that.

'I expect you'll be quite famous,' Pud went on. 'It's not every family that has a murderer!'

'I'm not a murderer,' I retorted. 'No one suspects me. Or you! We're just helping the police with their enquiries.'

'We're the star witnesses!'

I think you two should stop talking about it now,' Mum said.

We were beginning to get to her.

'But we've got to make sure we've got the same story, Mrs Thomas,' Pud said winking at me. He could see how Mum was beginning to lose it. 'I mean, if we get our stories wrong they may send us away to Borstal.'

Unfortunately we didn't have time to wind her up any more because we heard a knock on the front door. Mum went and opened it. We could hear her speaking to a man. A moment later she showed him through to where we were. He looked at us and all of a sudden everything began to look more serious.

'They're young, Mrs Thomas,' he said. 'Are they all right?'

It was the first time that anyone had asked if I was all right. Not even Mum had asked when we first got home.

'I'm fine,' I said. 'It's not the first time I've come off my bike,' I added with some pride.

'But it's the first time you've landed on a dead body,' he said with a twinkle in his eye.

I liked him instantly. Perhaps he's not so frightening after all, I thought. He asked Mum to tell him what she knew and then he turned back to us.

'I think we need to look at the scene,' he said, 'and then I'll have to ask you some questions. I'll write it all down and you and your Mum will have to sign it to say that what I've written down is what you said. Do you understand? There's nothing to be frightened about.'

I nodded and Pud swallowed hard. I heard his gulp, halfway between a swallow and a burp.

'Right, let's go,' the sergeant said. 'We'll go in my car.'

There was a shiny, black police car parked outside our gate.

'Can you ring the bell and flash the lights,' I asked.

He looked rather straight at me and I thought I'd gone a bit too far. I was going to say it was only a suggestion but he spoke before I had the chance.

'I don't see why not,' he said, smiling. 'After all, it is a murder enquiry and you are very important.'

'Cool!'

Mum went quite pale and I could almost hear her asking what the neighbours would think if we were 'arrested' and driven away in a police car with flashing lights! I wondered if I could make a dash for it as soon as we were outside so that they could chase after me. Perhaps they'd handcuff me! As it turned out I didn't have the chance because the sergeant chatted to me all the way out to the car, asking me how often we played in the woods and how many other people we saw there. I told him that we played there most days when we weren't playing out the back on the green, and that we seldom saw anyone.

'And you're in the church choir, too?' he asked me.

I said I was and wondered how he knew that.

'Your Mum told me,' he said as if he had read my thoughts. 'She wanted me to know you would be a reliable witness.'

More like she was trying to get me off, I thought, just in case he believed I'd done it. Mum, Pud and I sat in the back and the sergeant told the constable to put the bells and lights on. It only took us a couple of minutes to get to the woods but it was worth it. The Vicar was walking down the road and I saw him stop when he heard the bells and saw the car. And when he saw us sitting in the back I thought he was going to drop to his knees and pray for us – his face was a picture!

PC Norris was waiting for us at the road edge in the woods.

'I'd like you to imagine that you're on your bike,' the sergeant said, 'and do exactly what you did earlier.'

I led the way and he followed. I told him how you had to be careful not to scalp yourself on the low branch and how you had to judge your speed just right up the second hump. He seemed quite impressed.

'And so you managed all that and everything was fine until your front wheel hit a branch?' he said.

I nodded.

'Are there often branches like that on the ground?' he asked.

I hadn't thought about that. At the time I was so surprised that I'd fallen off, and then there was the dead man, so I hadn't had time to think about the branch.

'I don't think so,' I said. 'If we come off it's usually because we've got our speed wrong or because we twist the handlebars.'

'Would you recognise the branch?' he asked.

'I don't know,' I answered. 'But it must have been quite big if it threw me off.'

'Let's look for the branch,' he suggested. 'But don't touch anything. It might have been used to hit the man and it might be important.'

I was impressed once more. He was good, this sergeant. He knew what he was doing. I wished I'd have thought about it a bit more before we called the cops. We might even have found the branch or some other murder weapon.

We walked down the other side of the second hump and I showed him where I'd hit the branch. There were several other branches on the ground and he made the constable pick them all up and check them for blood stains. He put them in a pile and then we went on to the body.

'Now, I know you didn't have time to see him before you landed on him,' the sergeant said, 'but can you remember if the body was hidden or if it was just lying there?'

I thought for a moment or two, trying to remember exactly what had happened in the split second after my wheel hit the branch.

'My wheel hit the branch,' I said, 'and I knew I was falling off so I let go of the bike. If you hang on it usually lands on top of you and it hurts. I remember going through the air and landing on the bushes. He must have been partially hidden because I felt the bushes first then my feet touched something soft and spongy and then I landed on my bum,' I saw Mum wince, 'on my bottom, and I only just kept my head off the ground. I was shaken and I think my eyes must have been shut because I remember opening them and seeing him looking at me.'

I paused, trying to remember exactly how it had been.

'I must have shut my eyes again. I think I was still a bit shaken up and I was only too glad I hadn't hit my head. When I opened my eyes again he was still looking at me. I turned over and knelt up.' I looked at my knee. 'I must have scraped my knee at some point because I remember it hurt. I saw he was still staring at me and I realised he was dead. He hadn't moved at all. And when I got up I could see the blood under his head and the bit where he'd been hit.'

'And you didn't touch him? He asked.

'I poked him with my toe, just to make sure he was dead, but I didn't move him or touch him with my hand.'

He seemed satisfied with what I'd told him and he said I could go and stand with Mum while he inspected the body. It was beginning to get busy now. The next person who arrived was the doctor.

Doctor Maclean was our family doctor and we knew him quite well.

'So, what have you been up to?' he asked me as he came up.

I saw he had his bag with him.

'Nothing,' I said. 'We just found a dead body.'

The doctor went up to Sergeant Marks and they spoke for a moment or two and then the doctor went across to the body. I watched as he felt for a pulse at the man's neck and then he lifted one of his arms before he rolled him over to look at the man's head. He stood up.

'He's certainly dead,' Doctor Maclean said. 'And by the look of the ground and the wound on his head I'd say he'd been hit with something heavy and blunt. It may have killed him or he may have bled to death from the wound while he was unconscious. Judging by the state of the rigour I'd guess he was killed some time last night. Definitely no later than early this morning.'

The doctor lit his pipe and puffed clouds of smoke for a moment or two.

'So you think it's safe for us to move the body once we've done our work?'

'I can't see why not, sergeant. We'll know more after the post mortem, of course, but I don't think there can be much doubt. Is that all you want from me?'

'Yes, thank you doctor. I know you were on your rounds so I won't keep you.'

The sergeant turned to PC Norris.

'I'll have to radio for the CID,' he said. 'Make sure no one touches anything and don't let anyone near.'

It seemed an age before the next car arrived. Mum was getting more and more agitated. At last she couldn't keep still any more and she got up and went to find the sergeant. We could hear her talking to him on the other side of the hump.

'It won't be long,' I heard Sergeant Marks tell her. 'I really think it's best if you wait until the Detective Inspector gets here. I'm sure he won't keep you, but he'll want to see the kids here before we take their statements.'

When he arrived the Inspector had a team with him. One of the policemen took photographs with a big camera that had a flash gun, and another took over from PC Norris who was standing guard over the body. I couldn't really see why that was necessary because the bloke was dead. He wasn't going to run away. And if anyone had wanted the dead man they wouldn't have dumped him in the bushes in the first place. I suppose it was all part of the police procedure – what they call keeping the crime scene safe. Another of the policemen started looking through the bushes. He was a lot more thorough than PC Norris had been.

Inspector Johnson introduced himself.

'I know you've already told the constable and the sergeant what happened but I need you to tell me now. Try and remember exactly what happened.'

I went through it all again, right up to the time when Pud saw me and the dead body. He asked me more questions, just like Sergeant Marks had done. He was particularly anxious to know if we'd ever seen anyone hanging about in the woods, but we were both able to say with complete honesty that we seldom saw anyone. After all, that's why we liked playing there.

Another couple of men arrived – they looked like ambulance men because they wore a different sort of uniform, not like the police ones. They brought a stretcher and lifted the man on to it, covered him with a grey blanket and took him away. Inspector Johnson detailed one of his constables to go with the body.

Everything seemed to be happening a bit faster now. The Inspector told Mum that she could go home if she wanted. He told his driver to take us back in the police car.

'Don't go anywhere,' he said, 'because I must take a statement from you. The constable will stay with you until I arrive.'

When we got home Cath was outside. She didn't have a door key and when she saw a police car bringing me home with Mum I saw a positive gleam of satisfaction on her face.

'What's it been up to this time?' she asked as soon as Mum was on the drive.

'I'm the major witness in a murder crime,' I told her rather smugly.

That wiped the smile off her face.

'That's right, Miss,' the constable said. 'And we've got to make sure that these two come to no harm,' he added, pointing to Pud and me.

'Be a love, Cath,' Mum said, 'and nip round to John's Mum and ask her to come round for a bit. Don't tell her why. Just say I need her to come right away.'

Chapter 13

The Inspector finally came back and explained to Pud's Mum that he needed each of us to tell him exactly what had happened. She didn't believe him when he told her that we weren't in trouble and he had a bit of a job calming her down. Eventually he asked Cath to make us all a cup of tea and that seemed to work. Then Mum and I had to go with him into the lounge while Pud and his Mum stayed in the breakfast room.

'I want you to tell me exactly what happened,' he said. 'Use your own words and I'll write down what you tell me.'

This was the fourth time I'd done it now and I think I made quite a good job of it. He asked me some more questions and after he'd finished writing down my answers I had to read what he had written. Then Mum and I had to sign both pages of the statement. He signed them underneath our signatures and added the date and time.

Then it was Pud's turn, and he and his Mum went into the lounge to make their statements. It was quite late when he'd finished and soon after that Dad came home. Cath was jumping up and down with frustration by now because I wouldn't tell her what had happened. I think she still thought I was in trouble.

The Inspector left when Dad came in and he said now he'd got our statements, I could tell them all what had happened. Pud and his Mum went home, too. Well, after all my practice I did a really good job. Cath even turned green when I described what it was like when I landed on the dead body and saw his eyes staring at me.

'Do you realise,' I said, looking at Cath, 'that if I'd have been a bit heavier, he might have popped when I landed on him. His eyes might have shot out like corks from a bottle.'

I realised I might have gone a bit too far when Mum said I ought to go and have a bath.

'And I'll come and wash your hair with my nice shampoo.'

She must have really been spooked because she didn't let Cath use her shampoo, not even on special occasions.

We had a late tea and Mum opened a tin of spam and we had

baked beans, too. She said after all our ordeals we needed something to cheer us up. I would have asked what Cath had done but I suppose making the tea for the Inspector had been her part, and since I had kept her waiting to find out what had happened she had probably suffered more than any of us, so I kept quiet.

We had a thunder storm that night but it was weird. There was no rain, just lightning and thunder. I must have been dreaming and I woke up with the first crash. I felt the noise in my head and I put my hand up to check that I hadn't been hit. I expected to feel a gaping hole and sticky blood, just like the bloke I found in the woods. My heart was thumping away but I didn't have time to do anything because a flash of lightning ripped through the air. It must have been close because I hadn't even started counting when the thunder shook the house.

I leapt out of bed and pulled the curtains back. The lightning was making patterns in the sky. In the dark it looked as if the heavens had split apart and light was coming in through the cracks. I heard Dad moving about. He went into Cath's room. A bit later he came into mine.

'I might have guessed you'd be out of bed watching it,' he said. 'Cath's got her head under the sheets.'

'I bet she's snivelling,' I said. 'She's a cry baby.'

'She doesn't like thunder, that's all. Are you all right?' he asked.

'You bet! I thought I'd been hit when the first one went off.' Another crash shook the house and the horizon was bright with sheet lightning. 'I thought it always rained with thunder.'

'Not always,' Dad said. 'It's safer when it does but it's not the rain that makes the thunder – it's the clouds and the air currents.'

We watched for a bit and the storm began to move away. The flashes were getting further apart and there were longer gaps between the flashes and the crashes.

'You ought to get back into bed,' Dad said. 'And I'll go and see if I can calm your sister down. Are you sure you're all right? You're not having bad dreams?'

'What about?'

'About this afternoon.'

'Oh, that,' I said, trying to sound casual. 'No, I'm fine. It'll take more than one dead body to worry me.'

All the same, I was glad he'd come. I didn't tell him the thunder had woken me up from a bad dream.

'I'll bring you up a cup of tea in a minute.'

Next morning Dad stayed home. His work had given him what they called compassionate leave so that he could be with me. Cath was pale and looked dreadful but that was nothing new – I thought she always looked dreadful. Her eyes were puffy and had black rings round them. I suppose it was from where she'd been crying through the thunder. Mum was tight-lipped. I don't think she was happy at all. But I was cheerful. Well, I was until Mum said I couldn't go out.

'Why not?' I asked.

'There's a murderer out there, and now he knows the body's been found he'll be angry. I don't want you to be his next victim.'

'It might not have been a man,' I suggested. 'It could have been a woman.'

'You're not going out and that's an end to it!' she snapped.

I reckoned that if Mum had lost her cool by nine o'clock I'd better keep out of her way so I asked if I could go out into the garden.

'Check the shed first,' Mum ordered Dad.

I could see Cath was shaking and I began to feel sorry for her. I thought Mum was over the top and she was only making everything worse.

'Nobody knows it was me who found him,' I said.

'Don't be so sure of that,' Mum said. 'Most murders are done by members of the family or people who live near by. I wouldn't be surprised if it wasn't Mr Harris. He's got a terrible temper and if he thought this man was stalking Sandy ... well, I wouldn't like to say what he'd do.'

'If it was PeeDee's Dad,' I said, 'he's hardly likely to murder me.'

Dad finally worked out that it was time for him to do something.

'I'll check the shed if it makes you happy,' he said to Mum, 'but I'm sure we're all quite safe.' He turned to me. 'I think you should stay in because the police might want to speak to you again. It's not a punishment. We're very proud of the grown up way you dealt with it all.'

Trust Dad to talk me round. It had never occurred to me that they were proud of me. I always thought that when Mum said she liked to watch me going into church it was just her way of checking up on me in case I did a runner. I went out with Dad.

'Shouldn't you check first?' Mum said.

'He might need me to give the murderer a good kicking,' I said, ignoring her.

When we were going down the garden Dad talked to me about it all.

'This is serious,' he said. 'You found a dead man and his killer is still out there. I'm worried about you. I'm worried about all of you kids.'

'He won't hurt us if we're together,' I said. 'There're always at least two of us and we always take our bikes.'

'I know you think you're tough,' he said, 'and so you are but you'd be no match for a man who was intent on catching you and hurting you.'

I thought of the way we'd played bank robbers and the way we'd split up. It was true – if someone was lying in wait he could have taken one of us and killed us without the rest of us knowing. I resolved to make sure I always had my penknife with me – you never knew when it might be needed. The shed was empty, of course, and Dad asked if I wanted to kick a football around for a bit. He looked so lonely that I agreed just to give him something to do. We used Cath's deck chair, which was still on the lawn, and the apple tree as goal posts and took turns shooting goals. Dad beat me easily.

'Right,' he said. 'We've got a job to do. The Vicar wants me to paste up a new notice and I need you to help me.'

Because we lived near the main road, and because the church had a notice board on the corner, Dad was in charge of pasting up the notices. Usually we did it just before the main church festivals or if there was going to be a fete. This one was about the holiday ramble. Every year the Vicar took anyone who wanted to go on a ramble through the woods and we had a picnic, played cricket and came back in time for tea. It was quite fun because there was plenty of time for us younger ones to go ahead while the oldies caught up.

The posters were written by a man in the village and he did

them on four huge sheets of paper which Dad had to line up so that it looked as if it was just one huge page. We mixed up the paste in a bucket and I had to keep stirring it until all the lumps were smashed up. Dad fetched the ladder and the long handled brush he used to spread the paste and we loaded it all on to the wheel barrow and set off.

The notice board was on the corner of the road behind a patch of brambles and rough grass and we had to climb over the fence and tread the grass down before we could begin. The poster on the board was about the regular weekly services and it was still stuck quite firmly so we didn't have to peel it off. Dad started pasting the board and I found the top left hand piece. We managed to get it up without any trouble because there was no wind or rain. Sometimes, in the winter when it was cold and raining and if the wind was blowing, it was almost impossible to get the paper straight. And sometimes it tore and if it was raining the rain made the paste even more slippery so the poster wouldn't stay in place.

As soon as he was happy that it was straight he slapped another coat of paste all over it. He said it helped to make sure it was properly stuck. The second piece was always the most difficult because you had to line it up properly and it was at the top of the board. You could put the ladder on the side you weren't using for the first piece but you couldn't do that for the second because the ladder would tear the bit you'd just stuck up so it had to be balanced on the edge. It was not unusual for it to slip and Dad had even fallen off once and torn the poster. He managed okay today. The last two pieces were simple because you could reach them more easily. He tucked them under the top sheets and gave them a good coat of paste.

After we'd done it we crossed the road and looked at our handiwork. It didn't look bad. The lettering was almost straight and it had been done in a bright red with a few trees in each corner just to make it look eye–catching. Dad went into the sweet shop and we chose some sweets as a reward for our efforts.

Just as we were collecting our stuff together to go home Mrs Painter came round the corner. She looked up at the poster.

'You won't catch me letting Jenny go on that,' she said. 'Not while there's a murderer out there.'

News travels fast I thought, wondering how she'd found out.

'I think she'll be perfectly safe,' Dad said. 'There will be a whole lot of us. Plenty of adults to watch the kids.'

Mrs Painter humphed and half turned away as if she was going to go on down to the shops.

'I didn't think you'd be the sort of family that would let their children play with dead men,' she said as she stumped off.

'I wasn't playing with him,' I muttered angrily.

'Let it go,' Dad said. 'Some people will find any excuse just to try and be better than everyone else. If it makes her happy keeping Jenny in then let her do it.'

'You're not going to keep me in, are you?'

'We'll all go on the hike, just like we always do,' Dad said. 'Now, let's get these bits back home and washed up.'

We loaded the paste bucket and the brush back in the wheel barrow and Dad put the ladder on his shoulder.

The rest of the morning was dull as ditch water. I wanted to do something but Mum and Dad wouldn't let me go out so I ended up digging in my hole behind the bonfire. They did their best to cheer me up over lunch but they failed miserably. The long afternoon loomed ahead and I was beginning to feel more and more like a prisoner. I went back to my digging but I'd only just started digging when I heard Dad calling down the garden. I went to see what he wanted.

'Mr Robinson wants to speak to you,' Dad said, indicating a tall man in the hall. 'He's from the Portsmouth Evening News and Sergeant Marks has given him our address because you found the man in the woods.'

'If it would be all right, Sir,' Mr Robinson said, 'I'd like to get a picture in the woods. I've brought my photographer, he's in the car outside.' He turned to me. 'Then I'd like you to tell me the story just as it happened.'

I looked at Dad. He smiled.

'I think that would be all right but I'll need to come as well.'

'Of course, sir, and I'd like you and your wife to be present for the interview.'

Dad and I rode up to the woods in the reporter's car, and I showed him exactly where I'd found the body and the photographer took a photograph. It surprised me how bright the flash was and it went off with quite a loud noise which made me jump.

'You'd better take another one, Alf,' the reporter said, 'just in case.'

I had to point to the bushes where I'd found the body and I had to look at the camera as well.

'Pretend that you're just telling Alf where you found him,' the reporter said.

After that we went home and Mum made them a cup of tea and I had to tell my story yet again. He said the story would be in today's paper because it was hot news. They were holding the front page for it and he was rushing back to file his copy.

Chapter 14

'You're famous,' PeeDee said when his lot came round on Saturday morning.

He was unable to keep the envy out of his voice as he held up a copy of the Evening News and there I was, splashed right across the front page. 'Cowplain Girl Finds Murdered Man' the headline said. And next to the headline there was a picture of me pointing to where I found him in the bushes.

Of course I'd already seen the newspaper but I took it and read it just to make him feel as if he'd brought me the news. Dad had bought one the night before. Well, actually he'd bought seven: one for each of my grandparents, one for his sister, two for Mum's brothers, one to keep and one for me.

'What on earth have you wasted all that money for?' Mum asked him when he got in and showed them to her.

'It's not every day that my little girl is famous,' he said, winking at me.

And it wasn't just Dad. I was going down to the shops on my bike when the two March sisters saw me. They flagged me down outside the paper shop and said all sorts of silly things like how brave I must have been and they asked me if I was scared. They didn't seem to get the point that finding a dead body was the best thing ever.

I handed the paper back to PeeDee.

'Could have been any one of us, PeeDee,' I said, trying to sound modest.

I tried to act as if it was the sort of thing that I did every day. I didn't want to give him the excuse for saying I'd been too 'girlie' about it. I'd sworn Pud to secrecy about how I'd screamed out. He didn't think it was anything to worry about but I knew that if PeeDee heard about it I'd never hear the end of it.

Cowplain Girl Finds Murdered Man
Children find body in Padnell Woods

This is the season of the school holidays and it's the time when children go out to play. But beware, in the words of Henry Hall's famous record, *'If you go down to the woods today, you're sure of a big surprise ...'*

'Ten' Thomas, the leader of The Bramble Gang, agrees. *'I was riding up the track on my bike,'* Ten told us, *'and I was doing okay. But then my front wheel hit a fallen branch, and when my bike twisted I came off.'*

And we can picture Ten, like that daring young man on the flying trapeze, flying through the air with the greatest of ease. But what broke Ten's fall? And why wasn't Ten hurt? That is the 'big surprise' because the leader of The Bramble Gang landed on a dead body.

Inspector Johnson has informed us that the police have not as yet been able to identify the corpse but there can be no doubt that the man was murdered.

'He seems to have lost a great deal of blood from the wound on his head,' the Inspector said, *'and the post mortem confirmed that this blow to his head was clearly not accidental and led to the man's untimely death.'*

Even as we write, the police are checking finger print records to see if the man had a criminal record.

The Inspector went on to say, *'This is a murder enquiry and we are treating it as a matter of the greatest urgency. If anyone has any information that can assist us in our enquiries we ask them to contact us without delay.'*

And what about Ten? She is fine and seems to have suffered no more harm than a grazed knee.

'She is a very brave girl,' the Inspector told us, *'and a credit to the youth of today.'*

What is wrong with our society, we ask, when a twelve year old girl can no longer ride her bike in the woods in safety?

The trouble was I was still under house arrest. At least, that's what it felt like. Both Mum and Dad said I wasn't to go out unless one of them was with me or unless it was just to the shops. Pud was also having difficulties getting out. For the time being I'd had to rely on Merlin and Oz. They'd come round as soon as they'd heard and we'd reached a compromise – the headquarters of the Bramble Gang was temporarily moved to the shed at the bottom of our garden.

I'd called a council meeting and Merlin and Oz had gone to Pud's house. His mum gave in and said that so long as they left their bikes there and walked straight round to my house she supposed it would be all right. Tod came round later. Merlin and Oz had used their brains for once and had called on him before they went to Pud's house.

PeeDee's lot were here, too. When we were all finally in the shed we couldn't close the door so most of PeeDee's lot had to sit outside. At least it meant they could keep an eye open in case Cath tried to sneak up on us and eavesdrop. It was the sort of sneaky thing she'd do. I'd caught her at it before and I knew she was envious that I was a hero.

'The first thing we have to do is to find out if anyone has seen the Prowler,' I said. 'We don't yet know if the corpse is the Prowler or if the Prowler is the murderer. If anyone saw the Prowler last night then we can assume he's the murderer.'

'Plod was round our house last night,' PeeDee said. 'He wanted to know where the old man was on Wednesday night.'

'Why? Did they think he'd done it?' Oz asked.

'Someone'd heard him say he'd kill the Prowler for chasing Sandy. I don't know how, but it got back to the police. I think it was Mrs Harris next door. She hates him 'cause he sings a bit sometimes. Mum told her it's only the Irish in him and she says it's not the whisky, it's the beer.'

'So where was he?' Oz asked.

'In the Spotted Cow until closing and he came home with Bunny's Dad. He wasn't even drunk, they'd had a darts match.'

'So Bunny's Dad was his alibi,' I said. 'It's important to check everything. 'Has anyone checked with Monkey? He'd know if PeeDee's Dad was in there.'

'You saying my Dad's a murderer?' PeeDee said, turning on me.

'No. Course not, but if we can rule him out then we can move on. We've got to check his story to prove he's innocent. That's how police work is done.'

I got out a notebook. It wasn't as posh as Plod's but it was all I had. I made an entry. PeeDee looked impressed.

'Who's going to check with Monkey?' I asked.

Tod said he would on his way home. I noted that down, too.

'Good detective work has to be methodical,' I said, 'particularly if we're going to solve this crime.'

'What does your Mum think about all this?' Roller asked. 'He was still in awe of me for landing on a corpse.

'She'd go ape if she thought that we were going to solve it,' I said. 'In fact, she'd probably chain me to my bed.'

PeeDee snickered.

'I'd like to see my Mum try it,' he said. 'I'd give her a right mouthful.'

'My Mum's got a cane,' Chris said. 'She'd give me what for if I yelled at her.'

'Last time I yelled at my Mum,' Beaky said, 'she clipped my ear and I couldn't hear anything for days. It was all right, though, 'cause when she said I couldn't go out I just went. She moaned at me like nobody's business when I got in but I ignored her – I said I couldn't hear. I think she got the point.'

I found this all quite interesting, but it wasn't getting us anywhere with the matter in hand so I called the meeting to order.

'We must get organised,' I said. 'PeeDee, you go and look at the dirt track and see if the police are still there. Check your den, they might have raided that as well. Merlin, you check ours. I don't expect they found it 'cause it's not so obvious as PeeDee's but we can't take anything for granted. You'd better take Oz with you in case the murderer's using it as a hide–out.'

I'd only thought of that on the spur of the moment. It was a stroke of pure genius, the sort of thing I was famous for coming up with, and everybody suddenly went quiet.

'Do you think he's still out there?' Goat asked.

'I'm sure he won't be,' I said trying to sound doubtful. 'But if he is, Merlin and Oz can handle him. Perhaps you should go with

PeeDee, just in case. It's a pity I can't go out or I'd give him a kick or two for ruining my holiday. The thing is, I may have to speak to the papers again. My reporter said it might go national!'

I was making all this up as I went along. I'd had plenty of time to work out how we were going to play this and I wasn't going to let them know what I was up to. And you never knew – we might just find the murderer.

'Cath alert,' Chris said.

We immediately started talking about PeeDee's last football match. We always did this if we thought someone was going to listen. It was foolproof. They always went away again.

'Mum says you've got to come in for dinner,' Cath called out from halfway down the garden. She didn't like the look of PeeDee's lot and wouldn't come any nearer.

'That's it for now, then,' I said. 'Try and report back this afternoon. I'll be here.'

But I wasn't there when they called back later that afternoon. Fate had pulled another trick. As soon as I'd seen the gang off I went in, and Mum dropped the bombshell. The March sisters had called in when I was in the shed and had invited Mum and me to tea! Mum was dead chuffed and accepted immediately without even asking me.

'You may as well have your bath early,' Mum said.

Now I know Saturday was bath day but I'd already had a bath on Thursday. I tried to protest but she'd have none of it.

'And you'll have to put your best dress on,' she said, just to clinch the matter.

It was all I could do to stop myself from throwing up on the spot.

'And they've invited Cath, too.'

The urge to throw up became even more pressing. I could see Cath was looking better. She was on cloud nine, bathing in my reflected glory. I had to do something.

'Wouldn't it be better if I wore the clothes I was wearing when I found him?' I asked. 'You know, it would give my story a bit of authenticity when I tell them about the blood.'

Cath winced but even that didn't wipe the smile off her ugly face.

'Wouldn't it be nice,' she said, 'if you pretended you were a normal little girl for once. I can't think why the March sisters want to make a fuss of you.'

'So,' I said, 'what have you done for them? All the time the Prowler was ravaging people it was me who risked my life doing their shopping. I could have found them dead on the floor with their throats cut while you were sitting here doing your needlework.'

Mum wasn't listening.

'That's enough,' Mum said firmly. She had no idea what I was talking about but she wasn't going to let me spoil her afternoon. 'You will wear your best dress and you are going to behave like a well brought-up girl for once.'

'But, Mum ...'

'There are no buts, not unless you want to stay in for the rest of the holidays.'

I recognised the tone in her voice and shut up. She even made me wash up after dinner. She fussed so much you'd think I was going to see the queen. And she checked my finger nails after my bath for dirt, scraping the last bits out with some evil weapon from her nail kit. I thought she was never going to stop brushing my hair and she made me wear a blue Alice band. She said it matched the colour of my eyes and made me look pretty. Pretty! I ask you!

'Remember your manners,' she said, 'and make sure you say please and thank you.'

'I'm not completely ignorant,' I said.

'You could have fooled me,' Cath muttered.

She was beginning to bug me and I couldn't resist baiting her.

'Do you think they were frightened by the thunder storm?' I asked. 'You know how it is for the infirm and mentally deficient, they get scared at the silliest things.'

Cath shifted uncomfortably and I poked my tongue out at her.

'You won't be doing that this afternoon,' Mum said. I hadn't realised she was watching me. 'And I don't think the March sisters are infirm or mentally deficient. I'd say they were pretty sharp if they've survived all this time on their own.'

I played what I hoped would be my master stroke.

'They told me they were waiting for Mr Hitler to come and visit them,' I said. 'They've got a big club inside the front door ready to bash his head in. Perhaps the Prowler called and they did him in and dragged his body up into the woods and now they're waiting to finish us off, too. Will you help me check for blood spots?' I asked Cath. 'You could keep them talking while I have a quick look.'

'You can talk all the rubbish you want, Theresa, but we're going to tea and you're going to behave and that's all there is to it. If you can't wait nicely you can go to your room.'

I gave up. Even I know when I'm beaten.

But there was worse to come. Just as we were walking up the road, PeeDee came by on his bike. He looked straight at me and nearly fell of his bike. He gave me such a stupid stare that I just knew he was going to give me a hard time on Monday.

Chapter 15

The Misses March did me proud. They'd really gone to town and made all the party food that they thought someone my age would like. I thought it was a bit sad that they didn't have children of their own because the spread they put on was fantastic. There were egg sandwiches, liver and bacon paste sandwiches and ham sandwiches cut into triangles for the adults. There was a red jelly in a glass mould and a pink blancmange in a white china mould – and they turned them both out perfectly. There were fairy cakes with butter icing and an iced cake with my name on the top in fancy lettering. They had bottles of ginger beer for me and tea for the grown ups and, best of all, it was served on a table in their sitting room on a white cloth. We even had white napkins.

I was really impressed and for once I behaved properly. I said 'please' and 'thank you' without having to be prompted and I only ate what I was offered, even though I could have eaten more. As soon as Mum said she couldn't eat another morsel I said I was fit to bust and couldn't eat any more either. Mum looked shocked but the sisters laughed. They said I could go round and see them any time I wanted and they told Mum how kind I had been, doing their shopping and running errands for them.

I think Mum was a bit surprised but she laughed it off. Then the adults got to talking and I had a chance to look round the room. I heard Miss Eileen say how pretty I was. I suppose they were so used to seeing me in my comfortable holiday clothes that they didn't expect me to wash up that well! They had a massive old harmonium against the wall opposite the fireplace and it had shelves on its top with pictures in silver frames. Miss Eileen saw me looking at it and she got up and took me over. She told me the pictures were of her family. There was a picture of her parents. Her mother was sitting very straight-backed in a chair and was wearing a dress with lots of lace and frills down the front. Miss Eileen's father was standing just behind her mother. He had a heavy moustache which drooped down on both sides of his mouth.

'He was so handsome,' she said.

There was a picture of him in an army uniform from the First World War. There were pictures of Miss Eileen and Miss Barbara when they were babies and when they were young children.

'Theresa plays the piano,' Mum said.

Miss Barbara asked me if I'd like to try her harmonium but I said I didn't know how.

'She pumps the organ in church,' Cath said.

'Well, it's just like that only easier,' Miss Barbara said, 'because you use your feet to pump. It's just like walking along.'

They persuaded me, and at first I found it weird but I soon got the hang of it and picked out a couple of the pieces that I knew by heart. They clapped and said I was very good. I think Cath was annoyed. She'd only said I pumped the church organ because she was sure I'd make a fool of myself. Miss Barbara told me I should bring my music next time and she'd help me. I could hear Cath grinding her teeth. I smiled sweetly – it was fun being a girl for once!

When we got home I was glad I'd been – despite what I'd thought before I went, I'd had a good time and I hadn't thought once about the dead man or the Prowler. But later, in bed, as I went over the afternoon I remembered PeeDee and I suddenly went cold when I thought of what he was going to say and do on Monday. After that it took me ages to get to sleep.

Next morning, at church, I was the centre of interest. Even Bunny was dead envious.

'You always get all the good luck,' he said.

The Vicar even mentioned me in the prayers and we all had to say The General Thanksgiving for my 'safe delivery from the evil lurking in our midst'.

Mum said I didn't have to go to Evensong, but I said that of course I'd go. She came with me, just in case, she said although she didn't say in case of what!

I was still worried about PeeDee when I woke up on Monday morning. It was almost as if I'd had a bad dream. I could almost hear him telling the rest of *The Flag Boys* how *The Bramble Gang* had a sissy girl for their leader. We'd never live it down, no matter how many times we whipped his arse playing in the woods. I could even see him doing a 'girlie' walk to demonstrate what I looked like. I put on my oldest pair of shorts, the ones Mum had patched where I'd ripped them, and a baggy shirt that I left un–tucked. I looked in the mirror and un–tidied my hair. At least the person looking back at me no longer resembled the 'pretty' girl he'd seen on Saturday.

I went down to breakfast. Fortunately Cath was still in bed. She was the last person I wanted to see and Mum was dithering about so I crept through into the kitchen and had a Weetabix while she was busy. The tea was still warm in the pot so I poured myself a cup. Then I heard the door bell ring. Mum answered it and came through a moment later.

'There's a boy outside! He says he wants to speak to you!'

'Who is it?'

'I don't know. I think he's one of your friends. Go and talk to him, it might be important.'

I went. Reluctantly. If it had been one of my friends he would have come to the back door. Perhaps it was someone who wanted to join my gang.

And then I saw it was PeeDee.

'If you've come to gloat you can just keep your gob shut,' I said, bristling.

'I haven't,' he said.

'Well you can push off,' I almost yelled. 'I bet you have to do things you don't like. Just to please your parents. Well, that was what I was forced into doing!'

I stuck my hands in the pockets of my shorts and glared at him, daring him to say anything.

He shuffled his feet and looked nervous. That's cooked his goose, I thought.

'I came to bring you this,' he said, holding out a little parcel.

I was lost for words and my mouth felt as if it had dropped open.

'And to tell you how nice you looked yesterday afternoon,' he continued. And then, in a rush, he added, 'And to ask you if you'd like to go out with me.'

He was blushing furiously. Not a nice effect considering the colour of his hair. I didn't know what to say.

'Go round the back,' I said, 'and I'll come out.'

I shut the front door in his face. What was I going to do? I turned the little packet over. It rattled. I put it in my pocket and went back into the kitchen.

'It's just PeeDee,' I said as nonchalantly as I could. Mum was sorting the washing into piles. 'He's come on gang business. I've got to go out and talk to him.'

Mum seemed to accept that and I went out the back door and down to the shed where he was standing.

'You'd better come in,' I said. 'I don't want Cath gawping at you.'

I opened the shed door and we went in, out of sight of the house but I left the door open.

'And I don't like people taking the Mickey,' I said. 'And my lot will knock spots off your lot if you think you can take liberties. We're enemies, sworn enemies, for ever.'

I glared at him again. And he just stood there, all awkward. I almost laughed.

'I know all that,' he said, 'and nothing's changed. And your lot won't ever beat us again when we're in the woods.'

"We could always try another bank robbery!' I said.

'That was just a lucky fluke!'

He was beginning to sound more like PeeDee, now, and I felt relieved.

'Even if you are a girl,' he said, 'you're just as good as any boy! Better than most, I suppose. But isn't there any way you could just be a girl sometimes? I really like you, Ten. It wouldn't change anything in the woods! What with you being in the paper and then all posh yesterday ...'

He tailed off. I don't think he knew what to say. I certainly didn't know how to answer him.

'Why don't you open your present?' he suggested.

I'd forgotten about it and I took it out of my pocket where I'd put it before I went into the kitchen. It was done up in brown paper and tied with string.

'It's not beetles is it?' I asked suspiciously.

'I wouldn't do that to you, Ten,' he said.

'I'd do it to you,' I retorted.

'That's what I like about you,' he said, 'you're always ready to have a go.'

He was being so wet I didn't know what to say so I opened his parcel just so I didn't have to reply. There was a box inside and I opened it. Quite what I expected to find I don't know but what was there certainly surprised me.

'How did you know I collected these?' I asked.

'Pud told me. Don't worry, I didn't ask him outright, we were talking about them some time ago and I remembered he said you were missing two of the White Waistcoat ones.'

I was surprised that he'd thought so carefully about what to give me. It was a side of PeeDee that I'd never seen before. Usually he was the tough one, all big boots with his laces undone and his shorts a size too big because they were hand–me–downs from his older brother, Malcolm. It came as a shock, I can tell you, to realise that he had a sensitive side. I didn't know what to say. You see, I also tried to be tough.

Being a girl was a real handicap so I fought harder, thought quicker and generally outsmarted the others just to prove that I was at least their equal if not better than them. The trouble was I had to work at it twice as hard as they did and even then it was as if I was only half as tough. Now PeeDee had shifted the game away from being strong and I wasn't sure I liked it at all.

'Thank you,' I said. 'There's only one to go now and then I've got the whole series.'

PeeDee had given me the Footballer and the Bagpiper. We all collected the paper gollies off Robertson's jam jars and stuck them on our exercise books but I also collected the enamel golly badges. I don't remember when I started but I'd got quite a collection now and they were pinned on a cushion in my bedroom. I seldom wore them out of the house – it would be far too childish. And I'd never seen PeeDee wearing one, either.

'How many have you got?' I asked.

'Not many but my Gran gave me some and they were ones I'd already got. I thought you could add them to your collection.'

This was all beginning to sound a bit soppy and so I asked him if he'd heard anything more about the Prowler.

'Not a thing,' he said. 'It's like he never existed.'

'Perhaps the dead man was the Prowler after all,' I said. 'Now all we've got to do is find out who did him in.'

'How are we going to do that?' he asked. 'Won't the police get the hump if we interfere?'

'We'll keep out of their way. They don't know the village as well as we do. If he was the Prowler he must have been murdered by someone in the village.'

I know this wasn't logical but it would have to do for now until I'd had time to think out a proper plan.

'I know it wasn't the Misses March,' I told him. 'I had a good look at the club they keep inside their front door. There wasn't any blood on it and there was a cobweb between it and the coat stand so they couldn't have taken it out recently.'

'That's good,' he said, admiringly. 'I'd never have thought to look for the cobweb.'

I began to feel as if I couldn't do anything wrong. What had got into him?

'Look,' I said, 'I can't cope with you being all soppy. I'm Ten, leader of the Bramble Gang. Let's get back to being proper enemies.'

'I don't think I can,' he said. 'You see, it's really serious. I hadn't really thought about it until Dad was going on last night. It could have been your corpse in the woods. Or any of us. I'd be just as worried if it was Merlin – well, nearly as much.'

He and Merlin were not friends at all and they never missed a chance to pick on each other.

'Until this is sorted we've all got to stick together.'

I don't know what it was, but he was beginning to get to me.

'I'm still sure that we are safe, PeeDee. I mean, you don't go finding corpses every day so this has to be a one–off special. And I can't believe that anyone who killed a bloke would hang around and wait to be caught.'

'Not unless he lives in Cowplain.'

Now that really hit home. Not that I was going to let him know.

'Right,' I said, trying to sound business–like and efficient. 'We'll have an extraordinary meeting this afternoon and work out just what we're going to do. We can't let a chance like this go. We've got to do something. The honour of the gang is at stake.'

Chapter 16

PeeDee had given me a real problem. Not because he'd gone soppy and asked me out but because he'd suggested that the person who'd murdered the Prowler – well, we didn't know for sure that he was the Prowler but it was convenient to think he was – might actually live in the village. My mind was working overtime. If the murderer lived in the village he'd know by now that I'd discovered the body because it had been in the newspaper, and he'd know where I lived so I wasn't even safe at home any more.

I wasn't sure if PeeDee was serious when he'd asked me to go out with him but he came round again just after lunch and said that he'd checked with his Mum and she had suggested that we could go to the pictures at The Curzon, the cinema in Waterlooville, next Saturday morning. I said I'd think about it and let him know. I thought it would be better to let him down gently because I definitely wasn't going to go anywhere with him.

The rest of our gangs arrived and Tod was bursting with his news. He'd been round to Monkey's in the morning and couldn't contain himself.

'He's not the Prowler,' he said as soon as we'd crammed into the shed.

'Who isn't?' Roller asked.

'The corpse. Monkey told me that Plod had said that someone had seen the Prowler on Saturday night.'

For a moment we were all speechless. We'd been sure that the corpse was the Prowler. In some ways, of course, it was good news because now we'd got a mysterious dead body and nobody knew who he was. We'd also got a murderer who might or might not be the Prowler. So we were still looking for the Prowler and possibly someone else as well – we had two cases to solve now instead of just one!

'That means that the Prowler could have been the murderer,' PeeDee said, stating the obvious. 'This makes it all the more dangerous.'

'Did he say where the Prowler was spotted?' I asked. I'd taken out my notebook and was taking notes of what he said. 'Or who saw him?'

'I didn't think to ask,' Tod said. 'He didn't say, so he probably doesn't know.'

'That's not good enough,' I said. 'If we're going to solve this we have to have every bit of information that we can get. We must be thorough.'

'Go back and ask him,' PeeDee said. 'Ten's right. Our lives might depend on it!'

I thought PeeDee was laying it on a bit thick but I was glad that he'd backed me.'

'So what are we going to do?' Merlin asked as soon as Tod had gone. 'I mean, most of us are under house arrest and there's the evening curfew as well.'

'We've got to get the olds to think it's safe again,' Beaky said.

'And just how are we going to do that?' Oz said a trifle sarcastically.

'Don't know,' Beaky said.

'It's up to the police,' PeeDee said, sensibly. 'When they catch the murderer we'll be off the hook.'

'What if they don't catch him?' Oz asked.

'It'll die down in time,' PeeDee said.

'Why don't we just start being such pains that the olds throw us out just to get some peace?' Goat said.

'You mean just carry on like usual?' Pud said.

'Why don't we start a new project right here,' I suggested. 'PeeDee and I were thinking that it might be fun to build a couple of rafts and have a sea battle on the big pond.'

There was a stunned silence. They weren't prepared for a new idea. They were so taken up with the dead body that they'd almost forgotten about our normal lives and the way PeeDee and I were always at war.

'I'm going to be Calico Jack,' PeeDee said.

'Who the hell's Calico Jack?' Merlin asked.

'Jack Rackham, one of the most famous and dangerous pirates who ever sailed the seas and Ten can be Anne Bonny, the notorious woman pirate.'

'I thought I might be Captain Nancy Blackett.'

This time it was PeeDee who asked.

'Who the hell's she?'

'She's the intrepid Captain of the Amazon,' I said.

Then I had to explain about 'The Swallows and Amazons' books by Arthur Ransome.

'I've been reading them while I was under house arrest,' I said.

They seemed to accept that, so it was fixed that PeeDee would be Calico Jack and I'd be Nancy.

'How are we going to get the rafts up to the pond?' Roller asked, ever practical.

'We build them in bits,' PeeDee said, 'then assemble them up by the pond when we're ready.'

'And if the olds see us all getting on together,' Chris said, 'they might let us all off the hook to float our rafts. We don't have to tell them we're going to have a battle.'

'Danger,' Roller said. 'Your mum's coming down the garden.'

We started talking about the Bank Holiday ramble. Even though it was a church activity lots of the rest of the village came along too. Our gangs nearly always turned out in force. Like PeeDee said, we needed to be on hand in case they wrecked our dens. Mum walked down the path checking the washing to see if it was dry. She came on down to the shed. She wasn't scared like Cath.

'Would you like some squash and biscuits?' she asked. 'I know it must cramp your style having to hang around here like this.'

'It makes a nice change, Mrs Thomas,' Chris said. 'Anyway, I expect the police are finishing up in the woods so we'll soon be able to go back.'

'We'll see,' Mum said. 'But for the moment it's better to be safe.'

Tod came riding down the garden just then.

'You're just in time for orange squash,' Mum said as she passed him.

'What did Monkey say?' PeeDee asked.

'Plod didn't say,' Tod said. 'I knew Monkey would have said if he'd known.'

'Come on, let's get a drink,' I said.

I made an entry in my notebook and closed it. The rest of the afternoon slowly drifted by. We couldn't settle to anything and eventually Pud left with Merlin and Oz. Tod rode off and then Goat went.

'What're we going to do now?' Roller asked.

'Don't know,' PeeDee said.

'We could start drawing plans for the rafts,' I suggested.

'Why don't you three go to the dump and see if you can sort out some planks for the rafts while Ten and I draw the plans,' PeeDee suggested. 'If you find any, bring them back here.'

PeeDee's lot went leaving just PeeDee and me.

'I'll get some paper,' I said, leaving him in the conservatory.

I felt strangely uncomfortable being on my own with PeeDee. It was all right in the woods but here it felt quite different.

'What's lover–boy doing here?' Cath asked as I went through the kitchen to fetch my note book from my bedroom.

'He's not my 'lover–boy',' I said. I hurried on because I felt that I was beginning to blush. I stopped in the doorway, 'actually we're sworn enemies and we're just going to plot our next fight. I'm going to get some paper.'

I turned and went into the hall and up the stairs. I could feel her eyes burning into my back and I stopped in the bathroom on the way to my room and looked in the mirror. I couldn't believe what I saw. My cheeks were burning!

I took as long as I could sorting out some paper and pencils and on the way back down I splashed cold water on to my cheeks which were still a bit red.

PeeDee had settled down outside under the tree where Cath had been sitting earlier. He looked quite at ease and was chatting to Mum. She looked up.

'PeeDee's just been telling me that he's asked you to go to the pictures with him next Saturday morning.'

'I know,' I said. 'But what with being unable to go out and all, I don't think I'll be able to go.'

'What rubbish!' Mum said. 'I'll be quite happy if the two of you are together. I'm sure that PeeDee will look after you!'

This wasn't at all what I wanted to hear. Why is it that adults can be so unpredictable? They seem to have the knack of doing and saying just what you don't want and then they pretend that everything's fine when it really isn't. Why on earth was it all right for me to go out to Waterlooville with PeeDee but not safe to play in the woods? I gave up.

'Right, I'll leave you two to get on, then,' Mum said. 'And it was nice to meet you properly, Peter.'

PeeDee looked smug. I sat on the opposite side of the table and tried to give the impression that I was totally indifferent to him – which, of course, I was – but every now and then I looked up and each time I saw him looking at me. At last I couldn't bear it any more.

'What's the matter?' I asked.

'Nothing,' he said.

'Why are you looking at me?'

'You're pretty,' he said ingenuously.

'Pretty!' I tried not to sound too appalled. 'What's got into you?'

'We've never been together like this,' he said.

I was pleased to see that he was blushing now. It made me want to laugh – he was so easy to tease.

'Don't think it's going to happen again,' I said. 'And we're not together! You are my enemy and I don't want you to be anything else. Got it?'

Dad came down the garden. I hadn't noticed how the time had passed.

'You're in the paper again,' he said, holding it out to us.

We read it and I glared at PeeDee across the table, brushing my hair out of my eyes.

'Why don't you wear your hair band?' PeeDee asked. 'It looked ever so nice.'

I snorted with derision.

'Does that mean that we can go back to our den?' I asked Dad, ignoring PeeDee. I held up the newspaper. 'The Inspector says the woods are quite safe.'

'It means that I'll talk to Mum about it,' he said.

I looked at PeeDee and nodded towards the front.

'I'd better be going,' PeeDee said, taking the hint. 'Thank your Mum for the orange squash.'

Dad and I walked back to the house with PeeDee.

'He seems like a nice boy,' Dad said as PeeDee went round to the front drive.

'We're trying to plot out our next game,' I said.

I thought I sounded pretty non–committal but I didn't get away with it for long. We had only just settled down to tea when Cath started.

'Tess has got a boy friend,' she announced.

I nearly choked and Mum had to come and give my back a good slap.

'I expect she's got lots of boy friends,' Dad said.

'But Peter's asked her out!'

'Only to the pictures on Saturday morning,' Mum said, coming to my rescue. 'Lots of kids go to the Saturday morning children's showing. I expect all his friends will be there, too.'

I didn't think that was what PeeDee had in mind but it was a lifeline and I grabbed it.

'Both our gangs will probably be there,' I said. 'We haven't sorted out the details yet.'

I don't know if Cath believed me but she gave up.

'Can I have some water?' I asked. 'I think my bread's still stuck.'

I saw a glint of malicious delight in Cath's eye as she turned to me She hadn't given up after all and she fired her parting shot with consummate skill.

'Your cheeks are very red,' she said. 'Perhaps you're sickening!'

Dad grinned at me and came to my rescue.

'Be a love,' he said to Cath, 'and get her some water. Now she's famous we'd better look after her. We don't want the press back again asking what we've done to her.'

Cath's face took on the look of a martyr as she fetched me a glass of water. She knew she was beaten this time.

Chapter 17

'Mum, I think you need to come,' Cath yelled out at the top of her voice.

'Why?' Mum said rushing through into the kitchen. 'What's the matter? What's happened?'

'I think there's something wrong with Tess.'

Mum looked at me and I felt uncomfortable under her intense gaze. I looked daggers at Cath and tried to carry on eating my breakfast as if I hadn't a care in the world. Mum put her hand on my forehead.

'She hasn't got a temperature – perhaps it's the shock coming out,' Mum said without grasping what Cath was on about. 'Perhaps I'd better call the doctor just in case. But she looks all right.' Then the penny began to drop. 'In fact, I think she looks very nice,' she added, going back to the lounge with a smile.

'Pig!' I hissed at Cath as soon as Mum was out of the room.

'It's too late for you to try and join the human race,' Cath said.

'How would you know?' I retorted. 'You're not one of us – you're a monster from outer space.'

The reason for Cath's outburst was that I was wearing a skirt – not from choice mind you, but because I didn't have anything else that was clean. I finished my breakfast in stony silence, glaring at Cath whenever she looked in my direction, and then stomped back up to my bedroom.

Mum was vacuuming and the noise was dreadful. I sat on my bed until she'd finished.

'Are you all right?' she asked.

'I'm fine,' I said. 'When will my proper clothes be dry? I haven't got any shorts.'

'It won't hurt you to wear a skirt for a while,' she said, smiling. 'I'll start the ironing as soon as I've finished cleaning. Your hair looks a bit of a mess.'

'I think I need a new comb. I don't think my old one's much good any more.'

'I'll see what I can find when I go to the shops,' Mum said.

'What do you want with a comb?' Cath asked from the landing. I hadn't noticed she'd come up stairs. She turned to Mum. 'I shouldn't bother. I don't think she'd know what to do with it!'

'Don't be mean,' Mum said. 'Tess has lovely hair. It's time she started to look after it a bit more.' She turned to me. 'I could take you to the hairdressers if you want it cut,' she offered.

'I was thinking of letting it grow a little bit,' I said.

I turned my face away and bent down to scratch my ankle so that Cath couldn't see me blushing. For a moment it felt as if the whole world had stopped and everybody was looking at me.

'If you're going to let it grow you'll need a brush,' Mum said. 'It'll take the tangles out better.'

Cath went on into her bedroom and shut the door and Mum took the vacuum downstairs. I went into the bathroom and looked at my hair. Mum was right, it was untidy. I damped my comb under the tap and tried to flatten it but it insisted on springing out again. I don't know why I was suddenly thinking about my hair or how I looked. While I looked at myself in the mirror I remembered that Rita, one of the girls in my class, had said that my eyebrows were too close together.

'In fact,' she snickered, 'I don't think you've got two because they've quite joined up in the middle!'

Rita was very proud of hers and the way they arched. Personally, I thought they made her look as if she was on the point of asking a question. And she was always going on, endlessly, about what she had to do to keep herself looking pretty.

'It's not easy,' she said, 'having to keep up to such a high standard. My mother says that I should always look my best.'

She studied my eyebrows again.

'You look like a chimpanzee,' she had said. 'You should try plucking them.'

When she said it I had thought that the idea was sheer stupidity but now, as I looked in the mirror, I could see what she meant. They did come close together and there were some straggly hairs that looked as if they were trying to join up. I looked in the bathroom cupboard and found the tweezers we used to grab splinters. I gripped them but they twisted in my fingers and slipped out of my grip. I picked them up and tried again.

It was one thing to decide that I'd pluck the odd hair out but it was another thing altogether now I was in the bathroom with the tweezers in my hand. I chose a likely hair, just a small one and lifted the tweezers to my face. That was my first problem because, with the tweezers in my hand and hovering over my nose, I couldn't see what I was doing. I turned my face sideways, squinted in the mirror and tried again. By now my fingers were sweaty with panic and I dropped the tweezers again.

It took several attempts but at last I managed to grip a hair. I gave it a tentative tug but it didn't come out. In fact it felt as if it was rather too well attached to me to come out at all. I relaxed and looked at it again. There was a slight reddening of the skin above my nose where I'd scraped myself with the tweezers. I couldn't believe that I was so chicken. Here was fearless Ten too scared to pull out one measly hair from her eyebrow. The idea was preposterous.

I squinted sideways in the mirror again to make sure I'd got the right one. All was well. I closed my eyes. I'm not sure why I did that but perhaps I thought I could take it by surprise. Anyway, I took a breath, gripped the tweezers as hard as I could and pulled.

It was all I could do not to cry out. I couldn't stop my eyes from streaming. The pain was intense. I looked in the mirror expecting to see blood pouring down my face. It felt as if I'd pulled half my face off but there was nothing to see, just a slight red mark where I'd scraped it earlier. And worse, I couldn't see any difference at all.

I decided that it wasn't worth the pain just to end up looking the same and so I gave up on that idea. Clearly the beauty business wasn't something to be taken too lightly. Rita might be prepared to go through that just to look pretty but I wasn't convinced – there had to be a better way. Just then Mum called up.

'Are you all right? You've been a long time in the bathroom.'

'I'm fine,' I called down. 'I've just taken a splinter out of my finger.'

I squeezed the tweezers on one of my fingers until it was red and then put them back in the cupboard.

'Your shorts are ready if you want them,' Mum called up.

I dumped my skirt on my bed and went downstairs.

'Can I go out now?' I asked as soon as I'd put my shorts on. 'Dad said he was going to talk to you about it now the police say there's no danger.'

'I suppose so, but don't go up the woods on your own.'

I didn't wait in case she changed her mind but went straight out, fetched my bike and rode round to the green at the back. PeeDee was playing football with Chris and Merlin. I joined in until we were all stopped by Oz when he came round.

'What's up with Sandy?' he asked PeeDee. 'Has she broken up with Denis?'

'Not as far as I know,' PeeDee said.

'Well, she wasn't out with him last night.'

'I know, he goes to college on Monday nights. She never goes out with him on Mondays.'

'It's August,' Oz said. 'There ain't no college in August!'

PeeDee thought for a moment.

'Perhaps he was busy doing something else,' he said.

'Sandy was,' Oz said. 'She was snogging the lips of some guy in the bus shelter!'

'Must have been dark,' PeeDee said. 'You must have made a mistake. She's not like that!'

We all knew that Sandy had something of a reputation but we dared not say anything because we all recognised the edge in PeeDee's voice. He was just like his father in some ways and was intensely protective of her.

'And anyway,' PeeDee reasoned, 'if she was, she must have had her reasons.'

And that was that. We all knew that it was no good going on about Sandy.

'Did you find any planks for the rafts?' I asked Chris.

I thought it was time to change the subject before they started fighting. Oz wasn't very bright about things like that and if they started scrapping we'd never get anything done.

'We never got there,' Chris said. 'When we left Beaky remembered that he'd got to go up the shops for his Ma and Roller went with him so I just went home.'

'You're useless, you lot,' PeeDee said. 'I suppose I'd better do it myself.'

'No sweat,' Chris said. 'When Beaky and Goat get here we're going to do it this morning.'

PeeDee seemed satisfied at that.

'So, what are we going to do this morning?' he asked me.

'Well, if we're off the hook I thought I'd go and check our den. I haven't been there since, well, since I found the body.

'I'll come, too,' PeeDee said. 'I don't think any of us should be in the woods on our own until we know what really happened. If they're going to look for wood, I won't have anything else to do.'

We all agreed to meet up at the dens after lunch and went off to complete our various tasks. I said I'd ride round and let Pud and Tod know although I wasn't sure that Pud's mum would let him out yet. She was very protective and I think she thought that PeeDee was too rough so she'd probably try and use the murder as an excuse for keeping him in.

In the end we didn't go and check our dens because PeeDee suggested that we could go and check out the big pond ready for our pirate battle.

Chapter 18

We were sitting under the oak by the pond. When PeeDee arrived after lunch he'd found the rope had been taken down. Normally it swung out over the water but just close enough for us to be able to hook it with a bit of wood, there were always fallen branches lying around. But today it had been left neatly coiled on the ground by the tree.

'Probably those Teddy Boys,' PeeDee said. 'I bet they couldn't think of anything better to do so they came up here and spoilt our fun.'

'Perhaps the farmer took it down 'cause it wasn't safe,' Chris suggested.

'He'd have taken it away if it wasn't safe,' PeeDee said grumpily.

'You get out of bed the wrong side?' Chris asked.

PeeDee didn't rise and just ignored him. That's how out of sorts he was.

I pulled the back of Goat's braces for a diversion, and let them go. The resounding thwack was rewarding but his yelp of pain was even better.

'Ow!' he wailed. 'That hurt.'

'Not my fault you're a sissy,' I taunted.

'Bet it's made a mark,' he said, pulling his shirt up and showing Beaky his back.

It had, too. I didn't feel like saying sorry so I suggested that I could do the same on the front so that he had another set of marks to make it even but he wasn't interested.

'You should wear a belt,' I suggested.

'Doesn't work,' he said. 'Mum says me hips are too thin and me trousers just fall off.'

'You need to pull it up tight,' Beaky said.

Beaky had a blue elastic belt with a fastener shaped like a snake that hooked into a loop on the other end. You could adjust the tension with a sliding clip and he always wore his belt so tight that it made the top of his shorts ruck up like a frill.

'What are we going to do now?' PeeDee asked.

'We'll just have to tie it back up,' I said.

'And just how are we going to do that?' PeeDee looked glumly at me.

'Climb up, edge along the branch and tie it back.'

'Just like that?'

'Just like that!'

Of course, PeeDee had a point. The tree leaned precariously out over the pond and the trunk was massive.

'You'd have to have arms the size of a gorilla to climb that,' PeeDee said.

'We could fetch Monkey,' Merlin suggested.

'You're the tallest,' I said to PeeDee. 'If you stood against the trunk you could give someone a bunk up.'

He looked up at the tree. From where we were sitting on the ground it looked impossible.

'Pud's the next tallest,' Oz said.

PeeDee turned his mournful gaze from the tree to Pud. Wonder of wonders, Pud's Mum had let him come out provided we all stayed together. I could see PeeDee gauging Pud's weight.

'He's too heavy,' I said. I thought it would come better from me. 'We need someone lighter. And there's the rope to think of.'

'Couldn't we just fetch a ladder?' Merlin asked. 'It'd be a lot simpler.'

'We've got a ladder,' Beaky said. 'But Dad'd never let me borrow it.'

'Couldn't he come and do it?' PeeDee asked.

'Don't think Mum'd let him. Last time I went home all dirty she said she'd stop me playing up here if I came home like that again.'

He had a point. I think most of our parents thought we were barbarians and they'd be only too pleased if they knew the rope was down.

'I could do it,' I said. 'I can climb trees. I spend half my life up in our apple tree.'

'She does,' Pud confirmed.

PeeDee looked sceptical.

'I don't know,' he said.

'Well we could try,' I said. 'If it doesn't work we'll have to think of something else.'

'I could get my brother,' PeeDee began.

Beaky cut him off.

'Give Ten a try. If it don't work then you can try your brother next. I mean,' he said looking round, 'we're all here now. We can probably catch Ten if she falls!'

'I don't know,' PeeDee said again.

'Are you chicken?' I asked him.

I know he saw the glint in my eye. The old PeeDee would have risen instantly to the challenge, but he still looked doubtful.

'You might fall and hurt yourself,' he said.

I saw the look on Merlin's face. I interrupted him before he could get stuck in.

'What you mean,' I said, 'is that you don't think I can do it.'

'No,' PeeDee began

'Or you don't think you can take my weight.'

PeeDee gave in.

'Okay,' he said. 'We'll give it a try.'

We looked at the rope. It seemed to be in good condition. Someone must have climbed up and untied it because the rope was still twisty where it had been knotted. Tod, being the expert, looked at the rope.

'It'd be easiest if we made a slip knot,' he said. 'Then all Ten's got to do is pass the end through and we can pull it tight from down here.'

No one had a better idea so we watched as Tod made a loop for me to thread the end through.

'You're sure it won't come undone?' PeeDee asked. 'It doesn't look much of a knot.'

'If it does,' Tod said, 'the worst that can happen is that whoever's on it falls into the water.'

There didn't seem to be any answer to that so PeeDee stood up and went to the tree. He stood about eighteen inches from the tree and leant forward, resting his arms against the tree. Suddenly he looked very small and the tree looked very big and I began to regret bragging that I could do it. He braced himself against the trunk and Merlin knelt down against him.

'You can step up on to me,' he said, 'and then climb on to

PeeDee's shoulders.'

'Still won't reach,' Oz said.

It was true, the first branch was a lot higher than I was likely to be able to reach. I played for time and slung the coiled rope over my shoulder and walked round to look at the other side.

'It's just as tall that side,' Goat said.

'Perhaps we could catapult Ten up into it with Goat's braces,' Chris suggested.

All of a sudden I had a brainwave.

It's fine,' I said. 'Dead easy.'

Merlin looked at me as if I'd gone mad.

'Get back into your positions,' I said.

Once more PeeDee braced himself against the trunk and Merlin made a step for me to climb up on. I made it on to PeeDee's shoulders without any problem although I thought he was going to buckle under my weight. He straightened up and I looked up into the tree. The branch was still too far for me to reach it. The bark on the oak tree was thick and I could grip it with my fingers but I knew it was too risky to use it to climb up on. There were ropes of ivy, too, but they were loose and I couldn't trust them to stay on the trunk. I looked up.

'Told you so,' Oz said triumphantly.

I looked over my shoulder – and nearly fell off. Everybody was looking up at me. I regained my balance and slipped the rope off my shoulder, gripping one end in the hand I was using to steady myself against the tree. Pushing myself away from the tree I threw the rope up with my other hand. Luck was on my side and it looped over the branch. I grabbed the other end as it swung towards me. It was easy to thread the end through Tod's loop and pull it tight.

'It's on the wrong side of the tree. The water's over there,' Goat said pointing.

The others laughed. But their laughter died as I began to climb up the rope. That was something I could do. At school I was the only girl in our class who could get to the top of the ropes in the gym. The secret is in the feet. You have to cross them before you grip the rope. All you have to do then is reach up with your arms and grab the rope, hold on and move your feet up, grip with your feet and move your hands up.

As soon as I could reach it I grabbed the branch and hauled myself up until I was sitting on it. They'd stopped laughing now.

I pulled the rope back up and teased the end out of Tod's loop. I had to climb up the tree until I could change sides and then I climbed down on to the branch that spread out over the water.

'How far out would you like it?' I asked, edging along the branch.

'Drop the end down and I'll tell you,' PeeDee shouted up.

I kept hold of Tod's loop and dropped the other end down.

'A bit further,' Beaky shouted.

I moved out along the branch another foot. The branch swayed a bit and some dead branches fell off as I gripped it with my knees.

'Be careful,' PeeDee called up.

I looked down. His face was a picture. Concern was mixed with admiration as I moved out another foot. He'd got it really bad!

'That'll do,' he said. 'Fix it there.'

I wrapped my feet together under the branch and hauled the rope up. It was much easier threading the end through the loop this time and I let the end fall.

'If the rope's there,' Merlin said, 'how's she going to get back down the trunk?'

That had occurred to me as well. There was nothing I could do but climb down the rope and try to swing it so that I could land on the bank. Climbing down was easy but the rope was now further out than it had been before and the bank was a lot further away than before. It took ages to get the rope swinging and it seemed as if it would never get any nearer to the bank. I gave up and leapt off on its next swing. I nearly made it but unfortunately my feet went into the water.

I scrambled up the bank and emptied my plimsolls. There was a cheer from the rest who were standing on the opposite side of the pond. I was too out of breath and my heart was beating too fast to enjoy the moment but I knew that, yet again, The Bramble Gang had saved the day.

We spent the rest of the afternoon testing out the new position. Now it was hanging out further we couldn't reach it so PeeDee brought a short piece of rope from his den and we tied it on to the end of the rope.

'Perhaps if it's that far out they won't be able to untie it again,' he said, 'so long as we remember to take our rope with us when we go.'

It was certainly more challenging with the rope further out and predictably we all got rather wet. The problems of the Prowler seemed far away and we even forgot about the murder. Life was getting back to normal and we all felt a lot better.

Just as we were beginning to feel that nothing could go wrong Pud interrupted us.

'Someone's got to come home with me,' he said tapping his watch.

He was the only one of us who wore a watch when we were out playing. Most of us had a watch, but we only wore them for school although I wore mine on Sundays so that I could time the Vicar's sermons. Mind you, it was more of a liability because I usually looked when I was bored and then I knew I had another twenty minutes to go!

'You don't have to stay or anything,' Pud went on, 'just as long as Mum sees you.'

We all knew how fussy Pud's mum was so Chris said he'd go

and Tod went with them since he had his bike. After they'd gone we kind of drifted back towards PeeDee's den with his short bit of rope which he hid in his secret place — although we all knew where it was. On the way home we decided to go over the recreation ground and we scrumped some apples from one of the gardens which backed on to the field.

'Don't forget to keep watch for the Prowler tonight,' I reminded PeeDee when we got to his house.

'I tried last night,' he said, 'but Mum wouldn't let me out.'

'Keep trying,' I said.

I jogged back to the end of Mr Looker's garden and ducked under the hedge into our back garden. I went to the shed and shut myself in. I was confused and I wanted space and time to think without anyone interrupting me.

Ever since I'd found the body everything seemed to have changed. And it wasn't just PeeDee! We all seemed to be getting on together. Before, we were always trying to get one up on each other but now we seemed to be doing things together. How on earth were we going to have good battles if we all liked each other? And what was the point of being rival gangs if we didn't have anything to fight over? Finding a dead body had had been one of the best things ever but what worried me now was how to stop it ruining the rest of our holiday.

I shut the shed up and went up the garden. Cath was on her chair under the tree doing her embroidery.

'Didn't take you long to revert to being a dirty little grub, did it?' she said sniffily.

I ignored her, it was better that way, and I went in doors. Mum handed me a new comb and brush set.

'It's a Mason Pearson,' she said proudly. 'Look after it because it's a good one.'

As if I knew what she was talking about! I looked at her blankly.

'The brush,' she said. 'It's a Mason Pearson brush. The bristles are set in a rubber cushion so that it doesn't tear at your hair.'

I thanked her and took it upstairs. I hadn't expected her to be that keen and rush out and buy me one that quickly but I felt strangely pleased. I didn't understand why because normally a new hairbrush was the last thing I got excited about. I took it into the bathroom and tried it out. My face was all muddy so I washed it and brushed my hair again. The brush worked well. It even smoothed down my hair which usually stuck out in a kind of static frizz.

Chapter 19

I didn't have time to let any of the gang know where I was on Wednesday because Mum decided that we'd all go and see Gran. I tried to get out of it but Mum said that Gran had written a note saying that she particularly wanted to see me after I had been in the newspaper.

'I didn't know Dad had sent her a copy,' I said.

'He hasn't,' Mum replied, 'not yet. But I expect she buys a copy anyway. I told your Dad he was wasting his money. Now, buck up and get dressed!'

Gran was old-fashioned. I knew I'd have to put a dress on, so I didn't argue and I even spent some time with my new hairbrush trying to persuade my hair to lie down. Cath took ages in the bathroom and so we nearly missed the bus. As it was, we saw it come across the end of the road as we turned out of the gate so I ran on to see if I could persuade the conductor to wait. I needn't have bothered because there were lots of people at the stop and there was plenty of time. We went upstairs and I sat on the last empty seat at the front. Mum and Cath sat together further back.

It took ages to get to Portsmouth because we stopped at every single bus stop on the way. I thought that we'd never get there because the bus got stuck behind a horse and cart on the bends towards Purbrook. I think it was a rag and bone man because the back of the cart was piled up with junk and there was a rusty stove in pride of place on top of all the old rags. We had a rag and bone man who called on us in Cowplain, but Mum never went out when he called. Mr Looker did though. He followed the cart all the way up the road, pushing his wheelbarrow, waiting for the horse to do his business. As soon as the horse obliged, Mr Looker scooped it up and took it back to his beloved garden. Perhaps that was why he won so many prizes for his dahlias.

As the bus came over the top of the hill into Portsmouth I could see the whole of the city laid out in front of me. It was magnificent. Once, when we took the bus to the pantomime at the Theatre Royal, we went in the dark and then the whole city glittered like a fairy tale and that was pretty magical, too. Today the sun was bright and I guessed that if I'd had a telescope I could have seen the sea in the distance. The bus paused at the terminal by the Lido while we changed our driver and conductor.

We got off at North End and walked through loads of side streets until we came to Gran's house. She lived in a semi-detached house which only had a small front garden. The path up to the front door was tiled in a red and yellow pattern with a black edging. The rest of the front garden was laid down to a patch of grass with shrubs round the edges. I always thought it looked damp and dark but Gran was very proud of the rose that grew in the middle of the tiny lawn.

She must have been watching out for us because as we opened the gate and went up the path, she opened the front door. She was wearing her usual pink jumper with a matching cardigan and a string of pearls at her neck. She was what Mum called well-built although Dad said she was tubby. I dutifully held my cheek up for her to kiss and went in while Cath had her kiss. The hall was narrow and the stairs went straight up from inside the front door. There was a room at the front and another at the back with the kitchen opening off it into the space behind the stairs. Gran always expected us to go into the front room which she called her drawing room. She had a big brown leather sofa and two leather arm chairs which took up most of the room. There was a sideboard against the wall opposite the front window and she had a little low table in front of the fireplace.

'Well, sit down in one of the comfy chairs and tell me all about it,' she said as soon as we were all in.

I really disliked her chairs because the leather was always cold on my legs and the seats were incredibly hard. And then, when you'd been sitting down for a while and had just got the chair warm, the leather stuck to you so that when you went to stand up it felt as if it was ripping the skin off the backs of your legs. It always made me giggle when she told us to sit down in one of the comfy chairs.

'Do we have to hear that dreary tale again?' Cath asked looking like a martyr.

'You might have heard Theresa's story before but I haven't,'

Gran said. 'If you want, you can go and put the kettle on.'

I saw Cath's chin jut out. She never won when she went up against Gran. She stood up and went out into the hall and into the dining room. A moment or two later I could hear the water running as she filled the kettle.

'Now,' Gran said, 'tell me all about your dreadful afternoon. Were you scared? Was it really frightening?'

I told my story again, putting in as much detail about the blood and the man's bashed in head as I could remember. When I'd finished Gran looked at Mum.

'I think she might be a writer when she grows up,' she said. 'She certainly tells a good yarn.'

'It's all true,' I protested.

'I'm sure it is but the way you tell it makes it sound exciting.'

'It was. It was ace!'

'And the police are still baffled?'

'There's no more news yet,' Mum said. 'But the police have said there's no danger for us.'

'So, you're out looking for clues are you?' Gran said to me, her eyes twinkling.

She seemed to understand what interested me better than Mum or Dad.

'I hope not,' Mum said before I had a chance to reply. 'But there is a nice boy, one of the ones she plays with, who's looking after her so I'm not too worried about her being out and about.'

I could have kicked Mum but she was sitting opposite me.

'A boy friend, eh?' Gran said. 'Don't get too serious – love them all and look for someone better!'

Gran turned to Mum and I guessed that I had done my duty. She saw me begin to fidget.

'Why don't you go out and see if you can find some biscuits,' she suggested. 'Your Mum and I have got things to talk about.'

Gran always had good biscuits and that made it worth going out into the kitchen with Cath. Today she had Garibaldi biscuits.

'Do you want a squashed fly?' I asked Cath.

Gran didn't have a toilet downstairs so I had to go up to her bathroom. It had big white tiles on the walls and always felt cold. She had one of those new toilets where the cistern wasn't up on the wall like ours but was down by the seat and you flushed it with a little handle that stuck out the front. It didn't seem to do much – not like when you pulled the chain on ours – but it flushed okay so I suppose it was all right. But if Gran's toilet was odd, her soap was great. She always had scented soap, usually Camay, not like the Wright's coal tar that we used, and when you'd washed your hands they smelt scented.

We stayed to lunch. Gran had bought Telford's meat pies and we each had one. Cath looked horrified, she and I usually had to share one at home.

'If you can't eat it all,' Gran told her, 'I expect Theresa will eat half. She looks as if she's a growing girl with a good appetite.'

'More like a dustbin,' Cath said.

'And what would we do without dustbins?' Gran replied.

Gran two, Cath nil, I thought. Cath, of course, would rather have died than let me have half her pie so we had to sit and wait while she finished it. Gran had opened a tin of Libby's peaches for pudding and we had Carnation milk to pour over them.

After lunch we went into the front room and listened to Worker's Playtime *'broadcast from a factory somewhere in Britain'.* Gran's radiogram was a posh affair with the wireless on one side and a turntable for playing records on the other side, all under a lid which you had to lift up. It was very old-fashioned and didn't play the new 45s, only the old thick plastic ones, but it still worked.

When the programme had finished Gran asked if Cath and I would like to go out into the park. She was dead cunning. I guessed that she knew Cath would say 'no' so she turned it round.

'They've got lovely new swings,' she said, 'but I suppose you're much too old for that sort of thing now.'

I saw Cath squirm.

'I don't mind going if Tess wants to go,' she said. 'She's still into that sort of thing!'

'So am I!' Gran said. 'When the children are back in school, I often have a swing!'

She was probably fibbing but it annoyed Cath so that I knew she'd have a go when we got there. Gran gave us sixpence each and told us to buy an ice cream. We left together – not talking, but side by side – and Gran watched us go.

The swings were huge, tall and wide with the swings on chains. I tried them out as soon as we got there.

'Keep your legs together,' Cath said as I zoomed up and over her head.

It wasn't long before she tried one and soon she was swinging just as high as I was. The park was very quiet. There were some little boys kicking a ball about on the grass and there were a few mothers with prams walking along the paths. After the swings I persuaded Cath to try the see–saw with me but she was so much heavier than I was that it didn't really work too well.

'Let's go and find an ice cream,' I suggested, rubbing my leg where the see–saw had scraped it as I got off.

I had a cornet and Cath had a slice, which the man cut from a block, between two wafers. We didn't get ice cream at home very often and it was a real treat. We sat on the grass in the sun in front of the kiosk and watched the gardener working his way along the flower beds, weeding and cutting off the dead flower heads. His wheelbarrow was made of wood and had an iron tyre round its wheel which was also made of wood.

It was quite late when we got back to Gran's and we were actually talking to each other! I think Gran must have thought that Mum didn't feed us because she'd made a plate of sandwiches for us. I was surprised to see that Cath tucked in just like me and she drank a whole glass of squash. Just before we left Gran fetched her purse and gave me five shillings.

'Keep it for your choir outing,' she said.

Then she gave Cath the same but said she could buy something for her sewing with it. The bus was empty on the way home and we all sat upstairs across the front so that we could see everything.

Because it was Wednesday I had to go to choir practice. When we were all in church the Vicar came into church and said that since Chris had the best attendance for the year he could bring a friend with him on the choir outing. We were going to the Isle of Wight next week. We all asked Chris who he was going to bring but he wouldn't say.

'I bet he brings his pesky little brother,' Bunny said.

I thought that it was quite likely since his Mum could have a quiet day to herself if they were both out of her way. We checked over all the hedges on the way home but there was no sign of the Prowler. When I got back home they were listening to the wireless, 'Educating Archie' was on.

'Goo d'evenin geach!' I said, doing my best impersonation of Beryl Read.

Almost as soon as I'd said it, she came on and repeated the catchphrase. Mum laughed.

'She's better than you,' she said.

They'd got the Monopoly board out ready to play. I think Mum must have been tired because she went bankrupt almost as soon as we'd started and became the banker. We had to keep reminding her to pay out when we passed 'Go'. I didn't do much better because Cath got her grubby hands on Mayfair and all the Stations and Dad had Vine Street and Regent Street, so I didn't really stand a chance.

I left them to battle it out. Neither of them would give in and they'd probably be at it for another couple of hours. Mum was knitting so I got out the tiddlywinks and practised my shots. If you played on the carpet it was more unpredictable and getting them in the cup was much more difficult.

Chapter 20

I thought that Mum would have things for me to do the next morning but she was up early and was already reading the paper when I came down for breakfast. I don't know what Gran said to her yesterday but she certainly seemed more cheerful that she had been for ages.

'I suppose you'll want to go out,' she said, looking up. 'Check the March sisters on your way. I think they like you popping in now and then.'

'They don't always have anything for me to do.'

'But I think they like to have someone to talk to. They're lonely. They don't get many visitors and you cheer them up.'

I said I would and got on with my breakfast.

'I thought we'd have sausages for dinner today,' she said.

'Great!' I said, trying to sound enthusiastic.

I couldn't be doing with this new chatty mood of hers but I didn't want to be rude. I put marmalade on my toast and stuffed my mouth full. At least she couldn't expect me to talk now.

'Make sure you're back by half-past twelve,' Mum said. 'I'm on cleaning duty this afternoon and I don't want to be late.'

There were all sorts of rotas at the church. Mum was useless at flower arranging so she took her turn on the cleaning rota. It was her turn once every two months and she swept the floors and polished the altar rail and the choir pews. She did the cleaning with Mrs Walker, Chris's Mum, who polished the brass and washed out the porch. Every spring we all had to go just before Easter for the annual spring clean and the men brought ladders and cleaned the windows and dusted off the light shades. Last year we even took out the book cases at the back where the hymn books were stored and dusted them all off and cleaned all the cobwebs.

I dropped in on the March sisters and they wanted me to go up the butchers and get them two slices of liver for their dinner.

'It's so much quicker for you on your bike,' Miss Eileen said. 'It'll take us an hour if we have to walk.'

It took me ten minutes and they gave me sixpence for my

troubles. I rode on up to the woods and took the dirt track to PeeDee's den to see if he was there.

All his gang were there and something was wrong. They were sitting outside and looked very angry. PeeDee saw me coming and immediately jumped up.

'Have your lot done this?' he demanded.

'What?'

'Don't act the innocent. I bet it was all your idea!'

'I don't know what you're talking about.'

I think he was beginning to calm down. At least he had stopped shouting.

'Someone's been in our den,' he said. 'Come and look!'

'You sound like Daddy Bear,' I said, laughing.

'Well, you're no Goldilocks,' he retorted.

He waited for me to prop my bike against a tree.

'I didn't think you came up here in the evenings,' he said.

'I don't.'

'Well, you must have come up last night and done it,' he said.

'We were all here yesterday afternoon.'

I went into his den. The inside had been painted bright red and there was a notice scrawled on a piece of paper pinned on the wall. 'Under new ownership! Keep out!'

'It wasn't our lot,' I said. Then, when he didn't look convinced, I added, 'We were thinking of waiting until you were all in and then tying the door so you couldn't get out unless you paid us a ransom.'

Suddenly PeeDee grinned.

'I thought it wasn't your style,' he said, 'but the others said it must've been you. Who else is there?'

'Doesn't look like the Teddy boys again,' I said. 'It's too crude and the writing isn't grown up. I bet it was kids.'

'They wouldn't dare,' PeeDee said. 'They know I'd flatten them.'

'Might be some of the new kids on the estate,' I said.

They'd been taking some of the big trees out of the woods along the back of the houses and there was a new road cut in that rumour said was going all the way to Horndean. There weren't many houses yet but there were kids — I'd seen them riding their bikes on the new road. But I'd never seen them in the woods. If they were getting that brave then we'd all have to be on our guard.

Everything was different. It felt as if the Cowplain we knew was changing so fast that we never quite knew what was going to alter next. The new shops were good, of course, but we didn't want loads of new kids on our patch.

'I think we ought to work on this together,' I said. 'We can't start building our rafts if they're going to keep pestering us. Have you seen any of them?'

PeeDee shrugged.

'There's never been anyone else when I've been here except your lot.'

'And I haven't seen anyone else, either.'

I sat with PeeDee's gang and we tried to think of a plan.

'If it is the new kids,' Beaky said, 'they're much nearer and can watch out for when we go, and then they can come in and destroy our den, safe in the knowledge that we aren't here.'

It looked as if we had a real problem on our hands.

'If they are doing things in the woods,' I said, 'they've probably left things. If we can find anything we might be able to work out who they are.'

'Tod might know something,' Goat said. 'Since he's a year younger he might have heard them talking at school last term.'

'Good point,' I said. 'I'll ask him. We're meeting this afternoon at my house.'

'This is war,' Roller said. 'Real war! Not like our challenges. We've got to exterminate them!'

'The thing is,' Beaky said, 'if we can't come out in the evenings we'll never be able to catch them at it.'

'Don't see it'll make any difference,' Chris said. 'We've all been looking for the Prowler and we haven't caught him yet. We haven't even seen him and he prowls our estate. We don't stand a chance up here.'

'We can't just give up,' PeeDee said.

'Why don't you fix the loose board at the back?' I suggested. 'And then we could get a lock for the door. At least you've got a door!'

'Have you checked your den?' PeeDee asked.

'Not yet, I was on my way when I saw you lot sitting out here.'

'Let's go,' Chris said.

We rushed over to our den. It looked all right from the outside. I checked the secret stone and inside. It hadn't been touched.

'Perhaps they don't know it's here,' I said.

'We could leave one of my lot in your den and then we could go,' PeeDee said, thinking out aloud. 'If we made a lot of noise they'd know we'd gone and then we could find out who it is.'

It seemed as if a plan was coming together.

'I think we ought to meet on the green after lunch,' I said. 'It's no use meeting here 'cause they might be watching us and we don't want them to know what we've got in mind.'

'There isn't time to do everything,' Chris said. 'We've still got to find the Prowler, we're still looking for clues about the murder and now there's this new lot, let alone our rafts.'

'We'll build the rafts at my place' I said. 'I'll talk to Dad, he'll help.'

'And I'll take over the Prowler,' PeeDee said. He's nearly always seen at dusk. I'll ask Sandy to help, she's usually coming home at the sort of time he's seen.'

'Perhaps this new lot have come to look for dead bodies,' Beaky said. 'It's all your fault, Ten. You've made our woods famous.'

I knew he was pulling my leg but it made sense.

'I can't stay now,' I said, 'Mum's cooking sausages and I've got to be in by half past, but we'll meet after lunch.'

I cycled off home. I knew there was something coming together in my mind but it didn't make any sense yet. I needed time for my idea to gel.

'You're quiet,' Mum said at lunch.

'I was thinking,' I said.

'Told you she was ill,' Cath said to Mum. 'Didn't think you actually had any grey cells,' she said, turning to me. 'Does it hurt?'

I stuck my tongue out.

'If you two can't think of anything nice to say to each other,' Mum said, 'perhaps you'd better not talk at all.'

'But I didn't said a word,' I protested.

The sausages were great and we finished in silence. The idea in my head wouldn't stop buzzing around and I wasn't really thinking about lunch at all. Suddenly, I realised that Mum was talking to me.

'Sorry,' I said. 'What did you say?'

'I asked if you went in to the March sisters,' she said.

'Oh, yes. I said I would. They only wanted some liver from the butcher's. It didn't take long. They said they might be going out tomorrow,' I added, 'so they won't need me.'

'I still think it's creepy,' Cath said, 'you looking after two old ladies.'

Cath was clearly feeling argumentative and I scuttled off as soon as I could. I offered to help wash up but Mum said she and Cath would do it. I don't think Cath was pleased but I didn't argue, I just made my escape and cycled round to the green to wait for PeeDee and the others.

I think finding PeeDee's shed like that had made us all a bit worried. Too many things were happening and we didn't have any answers. We held a war council on the green when everybody had come, but we didn't come up with any original ideas. Goat was all for abandoning Padnell woods.

'All the older kids go to the Queen's Inclosure,' he said. 'Perhaps now we're older we should make a move as well, leave Padnell to the little kids.'

'What about the unexploded ammo?' Beaky asked.

'I haven't heard about anyone being blown up,' Goat said. 'I bet it's all just a rumour to keep us out.'

'We've got to solve the murder first,' I said. 'When we've done that perhaps we'll go and look round.'

'Perhaps we'll find more dead bodies,' Oz said. 'We could start a collection!'

They started kicking the ball about and I guessed they'd run out of steam. I had something to do so I left them to it and cycled off.

I was late back and Dad had already arrived home when I came in.

'Are you going to tell her?' Mum asked Dad. She seemed a bit agitated.

'Tell me what?' I demanded, wondering what they were getting at now.

'There's been another body found,' Dad said. 'In Guildford. There's a chunk about it in tonight's paper.'

'Well, it wasn't me,' I said.

'Here,' Dad said, getting up, 'read it for yourself.'

> ### Lead on Murdered Man
>
> Inspector Johnson has revealed to your busy reporter that another murdered man was found this very morning in Surrey, his body having been dumped in woodland, much like the man found by schoolgirl Theresa Thomas in the woods in Cowplain.
>
> *'It's too early to say whether there is any connection between the two murders,'* the Inspector told us, *'but some of the details of each case are similar.'*
>
> Unlike our own police, the Guildford force is confident that it has a lead on the dead man. A van was seen in the vicinity last night and Mr Hurford, who was walking his dog, has been able to help. He said that the registration number was unusual and it stuck in his memory.

'What I don't understand,' Cath said, 'is why they keep mentioning her name. I mean, this has nothing to do with Tess.'

'Quite right,' Mum said, rather quickly. 'This has absolutely nothing to do with Tess.'

'But Tess is what links it to our local news,' Dad said. 'She's important because everybody remembers her name and it reminds them what it's all about.'

'Well I don't see how they are connected,' I said. 'I mean, all murdered men are dead and I guess lots of them are dumped out of sight.'

It seemed such a coincidence that I grinned as I remembered what Oz had said about starting a collection of dead bodies.

'Don't be so blasé,' Mum said. 'It's bad enough that you found one murdered man in our village. Now another man has been killed and it's only one week later. I don't know what the world's coming to.'

'I didn't mean it wasn't bad that someone else has been killed,' I said. 'It's just something Oz said. What I want to know is why the police think there may be a connection.'

'Thank God it's nothing to do with us,' Mum said with a shudder. 'And now I don't want to talk about it any more.'

Chapter 21

That evening I spent a long time looking at the bit of paper I'd taken from PeeDee's den after I left them playing football on the green. I'd been thinking about it ever since I'd seen what had happened to his den. I know I said it was probably kids but the more I thought about it the more it didn't seem like kids at all. Lots of things just didn't add up.

I mean, if they were old enough to paint the shed like that then it followed that they wouldn't be scared of us. And when had they done it? The paint was dry so it must have been done the day before, the day when I was visiting Gran in Portsmouth, but PeeDee said his lot were there all the afternoon which meant that it couldn't have been painted until after they'd gone home. So it must have been done in the evening, just like he said. And it was painted quite well. Better than I could have done it, better than little kids would have done it. And yet another thing, would a group of little kids who had never ventured into the woods before have been brave enough to come out in the evening and do it? Wouldn't their parents have noticed? And where did they get the paint?

But it was the note that bothered me most of all. How many little kids would use a word like 'ownership' I wondered? True the writing looked childish but it might not have been written by a child. It could just as easily have been written by someone who wanted us to think it had been written by a child and if that was the case ...

I was beginning to think that it was all a ruse to try and drive us away from the woods. First it had been the rope and now it was PeeDee's den. Who would want to keep us away? I could only think of one answer to that question and it made my flesh creep. It looked as if we really were involved in a mystery and someone was trying to frighten us off. But if that was true, the next questions were 'who' and 'why'?

It was the 'why' bit that I was thinking about now. We'd already found the body so that couldn't be it. And anyway, if they hadn't wanted the body found they'd have hidden it more carefully. So if it wasn't the body it must have been something else. Elementary, dear Watson, I thought, any fool could have worked that out.

If it was something they didn't want us to find then whatever it was it must be valuable. It couldn't have been another body so it must either be something quite big or something which they needed to hide for the time being. Something they intended coming back to collect or they'd simply have taken it last night when they painted PeeDee's den. So why hadn't they? That was the question that bothered me and I couldn't answer it.

I was still thinking about it when I went to bed and I didn't sleep much that night. I needed to talk about it with someone. I suppose in a normal family I'd have talked it through with my sister but I knew I couldn't do that with Cath. For one thing she'd go and tell Mum the instant I'd finished – and that would put an end to it all – and for another thing she wouldn't have a clue how to help me. There was Pud, of course. He always listened when I had something on my mind but he wasn't very bright and I couldn't see him helping me to come up with a master plan. The rest of the gang would get fired up and I'd have a job from stopping them running riot through the woods. I needed someone who was clever and cunning, someone who would think it through properly and not rush off on a wild goose chase.

It came as a shock when I realised I was thinking about PeeDee! Over this last week we had spent more time together and I was beginning to see that he was not as impetuous as I'd always thought. True he had a quick temper and was always too ready with his fists, but I felt he would understand what I was talking about. I knew I could rely on him because he was already worried about our safety. I could see the moon high in the sky through my window and it must have been the small hours before I went to sleep.

I was in the woods and someone was shaking me. I punched out. I was rewarded by a loud shriek – I had punched Cath!

'You needn't have done that,' she said, rubbing her cheek.

'Well, I didn't know it was you, I was asleep.'

'That's why I was waking you up, thick head!'

Mum came in to see what we were shouting about.

'She hit me!' Cath said.

'She frightened me, I was asleep.'

'No harm done,' Mum said.

'It's not you she hit,' Cath muttered.

'Get up now Tess,' Mum said, 'it's nearly ten o'clock!'

I rushed through my breakfast and went in search of PeeDee. I tried the green first but there were only some young kids playing there so I cycled round to the woods, scorched along the dirt track and drew up outside PeeDee's den. I went in. Now I looked at it more carefully I could see that the paintwork wasn't as good as I had previously thought. The den was deserted so I went on to our den. That, too, was empty. The last place I could think of was the pond but there was no one there either. I was beginning to panic, where were they?

I came back down Padnell Road and stopped off at the March house just in case they'd changed their minds and wanted something. Miss Eileen was in but she was on her own.

'Miss Barbara has gone to have her hair cut and set,' she said. 'She's bringing back a couple of pies for lunch so we're all right for now.'

As I cycled off I suddenly thought of Monkey. Perhaps they'd gone down to the Spotted Cow to see him. I turned out of Padnell Road and made my way down the hill, but his Mum said Monkey was out. I didn't have the cheek to ask where so I made my way back home.

'You're back early,' Cath said when I went into the kitchen.

I knew she was trying to find out why I was not out with my friends but I ignored her and went up to my room. It was time to do some serious thinking. It seemed to me that there were two separate problems. Firstly, there was the Prowler. He could have been the murderer but we had no proof. None of us had seen him so we didn't even know who we were looking for. Secondly, there was the murder. There was definitely a body, but we didn't know who he was, who had killed him or why they'd done it. And then there was the question of PeeDee's den but I was sure that it was tied up with the murder.

What we needed to do was to start making a thorough search of the woods. I know the police had already done it but they didn't know the woods as well as we did. We knew all the secret places where things might have been hidden and I was certain that we'd spot anything unusual, or at least anything that was not usually there. It was surprising what things we'd found in the woods. Once we'd found a set of false teeth and on another occasion we'd found a pair of corsets. I wasn't sure what we should be looking for now but I knew if it was there we'd find it.

I waited in after lunch and it wasn't long before PeeDee and Goat arrived with Chris and Merlin.

'Where were you lot this morning?' I asked.

'I had to go down to Waterlooville with Mum,' PeeDee said.

'I got up late,' Goat said.

'The thing is,' I said impatiently, 'we've got to make a thorough search of the woods.'

'Why?' Chris asked.

I really wished I'd had time to talk this through with PeeDee but it was too late now.

'Look,' I said, 'I don't think it was kids that did your den over.'

PeeDee's eyebrows shot up. I went through the things I had been thinking over last night. I must say, it all sounded quite convincing when I listed them all, one after the other.

'I bet it's all tied up with the murder,' I finished up. 'They don't want us in the woods and they're trying to frighten us off.'

There was a stunned silence for a moment or two.

'It's possible,' PeeDee said at last. 'It all adds up when you think of it like that.'

'What are we going to look for?' Chris asked.

'I'm not sure,' I said. 'Anything that isn't usually there or anything that catches your eye.'

'That's not much help,' Goat muttered.

'If they don't want us to find it,' I said, 'then they'll have hidden it and we know the best hiding places. Go and round the others up, we need to get started.'

We split up at the gate. PeeDee and I went straight to the woods, Merlin, Chris and Goat went in search of the others after arranging to meet us at PeeDee's den.

When we got to his den PeeDee went straight in and I followed him.

'I see what you mean about the painting,' he said. 'It's too good for little kids.'

'And there isn't any mess. Whoever did it was used to painting.'

'You're getting quite good at this detective stuff,' PeeDee said admiringly. 'I'd never have thought about the mess.'

'Neither did I until now,' I said, hoping that honesty would stop him from being silly.

We didn't have long to wait before Oz and Pud arrived.

'How are we going to do this?' Pud asked.

'It might be best if we split up into pairs,' Oz suggested. 'That way we can cover more ground.'

'Let's wait till the rest get here,' PeeDee said, 'then we can organise ourselves properly.'

I felt a curious pent up excitement. It was as if I knew that we were going to find something this time even though our previous search had turned up nothing. When everybody had arrived I went through my plan and PeeDee divided us up into pairs, one of his gang with one of my lot like we did last time.

'That way,' he said, 'we stand a better chance of spotting anything unusual. What seems ordinary to a Flag Boy might be unusual for a Bramble boy – we can check each other.'

We sorted out the routes that we would search and just before we set off I reminded everyone that the police had found nothing.

'And we found nothing last time,' I added. 'So this time we've got to think like the gang who dumped the body. If they didn't know the woods too well then they would have gone for the obvious hiding places that they thought were hidden. Don't overlook anything this time.'

PeeDee and I set off along the path that led on from where I'd found the body.

'If they dumped the body here,' he said when we came to the track where I'd come off my bike, 'then they might just have walked on in for a bit until they found somewhere they thought was well hidden.'

'It would help if we knew what we were looking for,' I said.

'It could be the murder weapon,' PeeDee suggested.

'Not very likely,' I said. If they were in the woods they would probably have thrown it in the pond.'

'That's a point,' PeeDee said. 'What if they did and then they took the rope down to try and stop us using the pond in case we found it.'

That was good thinking. I was impressed.

'But surely they'd have taken the rope away,' I said. 'They must have had a car or a van and they'd just have thrown it in the back.'

'Still, it might be worth searching the pond if we don't find anything else,' PeeDee said.

We worked our way along the path but not actually on the path.

'If they came this way and hid something,' PeeDee suggested, 'what ever they hid will be in the bushes on one side or the other. They wouldn't just leave it on the path.'

Working along the undergrowth like this took a lot of time and I was getting quite scratched but it made good sense. Unfortunately we didn't find anything unusual. We'd almost given up when I spotted a newspaper.

'Look,' I said, picking it up, 'it's not local. It's The Surrey Advertiser.'

'Wasn't the other body found near Guildford?' PeeDee asked.

'That's right.'

I looked at the newspaper's date.

'It's dated last weekend,' I said. 'And they dumped the body a week ago, probably on Wednesday evening. The paper wasn't out then.'

'That means they've been back since they dumped the body.'

We looked at each other. This changed everything.

'It could do. All we really know is someone has been here with a Guildford newspaper,' I said. 'We must keep looking. They must have come this way.'

We still didn't know what we were looking for but, since the newspaper hadn't been on the actual path, we felt confident that we were looking in the right place and sooner or later we'd find something unusual. We'd reached the top of the rise and were standing in front of a spreading holly bush. This appeared to be a dense, prickly bush but when you walked round to the back there was a small gap through which you could squeeze and hide. We'd all used it from time to time when we were playing Fox and Hounds.

'What do you think?' I asked PeeDee.

'It's a bit obvious,' he said. 'Worth a try, though.'

We walked round and PeeDee squeezed in.

'Hey, come on in,' he called out.

There wasn't much room inside and we were jammed in against each other.

'Look!' PeeDee said pointing to the far corner where the branches reached right down to the ground.

'That's it,' I said. 'I think we've found the missing link!'

Chapter 22

PeeDee was the best whistler in either gang and he crawled out and gave a piercing blast. I sat looking at what we'd found. I knew enough to know that no one must move it or touch it. Too bad I'd already touched the newspaper but that couldn't be helped now.

As soon as the rest had come over to us we had a quick pow-wow. We agreed that we had to keep guard so that no one could touch or remove the evidence. In the end we sent Pud to tell my Mum that we'd found something.

'Make sure she knows it's not another body!' I said.

And we sent Merlin and Chris to tell Constable Norris.

'He'll know what to do,' I said. 'Tell him we think it's connected with the body I found.'

'And tell him we think we've connected it with the Guildford body,' PeeDee added.

'And possibly the Portsmouth bank raid,' I called after them, 'or at the very least with some sort of illegal money stash.'

'And tell him we're keeping watch until he gets here!' PeeDee shouted out just before they vanished.

The rest wanted to stay and wait with us for the police to arrive but we managed to persuade Tod and Beaky to wait on the road edge to show Plod where to come.

'It's a very important job,' I said. 'Time is short and we don't want to waste time. Who knows, we might prevent another murder.'

We sat and waited for PC Norris to arrive.

'Perhaps there's money buried nearby,' Goat said. 'We ought to have a quick look.'

'Don't be stupid,' I snapped. 'We mustn't disturb anything. In fact I think you should all wait well away, just in case.'

'Okay,' Goat said. 'If I don't touch anything at all, can I stay?'

He looked so anxious that I would send him away that I almost laughed.

'We're all in this together,' I said. 'This time we'll all be in the paper!'

'But it was Ten who put it all together,' PeeDee said.

Goat looked at PeeDee as if he'd gone mad. Personally I thought PeeDee had gone soft in the head but I didn't say anything. Time began to drag. Roller was playing five stones. He nearly always had something in his pocket, marbles, five stones or a pack of cards.

'Move away a bit further,' PeeDee said. 'There might be important foot prints and with you scuffing up the grass and leaves you might be destroying vital evidence.'

Roller grunted and moved off a couple of paces.

'I can hear voices,' Oz said.

'What if it's the murderers coming back for their money?' Beaky asked.

'Don't be daft,' PeeDee said scornfully. 'They won't come in broad daylight. They work at night.'

We could all hear voices now and I recognised PC Norris's voice.

'I hope they haven't touched anything,' he was saying.

I heard Merlin tell him that I was in charge and we were all keeping the site secure in case anyone else came.

PC Norris arrived and looked at us all squatting down outside the holly bush.

'Good afternoon, Constable Norris,' I said in my best Sunday voice. 'We think we might have found a couple of things which might help in your enquiries.'

'Good afternoon, Miss Marples,' he said, grinning. He saw the look of surprise on PeeDee's face. 'Miss Marples is a female detective,' he explained. 'In Agatha Christie's books.'

I handed him the newspaper.

'I'm sorry I picked it up,' I said. 'But I didn't know what it was until I opened it out. I had to touch it to do that. But we haven't touched anything in there.'

I pointed to the holly bush and the tiny opening at its back.

'I think I'll wait for Inspector Johnson before we go in there. You're sure it's a money bag?'

'I'm sure it's one of the bags they put the money in when they're taking it to and from banks,' PeeDee said. 'It's blue and there's printing on it but we couldn't see properly because we didn't want to touch it.'

'It doesn't look as if there's anything inside it,' I added.

PC Norris chatted to us while we all waited for the Inspector to arrive. When he finally arrived he came with all the help he needed this time. He spoke to us and cleared us back from the crime scene.

'I'll need to talk to you all,' he said. 'Don't go away.'

As if any of us would have budged! We watched as they retrieved the cash bag from the middle of the holly bush and then undertook a painstaking search of the whole area.

'I don't want anything missed this time,' he barked at the police officers who were starting the search on their hands and knees. 'Now, young lady,' he said turning to me and speaking in a more gentle voice, 'show me where you found the newspaper.'

PeeDee and I led him back along the path.

'Ten said we ought to look in the bushes at the sides of the path,' PeeDee explained.

Inspector Johnson nodded.

'And we'd almost given up,' PeeDee continued, 'when she saw the newspaper. It was kind of screwed up. She picked it up and then we saw that it was the Guildford paper and it had a last week's date.'

'So it was only you two who actually found anything'

PeeDee nodded.

'We were all looking. The rest weren't lucky like we were.'

'There is one other thing,' I said when he came back. 'Someone's painted PeeDee's den and put a notice on it. That's what started me thinking and why we started our search.'

I explained about PeeDee's den and the note.

'I've got the note at home,' I said. 'I didn't think about finger prints and all that. We thought it was just little kids mucking about.'

'Right,' he said to us, 'let's look at the den and then we'll get your statements and I'll have a look at the note.'

A bit later the Inspector sent the rest away.

'You can all go back home,' he said. 'But don't talk about it. Just keep quiet. You can tell your parents but ask them to keep it quiet for now.' He turned to PeeDee and me. 'I'll have to take statements from each of you,' he said. 'It might be best if we do it at Miss Thomas's house. She knows the ropes and her Mum will vouch for your statement as well.'

Suddenly PeeDee looked nervous. I guess the police were not always welcome in his house.

'I won't get into trouble, will I?' he asked.

'Quite the contrary,' the Inspector said. 'If this gives us a break through you might even be in line for a reward!'

PeeDee sat down next to me, clearly relieved.

'I think I'll send a constable for your Mum,' the Inspector said.

He went back to his men and gave them some more instructions.

'We can all meet at number 10. It's always best to have both sets of parents present.'

We showed him the inside of PeeDee's den and he agreed that it didn't look like the work of kids. Then we went back to the road and we climbed into the police car. He didn't ring the bells or flash the lights but it was still quite exciting riding back home in a police car. PeeDee enjoyed it immensely. Mum was quite sanguine about it once she knew there were no more dead bodies. The Inspector was very reassuring and made it sound as if what we had done was very helpful. PeeDee's Mum arrived, still in her overall, and was about to lay into PeeDee but the Inspector stopped her.

'Your son is a good example of our modern youth,' he said. 'You should be very proud of him!'

That took the wind out of her sails and PeeDee began to relax. The Inspector took PeeDee's statement first. Cath was seething with envy. Again! She was back in the tea making routine and fussing about but no one paid any attention to her. After PeeDee came out it was my turn. It didn't take long and Mum and I signed like old hands. Back in the kitchen we offered the Inspector a cup of tea but he said he had to be getting back to his men.

PeeDee's Mum stayed though, and she and Mum chatted away like old friends. PeeDee and I hot-footed it out to the shed.

'This won't change our going to the pictures tomorrow, will it?' PeeDee asked.

The chance was almost too tempting to miss but something had changed. Suddenly I realised that I was looking forward to going out with PeeDee tomorrow.

'Can't see why it should,' I said in as off-handed a way as I could.

PeeDee looked relieved.

It was Cath who told Dad all about my new exploit. As soon as he came in she started burbling away like a lunatic.

'What is she talking about?' Dad asked me. 'Has she totally lost the plot?'

'You know they found another body in Guildford?' I said.

'You haven't found another?' he asked.

'No, it's nothing like that. But we found some more clues this afternoon and the police think it's all tied in with the Portsmouth bank raid.

'Oh, is that all?'

'Is that all?' Cath said. She sounded dead miffed.

'Well, it doesn't match being in the national papers, does it?'

He took a copy of a daily paper out of his brief case.

'Someone had a copy at work and they showed it to me. I thought you might like to see it!'

He handed it to me.

'It's not quite the headline,' he said. 'It's just a tiny paragraph on page four. I shouldn't pay to much attention to it,' Dad said. 'It's just typical of the stuff that rag prints.'

All the same, we did listen to the evening news on the wireless just in case there was a mention. But, of course, there was nothing about it so Mum and Dad listened to a couple of programmes and I read my book.

Is no-one safe?

Not one body but two have been found in the South of England and all our gallant police can say is that they are baffled! The first body was found by a young schoolgirl, Theresa Thomas, when she was playing in the woods near her home in Hampshire. *'I fell off my bike and landed on him!'* she said. The second body was found in Surrey by a man walking his dog. Both men had been savagely murdered and their dead bodies dumped in woodland. No attempt had been made to bury them and this suggests to us that whoever did this was in a hurry to get away.

Is no one safe any more? What is this country coming to? Is this the best we can do? Did the pride of our youth die in the war so that the young and innocent can find murder victims in the woods? We say that it's time the police did their jobs. Undetected crime must not be allowed to hold sway in this glorious country of ours. We want our young to be safe when they go out to play.

Chapter 23

PeeDee came early. I was already up and had finished my breakfast. I thought that if I got up before Cath woke up, I could probably get out without her poking fun at me. It took courage for me to dress as a girl. PeeDee wanted me to look posh but I didn't go the whole hog and put my best clothes on. I settled on my only other dress – apart from my school dress which, of course, didn't count.

It was a navy blue pinafore dress and had white piping at the neck and round the sleeves. I wore my white blouse with puff sleeves under it. I knew it was probably going to be a warm day but I wore the navy cardigan Mum had knitted me because I felt I needed something on my arms. It was a strange sensation. All the week I'd been wearing just shorts and a T-shirt but as soon as I put the dress on I felt exposed. The only concession I made to PeeDee was to wear my blue hair band.

Mum and Dad looked at me when I came down to breakfast but didn't say anything about my clothes. Well, not directly, but Mum did suggest I wore an apron in case I spilled anything and Dad offered to polish my shoes. That put me on my guard because normally I had to polish his shoes!

'If I'd have thought,' Mum said, 'you could have borrowed my clear nail polish.'

'Mum,' I said, 'don't be so Nancy!'

'Next time,' she said.

'There won't be a next time,' I said.

Fortunately we were interrupted by the front door knocker and Dad went to see who it was. He showed PeeDee through to the kitchen. I'd only just had time to take my apron off before he came in. I wouldn't have recognised him if it hadn't been for the colour of his hair. He was wearing a tidy pair of grey trousers and a grey shirt – probably his next term's school uniform, I guessed – and he was wearing black shoes (which had been polished) and grey socks, although the one on his left leg had rumpled down towards his ankle.

'Hi, Tess,' he said, grinning like a Cheshire cat, 'you look great!'

I felt a blush starting on my neck so I shrugged.

'Just what girls usually wear,' I said.

Dad gave PeeDee some money.

'For the bus fare,' he said.

'That's all right, Mr Thomas, my Dad gave me some for the fare and the tickets.'

'Well, buy some sweets, then.'

'Come on,' I said to PeeDee, 'we don't want to miss the bus.'

'It's very early,' Mum said. 'You could wait until the next one.'

But by then there would be too many people about. I didn't want to be seen dressed like this and going out with PeeDee.

'I think it will be better if we get there early,' I said. 'The bus might be full or there might be a queue at the cinema.'

'Right, off you go, you two,' Dad said, emphasising the 'you two' rather too heartily for my liking.

'Lunch at one,' Mum said. 'Do you want to stay Peter?'

For one dreadful moment I thought he was going to say 'yes' but he declined Mum's offer.

'Mum said the same thing to me,' he said. 'I'd better not disappoint her.'

I knew he was lying through his teeth because they had their main meal on Sundays and he usually had to go up the chip shop for Saturday lunch and sometimes he just had a sandwich. I knew this because I'd seen him eating at the recreation ground while he watched the football. Somehow his fib made him seem more thoughtful than usual and I was pleased that he'd avoided embarrassing me.

We caught the bus without being seen and sat downstairs. We got off at the Hulbert Road stop and walked on into Waterlooville. The Curzon Cinema was on our side of the town and so we knew we were unlikely to meet anyone and also, as PeeDee pointed out, it gave us a penny more for sweets.

'Do you come often?' I asked him as we started walking.

'Not often,' he said. 'Too expensive! But I come if Dad wants to get rid of me and he pays.'

I was having trouble with my shoulder bag. I didn't know whether to carry it, put it on my shoulder or round my neck. There were no pockets in my dress, although there was a pocket on the front of my green knickers. But since I didn't think I could hoist up my skirt to get my hanky or my money out I was forced to use the bag. It was the silliest thing and I resolved to make sure that any other dress I was forced to wear in the future had a pocket. In the end I wound the shoulder strap round the bag and carried it in the hand nearest PeeDee. That way, I thought, there would be no chance of him wanting to hold my hand. Not that he'd tried! But he did make sure he was walking on the outside like a real gentleman should.

There was a short queue when we reached the cinema so we joined the end of it and it wasn't long before we were inside. There seemed to be loads of silly kids everywhere, all shrieking and talking at the tops of their voices.

'Is it always like this?' I asked.

'Usually. It'll get worse when he starts.'

'Who?'

'The Club leader.'

'The what?'

'You haven't been before have you?' PeeDee asked.

I shook my head.

'It's not like when you come in the evening. On Saturday mornings there's a man who comes on and introduces the films and he tells jokes and we have to sing the Saturday song.'

This was all news to me and I didn't like the sound of it one little bit.

'Don't worry, you just have to put up with it. That's why the tickets are cheap.'

A spot light lit up the front of the curtains and a man walked on stage in front of the curtains. The kids in the audience started cheering like mad. The next half–hour was excruciating. The man tried to tell jokes but the kids shouted him down. He called some up on to the stage and tried to hold a competition with hula hoops. He said they were the latest thing but they just looked like the hoops we used in PE to me. The children cheated so he gave up that idea. Then the curtains went back and the words of a song were projected on to the screen and he tried to get us to sing them. It might have been worth the effort if they hadn't been so silly. He went off after that and we sang the National Anthem – at least everybody did that properly – and then there was a trailer about next week's films.

The first film was a cartoon and then there was a Lassie film. It was terribly sad and it almost made me cry – just as well the lights were off! After that there was a cowboy film which was much more fun and then the climax of the morning was a Superman cartoon. The audience seemed to have settled down now and we watched it with baited breath. Just as it looked as if everything was going to end in disaster we saw Superman in the distance ... and then the film faded. PeeDee said we'd have to come back next week to see what happened.

'But it's always all right in the end,' he said.

Then the little kids started shouting again and the lights came on again and they all started scrambling to get to the exits. It seemed as if everybody had gone mad and we were carried along with the crowd. For a moment I lost sight of PeeDee and then I felt someone grab my hand. I looked round and saw it was PeeDee so I hung on to his hand in case we got parted again. When we came into the foyer it was much calmer. PeeDee didn't let go of my hand and somehow it seemed to be all right.

It was earlier than I'd expected so, since there was plenty of time, we decided to walk home and save the bus fares. For the moment the pavement was wide enough for us to walk side by side. PeeDee changed sides so that he was on the outside and he reached for my hand again. I don't know why, but I didn't stop him and we walked back hand in hand. I don't know what we talked about but it seemed to take us no time at all before we reached the Queen's Inclosure at the start of Cowplain. PeeDee let go of my hand. It seemed the right thing to do. We didn't want anyone to see us like that!

Mum and Dad quizzed me about the films at dinner time.

'It was silly, not finishing the film,' I said.

'That's so that you'll want to go back and see what happens next week,' Dad said.

'Well, I guess Superman will come to the rescue,' I said.

'Don't you want to go back and find out?' Cath said pointedly.

'Don't think so,' I said. 'Even PeeDee thought it was all too childish. The little kids were screaming like idiots!'

I saw Mum look across at Dad.

'I didn't think you went to the pictures to look at the film,' Cath said.

'I can't think why else you'd go,' I said.

I knew what she was trying to get at but I wasn't going to rise.

'Perhaps you'd better go to a Saturday afternoon matinee next time,' Dad said. 'They show proper films then.'

'Why didn't anyone tell me that before?' I asked.

'I expect that now you're in the national newspapers they thought you were too grown up to need baby–sitting.' Cath said.

Chapter 24

It was late when we'd finished lunch and I was too tidy to go out. The sun had gone in and the sky was clouding over. Dad said it looked like rain.

'I hope the police have finished searching the woods,' he said. 'If it rains they'll lose all their clues.'

'I don't expect there was much left to find,' Mum said. 'Not after our sleuth had done her work!'

I was surprised that they both seemed so positive now. After I found the dead body they had been a bit strange. Still, perhaps they were getting used to it all now and my not having found another dead body helped to make it seem less awful.

'It's just as well you had Peter with you,' Mum said. 'He seems such a sensible boy.'

PeeDee sensible! She needed her head looking at! I was going to say just how sensible PeeDee usually was when I remembered that he had warned me to be careful in the woods. And he had insisted on going with me. I thought it had been so that he could share in my success if we found anything, but perhaps he had been looking out for me as well. Mum and Dad drifted off to look at colours for the paintwork in the living room. Dad had a week's holiday coming up and he was going to redecorate it. They'd already chosen the wall paper. It had what Mum called 'pastoral scenes' on it – trees and sheep and rolling hills. I thought it was a bit Yuk but there were only two big walls since one of the others had the French doors and the fourth was broken up with a big bookcase and the fire place.

I don't know why, but suddenly I thought about the Prowler. With all the excitement of yesterday's finds I'd completely forgotten to ask PeeDee if he'd seen anything last night. I suppose he'd have mentioned it if he had. Lying on my bed I realised that it was unlikely the Prowler had anything to do with the murder or yesterday's finds. If he lived in Cowplain he wouldn't need to hide things in the woods. And if he didn't live here he certainly wouldn't be prowling the village if he had murdered the man. We still had two completely different cases to solve.

The doorbell rang. I wondered who it was. No one called up to me so I guessed it wasn't for me. I felt let down. Of late nearly everything that had happened at home had involved me and I was beginning to like being the centre of attention. I tried not to be big-headed but the last two weeks had been extraordinary. I heard Cath talking to someone and guessed it must have been one of her geeky friends so I fished my book out from under the bed. I'd just finished *Secret Waters* and there weren't any other 'Swallows and Amazons' books in the library so I'd had to take out *Children of the New Forest*. It had taken me a while to get into it but now I was beginning to get caught up in the story. I could imagine it all so easily because of all the time we'd spent in the woods. I was just beginning to think there might be a game in it – PeeDee's lot would have to be the Roundheads and we'd be the Cavaliers – when Cath called up to me.

'Can you come down, Tess? Deidre wants to meet you!'

I wasn't sure I wanted to meet one of Cath's friends but I went down all the same. Deidre had jet-black hair and an incredibly pale face and was wearing slacks. Cath sat primly on the edge of the sofa and introduced me to Deidre.

'This is my little sister,' she said. 'Her name's Theresa but she only answers to Tess.'

'Hi, Tess.' Deidre said. 'I've been reading all about you in the paper. I didn't connect the name at first but then I remembered that Cath had a sister so I called round to see if it was you,' she gushed. 'And Cath's told me that you found some more crucial evidence yesterday!'

'The police still want it kept secret,' I said. 'Cath shouldn't have mentioned it. We were playing in the woods and we saw this newspaper in the bushes. Well, you know how it is, one thing led to another and we looked in this hiding place a bit further on and found something that the police think may help them in solving this case.'

'She sounds so professional,' Deidre said to Cath, 'as if she's been doing this sort of thing all her life.'

'Don't be taken in by her,' Cath said. 'She's really just a little snot bag and she's showing off dreadfully.'

'She's got something to show off about,' Deidre said. 'I've never done anything like that.'

'That's because you're a normal member of the human race,' Cath said, 'like me!'

'She sounds like a proper detective!'

'More like a mental defective,' Cath snorted.

Mum came in just in time to prevent me from shooting my mouth off at Cath.

'Now,' she said, 'I've put out a tray in the kitchen and there's squash and biscuits. Go and help yourselves.'

'Thanks, Mrs Thomas,' Deidre said. 'It's all so exciting isn't it?'

'We try to keep calm, Deidre,' Mum said. 'After all, it's the police who do the work. It's really nothing to do with us.'

The door bell rang and Mum went to answer it. She came back in a moment later.

'The police need you down at the station,' she said. 'Dad'll take you. They want Peter as well.'

I stood up and looked at Cath and Deidre.

'I expect they need your help again,' Deidre said.

'No,' Mum said. 'They need her finger prints to eliminate her from their enquiry.'

'All in a day's work,' I said, shrugging my shoulders as if it was nothing. It took an effort, though, because having my finger prints taken was nearly as exciting as finding a dead body.

Dad collected PeeDee and his father and we drove down to the police station. We could have walked but Dad said it would be quicker if we all drove together.

'We don't want to waste the whole of the afternoon, do we?' he said.

PeeDee's Dad was familiar with the station from his previous visits and he seemed a bit cowed so Dad went to the desk. We were shown through to the interview room out the back and Sergeant Marks came in with the finger print kit.

'We've managed to get several sets of prints from the door of your den,' he said to PeeDee. 'And we've got prints from the notice and from the newspaper so we need to work out which ones are yours so that we don't waste time with them. One of the others might give us a lead.'

He took my prints first, rolling my finger tips with black inky stuff and then putting them on the ID sheet. Then he did PeeDee's and showed us where we could wash our hands. We didn't want to wash the ink off – it looked kind of special so we didn't try too hard.

It started to rain while we were in the police station.

'That blows any chance I've got of going out this afternoon,' PeeDee said.

We took PeeDee and his Dad back to their home and his Dad invited us in.

'We seem to be thrown together a bit, don't we,' he said. 'Gwen would like to meet you. She met your wife yesterday. PeeDee's done nothing but talk about it ever since Tess found the body.'

Dad hesitated a moment. I guess he was thinking what Mum would say! He looked at me and I nodded.

'We'd love to,' Dad said, pulling up outside PeeDee's house.

The front garden was quite neat, just grass with a narrow flower bed along the wire fence which separated their garden from their neighbour's garden. There was a narrow path leading to the back with shrubs planted close against the house wall and there was a little gate at the end, leading into the back garden. PeeDee's Dad led us round the back.

'I haven't got the key with me,' he said. 'Anyhow, we always use the back door.'

He opened the gate and led the way through a little covered passage way between the house and what looked like two brick sheds.

'That's the coal hole,' PeeDee told me, pointing to the first door on his left, 'and that's the outside lavvy.'

We went in through the backdoor, which was opposite the toilet door, and found ourselves in the kitchen. It was quite small but had everything that they needed. The boiling copper for the washing was tucked inside the door next to the white butler's sink which had a stainless steel sink clipped to it. I thought it looked much better than our wooden one which always looked dirty, no matter how much Mum scrubbed it. The gas cooker, much more up to date than ours, was next to the sink and then there was a larder cupboard. There was a little wooden table as well. There were shiny red floor tiles which continued through into the dining room which was next to the kitchen, separated from it by a wall which didn't reach right up to the ceiling but was too tall for me to see over. There was no door, just an opening. On the wall opposite the window in the dining room there was a free-standing coke boiler.

'It's hot this time of year,' PeeDee's Dad said, 'but it does the hot water so we only have it on at the weekends in summer. There was a table and chairs in the tiny dining room and next to the boiler there was a tall cupboard which reached right up to the ceiling.

'Come through,' PeeDee's Dad said, opening the door into the front room.

It was a bright room. There was a tiled fireplace on the wall from the dining room and a big rug on the floor. They had lots of pictures hanging from the picture rails in here. The window frames were metal and much thinner than our wooden ones and, even though there were net curtains, the room looked much brighter than ours. Perhaps the mirror over the fireplace reflected the light. There wasn't much room to move, though, because they had a big sideboard against one wall, two settees as well as an old armchair, and there was a record player in one corner with a radio on a shelf above it.

PeeDee's mother came in from the other door. She had been upstairs. PeeDee's Dad introduced my Dad to her.

'Please do sit down,' she said, clearing a newspaper from one of the settees. 'Would you like a cup of tea?'

'I'd love one,' Dad said.

'Why don't you show Tess your card collection?' his Dad suggested to PeeDee.

'I don't think you should take Tess upstairs to your bedroom,' his Mum said. 'Why don't you bring them down?'

'That's all right, Mrs Harris,' I said. 'I'd like to see the rest of the house.'

'Well, leave the door open, then.'

The front door was on our left as we went into the narrow hall and the meter cupboard was beside the front door. The stairs were quite steep and rose on the end wall with a cupboard beneath them. At the end of the hall there was a door which led into the kitchen.

The stairs were carpeted and turned at the top. The upstairs hall was carpeted, too. The bathroom was in the back corner of the house and next to it was the bedroom which PeeDee shared with Malcolm, his older brother. It looked out over the back garden and had a large brass double bed in it. The lino on the floor was worn but clean and there was a built in cupboard in the corner beside the window. There were shelves on the wall and books, boxes and piles of paper were stored on them together with their games. PeeDee took down one of the boxes and took out his cigarette card albums.

'Where does Sandy sleep?' I asked.

'In the little front room,' PeeDee said. 'The house is too small, really. There's only room for her bed in there so she has to put her things in Mum and Dad's room. She wants this one and Dad says if she's still here when Malcolm goes then I'll have to move into the front room so that she can have this one.'

'Is Malcolm leaving, then?' I asked.

'He's got to do his National Service next year,' PeeDee said. 'He might join up, anyway. Says there's nothing else he wants to do.'

'Tea's made,' his Mum called up.

'We'll take these down,' PeeDee said. 'She doesn't like me up here during the day.'

Chapter 25

It was still raining on Sunday morning so not only was I all togged up in my Sunday best, I also had to stay indoors with Cath. I don't know what Deidre said to her yesterday but she seemed to be a lot better tempered today than usual. Still, I kept out of her way just in case she reverted to normal and she seemed happy to help Mum in the kitchen. I picked up some bits and pieces from the living room ready for Dad to start redecorating – we were going to clear it after lunch. He'd promised that I could help him strip the old wallpaper and I was looking forward to that. I guessed that since we were the 'paste team' for the church notice board we'd also be putting the new paper up so it only seemed right that I should help him take the old stuff down when he started tomorrow.

PeeDee came round after lunch. It was just as well that there was no Sunday school or I'd have missed him. I took him up to my room and showed him my Golly Badge collection. I don't think he was very impressed – well, he's a boy! He was surprised that I had my own room, though, and my own bed.

'I suppose when Malcolm goes I'll have my own bed as well,' he said.

'Isn't it strange sleeping with your brother?' I asked.

'Don't know,' he said. 'We've always slept in the same bed. You know Graham Barnes?'

I nodded. We'd been in the same class at junior school.

'Well, he's one of eleven kids in his family and they all sleep in just two beds! They've only got the one bedroom between them. His Mum and Dad sleep in the other one.'

I couldn't begin to imagine what that was like. The thought of sharing my room with Cath was bad enough let alone sharing a bed with her. Sharing with ten other kids must be awful. I had no idea people lived like this in our village.

'It's what they're used to,' PeeDee said. 'Graham says it's great fun! The little ones go straight to sleep and the older ones are always scrapping and chucking each other out of bed and getting up to mischief.'

'Let's go down,' I said.

All this talking of getting up to mischief was making me feel strange and I didn't want to talk about that sort of thing with PeeDee. All the same, it made me think. PeeDee didn't stay long and we agreed to meet next morning on the green.

'Try not to be late,' I said. 'Get there at ten, then we can do something.'

'For someone you don't like,' Cath said, 'you seem to spend a lot of time together.'

'Don't be daft,' I said. 'We've got gang business to sort out. The murder is not the only case we're working on.'

Cath raised her eyes in despair and I took the opportunity to go and find Dad. I wanted to discuss the idea of making a raft with him. If he was home next week I thought I might even be able to persuade him to help us.

The afternoon was beginning to drag but at least it had stopped raining. I found Dad and he seemed to think that it might be possible to make a raft that would float.

'What you want to do is to go up to Hadaway's Garage and see if he's got a couple of old tyres that he doesn't want. He might even have an old inner tube. You need something that's going to make a float to keep you up.'

'I thought wood floated.'

'It does. But with your weight on top it'll need some extra buoyancy. That's where the inner tube would come in. Or an old oil drum. He might spare you a couple. That would be ideal.'

I could see he was getting interested.

'Perhaps you could ask him?' I suggested.

'I think he'd be more likely to give 'em to PeeDee if he asked.'

'PeeDee?' I said incredulously.

'Hadaway was a boy once,' Dad said. 'He'd understand if a boy wanted to make a raft.'

'What about a girl?'

'He'd laugh. He's got daughters. He'd never believe you!'

So much for the brave new world we were building after the war, I thought.

'But women worked in the factories in the war,' I protested.

'And after the war men wanted to spare their women that sort of work. It'll change in time. I still think it's best if PeeDee asks. You'll just have to settle for being the brains behind it all!'

'When are you going to start taking the old paper off?' I asked, changing the subject.

'Not till tomorrow. Mum doesn't like me doing that sort of work on a Sunday.'

But he did look at my plans for making a raft and he helped me with some improvements. Eventually it was time for tea and then I went to Evensong. Sundays were like that, you could do some things but not others. I came home over the recreation ground after church and they were still playing cricket. I found PeeDee who was watching over on the council house side.

'Nothing better to do,' he said by way of an excuse.

'I can't stay, I'm already late home from church.'

'I'll walk with you,' he said. 'Don't want the Prowler chasing you when you're all smart.'

'It's funny that we haven't heard anything more about him,' I said.

'I asked Sandy but she said she didn't know anything,' PeeDee said. 'But I don't believe her,' he added. 'Normally she's got lots to say about everything. I think it's suspicious. He's supposed to have chased her so she ought to have some ideas about him. I'm going to watch out for her, not the Prowler.'

I told PeeDee what Dad had said about asking for a couple of oil drums at the garage and he said it was a good idea.

'I'll go and ask him first thing tomorrow morning. I can let you know when we meet up.'

We'd got to the green out the back.

'I'll have to walk round,' I said. 'I can't do the ditch in my best dress. Not when there's water in it. You can go back if you want.'

'No, I'll see you to your gate.'

As soon as we'd got past the green and were walking round the bend towards Padnell Road I felt PeeDee reach for my hand. Normally I'd have clouted him but it felt nice that he still wanted to hold my hand. So much had happened since yesterday morning. When we came to the hedge outside Mr Looker's house I felt PeeDee squeeze my hand and then he let go. I wasn't upset – I didn't want Cath to see me being wet and holding hands with any boy, let alone PeeDee!

'Thanks for walking me home,' I said.

'That's all right. Didn't have anything better to do!'

I wondered if he'd have walked me home if he was watching a football match, but I didn't say so.

'See you in the morning.'

I went in without looking back, straight down the side of the house and round the back.

'You're late,' Mum said.

'I walked over the recreation ground,' I said. 'They were still playing cricket and then PeeDee walked round with me.'

Why did I tell her that, I asked myself as soon as I'd said it? A moment ago I'd been worried about being seen and now I was blabbing my mouth off. Just as well Cath wasn't in the room. I didn't understand why I felt so mixed up. This business with PeeDee was really beginning to spook me. It's not as if he was my boyfriend and yet I found that I quite liked him despite the fact that we were sworn enemies!

The evening had turned quite chilly and I stayed in and we listened to the wireless. I finished 'The Children of the New Forest' and then made a mug of Ovaltine. Cath seemed distracted and spent the evening unpicking her embroidery.

'I don't like the colours,' she said.

The room echoed because Dad had rolled the carpet up ready to start work in the morning. Mum had put out a pile of old sheets for him to cover the furniture.

'Are you going to start stripping the wall paper tomorrow?' I asked.

'Maybe. But I've got to do the ceiling first. There's no point in making the walls ready if I splash distemper all over them. We'll strip the paper when the ceiling's done. Less work that way.'

'Perhaps you and PeeDee could do it together on Tuesday,' Mum suggested.

I was going to yell at her but I bit my tongue instead. Think first, I reminded myself. Play it cool!

'I don't think he'd want to hang around with me,' I said as nonchalantly as I could manage. 'He's got things to do. He's making a raft.'

'You could ask,' Dad said. 'It's quite fun sloshing water on and then scraping the old paper off.'

'I'll see,' I replied, picking up my mug.

Cath didn't say a word! What was up with everyone?

'You could try the pumice stone on your fingers,' Mum said.

My fingers still had a bit of the finger printing ink left on them. No one had noticed at church. I felt quite let down.

'It'll wear off soon enough,' I said.

I was bored. I'd finished my book, there wasn't anything on the wireless and Mum and Dad were busy so I went up to bed.

I quite expected to hear something from the police on Monday morning but there was no news. Dad was washing the lounge ceiling off and splashing white water everywhere, Mum and Cath were doing the washing and so there was nothing for me to do. I checked on the March sisters but they didn't need any shopping so I went round to the green and sat and waited for PeeDee. It was nearly eleven before he appeared.

'I've got two oil drums,' he said. 'Only thing is, we've got to go and get them.'

'Great!'

'He asked me what I wanted them for and when I told him he picked two that still had their caps. He said they'd make better floats, particularly if we kept the caps at the top.'

It wasn't long before the rest showed up. We had a quick confab to make sure no one had seen the Prowler and then we headed off down to the garage. The oil drums made a terrible noise and they proved quite difficult to roll up the hill – they kept twisting first one way and then the other. We took turns to push while two of us tried to steer them straight. Dad came out when he heard the noise. He looked a bit like the abominable snowman where the distemper had splashed him. We put the oil drums by the shed ready for when we needed to tie them to the raft.

'I'll tell you what,' Dad said. 'If you lot help Tess and me strip the wallpaper tomorrow morning, I'll help you make a raft tomorrow afternoon.'

They were only too pleased to have a job to do and so it was agreed, they'd come round in the morning and help, then Dad would help us in the afternoon.

'Looks like you've got permission to get wet up at the pond,' PeeDee said when Dad had gone back in.

'Don't tell him we're going to have a pirate battle,' I told PeeDee. 'He might let on to Mum and I don't think she'd approve.'

Chapter 26

PeeDee was the first to arrive next morning, followed by Merlin and Oz and then Chris. Dad had filled two buckets with water and had found two paste brushes – the ones we used to stick the posters up on the church notice board.

'The thing is,' Dad said, 'you've got to make the paper wet but we don't want water everywhere. Think of it as if you're painting the paper. Give it two or three coats and it'll soak in. As soon as it's really wet you can scrape it off but you must keep the scraper flat on the wall. If you dig it in you'll gouge the plaster and then we'll be in trouble.'

'If we start at the top,' Chris said, 'it'll run down and do the bottom for us.'

'I've only got one pair of steps,' Dad said. 'You'll probably be able to reach off a chair, though.'

I went into the kitchen and fetched a couple of our wooden chairs. PeeDee, as usual, had organised the rest. He put Merlin and Oz to work on the wall which usually had the piano against it, and he was on the steps on the other long wall, the one opposite the French windows. Chris was helping Dad on the fireplace wall so I held the bucket up for PeeDee and he started 'painting' the wall but he was getting more on me than on the wall so we changed over. I wasn't much better at it and soon we were all soaked.

We let the first coat soak in and then we did it all again. We'd just finished when Mum called through and said she'd made us all a drink. We went out into the conservatory and the boys hung their shirts on the line to dry. After our drinks we painted the walls one more time and then Dad said they'd be ready for stripping. We all did some. It was quite tricky keeping the scraper flat and there were quite a few gouges by the time we'd finished. Dad seemed pleased, though, and said he could mix up some filler for the holes and they'd be good as new.

Then we had to let the room dry out so Dad said he'd help us with the raft after lunch. He told the boys to bring any planks of wood they had scrounged from the dump and any old bits of rope. The boys went home. The smell of damp paper had gone right through the house so we had lunch outside, under the apple tree, and Mum propped all the doors open so that the house could have a good blow through – not that there was any wind.

'I'll paint the woodwork tomorrow,' Dad said. 'I might even be able to start tonight. We'll put the paper up on Thursday.'

Mum was quite pleased that we had done so much already so she didn't mind Dad taking the afternoon off to help us with the raft. Like PeeDee said, having them both involved would make it a whole lot easier when we came to float it up on the big pond. Cath went out to visit Deidre so we had a quiet afternoon. Dad was very good. He made the boys do the work themselves. He showed them how to use the tools and sorted out the wood and nails. We worked from my plan which Dad had altered a bit. Pud hit his thumb with the hammer and Merlin got splinters in his knee but we managed it pretty well. In the end it looked very good. All we had to do was to lug it up to the pond, tie on the two oil drums for floats and climb aboard. At least, that was the theory!

There was still no news from the police. After giving them such good clues I thought they ought to have solved the case by now. And there was no news of the Prowler, either. I asked PeeDee how he got on watching his sister and he said that he was sure something fishy was going on because she hadn't gone out at all last night.

'She always goes out,' he said. 'Every night. And she just stayed in all Sunday night and sat in the front room with Mum and Dad. Last night Denis came for her and they went out. She was dead sulky and she came back early.'

'Perhaps they had a row,' I suggested.

'I didn't hear anything but she did come straight in. Normally she snogs him in the passageway between Mrs Harris's house and ours. There wasn't time 'cause I saw her come past the front and then the back door opened and she was back.'

It was quite late when we'd finished the raft so Dad said it might be best if we left its launch until tomorrow. He offered to help us carry it up to the pond. It was quite heavy but if there was one of us on each corner we reckoned we could manage. Dad looked disappointed. I think he was looking forward to seeing it launched.

'You can always help us Mr Thomas,' Merlin said. 'You might be better at tying knots than we are, even though Tod was in the Cubs.'

That seemed to cheer Dad up and he went in to look at the paintwork, leaving us to clear up our mess. We sorted out when we were going to meet and PeeDee reminded us that we had to carry the oil drums as well.

'If you're carrying the raft we can just put them on top 'til we reach the pond,' Oz pointed out.

We carried the raft up to the back of the house and it was really a lot lighter than we'd thought. We left it there ready for the next morning. Mum came out and had a look.

'Make sure you've got your bathers on,' she said. 'I wouldn't trust it not to capsize!'

PeeDee winked at me. Everything was going to be all right.

Next morning Dad was busy painting when they arrived.

'We'll carry it up ready,' I told him, 'and then we'll wait 'til you come to help fix the oil drums.'

He was well into the new painting. He'd started early and had done the picture rails and had nearly finished the dado rails as well. He just had the skirting boards to do and down the sides of the doors and windows. He was going to leave the rest until after we'd done the papering. He said they were big surfaces and would take longer to dry.

I wasn't sure about the colour. We'd always had cream paintwork but Mum wanted something a bit more modern and had chosen a colour halfway between green and grey. 'Eau–de–Nil' she called it.

'It'll cheer the place up a bit,' she said. 'And it tones with the new wallpaper.'

The walls were such a mess and the paint looked so green that I was expecting the worst.

'We're off now,' I said.

'Be careful,' Mum said, 'and don't go in the water until your Dad's checked it out.'

Although the raft was light enough for us to carry, it was actually quite awkward to manoeuvre. For a start, we had to tip it sideways to get it through our back gate and then it was too wide for the path so we had to try and keep it at an angle. It was better when we got to the road, though, because we just walked up the middle of the road. But if it was easier to carry on the road it was a long way and we had to keep changing over because the wood cut into our fingers.

We tried to match our sizes because PeeDee was a lot taller than Pud and when they had it with Merlin and Oz the raft was at such an angle that the oil drums kept falling off. It took a good half hour to get it up to the pond and we were all sweating by the time we got there. PeeDee was all for jumping in to cool off but Chris persuaded him to wait for my Dad.

'It won't look good if you're all wet,' he said.

While we were waiting we talked about the murder and the Prowler. There was still no news from the police. Merlin had told Monkey to keep his ears open if Plod came into the Pub and he'd been round early to check. Monkey said Plod hadn't come in lately.

'Did Sandy go out last night?' I asked PeeDee.

'She went out and was quite late back,' he said. 'But I didn't see Denis. Perhaps they went out to the pictures and he stayed on the bus. Mind you, they don't usually go to the pictures on a Tuesday.'

Dad arrived just before lunch and we lifted the raft on to the oil drums and Dad lashed them into place with the rope that Goat had brought. It looked very high and unstable but Dad said it would be all right when it was in the water.

'All you have to do is to remember to keep it balanced,' he said. 'If you're on your own stand in the middle and if there's two of you make sure you don't tip it over.'

PeeDee and Goat took their things off and lifted the side that was going into the water.

'It's all squidgy!' Goat said as he waded out in the mud.

'Probably all the cow poo washed down from the farm,' Beaky suggested.

Much to our surprise the raft floated. We'd nailed two bits of wood on the back to make a cleat and fixed a long piece of rope to the cleat end so that the raft didn't float away from us. Dad tied the rope to a tree near the edge of the pond.

'Don't leave it unless you tie it up,' he said. 'It'll be quite light when there's no one on it and the wind'll carry it out to the middle if you don't tie it up.'

It was lunch time so I had to go back home with Dad, but Chris said he'd stay with the raft until the rest got back. PeeDee said he'd bring his lunch up and share it with him. Merlin and Oz shot off so that they could be back early as well.

The afternoon was great but we really needed another raft if we were going to be able to have a real battle.

'I don't see why we can't build another one,' Beaky said. 'We've got more wood.'

'We ain't got any more oil drums,' Goat said.

'Don't think Mr Hadaway will give us any more, either,' PeeDee said.

'Why don't we try Foden's?' Tod suggested. 'They must have lots.'

Tod was delegated to go and find out. As soon as he was dry enough he put his shirt and shorts back on and cycled off to see what he could scrounge.

'I mean,' Oz said, 'natives use dug out canoes – they haven't got any oil drums.'

'Let's try,' Merlin said. 'The worst that can happen is it sinks. And we get wet anyway, even if it don't sink.'

Chris went off to borrow a saw and a hammer from his Dad's shed and Pud went in search of nails.

'Where's Roller?' I asked.

'He had to go out. He'll be dead narked that he missed this!'

Beaky and Goat went off to bring the extra planks that they had stashed round the back of their den.

'You ain't heard anything from the police yet, then?' PeeDee asked.

'Not a word. I thought they have solved it by now, what with the extra clues we gave them.'

'Police move very slowly. 'cept when they're nicking my Dad for being a bit merry!'

'I s'pose they've got to be sure. Takes time to go through the evidence.'

We lapsed into silence. It was nice sitting there in the late afternoon sun. It was quiet up by the pond.

'It's strange,' PeeDee said. 'Four weeks ago I couldn't have imagined that we'd be sitting here together and not fighting!'

'I'll punch you out if you want!' I offered.

'Don't want,' PeeDee said.

'Tell you something else,' I said. 'Everything seems a bit dull up here now. I mean, after the murder, nothing seems the same. I can't even get excited about the so called Prowler. He just doesn't seem important any more.'

'I'm still working on him, though,' PeeDee said. 'I'm keeping watch on Sandy. I think she might have broken up with Denis. She don't talk about him much any more.'

We could hear Goat and Beaky coming back through the woods with the planks and a moment later Chris arrived. We waited for Pud.

'If he ain't here in a minute,' Goat said, 'I'll have to be off.'

'There's always tomorrow,' Beaky said.

'When are we going to have this battle then,' I asked. 'Chris and I won't be here on Friday. It's the choir outing.'

Chris looked up at PeeDee.

'That's right,' he said. 'We won't be here.'

'If we start the next raft tomorrow,' PeeDee said, 'we can finish it on Friday and have a battle on Saturday.'

'Don't forget it's the church ramble on Monday,' I reminded them. 'I think we all ought to be on duty for that. You never know, we might find more clues.'

We were a bit late getting up on Thursday morning. Dad said

we'd all earned a bit of a lie in. As soon as we'd finished breakfast Dad and I carried the kitchen table into the lounge and I started mixing up the wall paper paste. When we did the posters we pasted the notice board because it was easier to handle the poster sheets if they were dry. But indoors we pasted the paper because there wasn't any wind to blow it about.

The lengths were quite short because we only had to do down to the dado rail. The bit below was a separate piece even though Dad had to try and match the pattern up so that it looked as if the rail was put over the paper. It took us a while to get going because Mum and Dad couldn't decide where to start the pattern. Either they had it looking right at the top or they had it looking right at the dado rail.

'You won't see the bit by the dado rail much,' I said. 'The piano covers one bit and the sofa another. It'll look better if the top is neat. You'll see all the tops.'

Even Cath agreed with me. She was quite un–nerving me, this new 'pleasant' Cath. But that wasn't the end of it because Mum still couldn't make up her mind. In the end Dad said it would have to be done from the top because there wasn't enough paper to cut it the other way.

'It'll waste nearly a whole pattern on each piece,' he said. 'I don't think we've got enough to do it that way.'

Mum and Cath left us to it then. Dad used a plumb line to get the first piece straight and then it was quite easy to do all the top pieces. I had to wash the table down in between pasting each piece so that we didn't stain the paper. I must say, with the paper up, the green paint looked quite all right, nothing like as bad as I thought it would. We did two walls before dinner time.

Dad said I could go out after dinner if I wanted but I said I'd stay and finish it with him. Pud came by and said they'd been busy up in the woods and a bit later PeeDee dropped in to say they'd finished it. Tod hadn't managed to get any more oil drums so they had to do without.

'It sits a bit low in the water,' PeeDee said, 'but it floats if you're careful.'

Dad said I could go and have a look if I wanted but I said it would keep.

'See you Saturday, then,' PeeDee said as he left.

I thought he could have wished me a good trip to the Isle of Wight but he seemed to be in a hurry to go. Boys, I thought!

We finished the papering – all but the fiddly bits round the fireplace which Dad said he hadn't the patience to do.

'I'll do them first thing in the morning,' he said, 'when my fingers have had a rest and my eyes aren't tired.'

Even though there was still a lot of mess in the room I thought it looked very good.

Chapter 27

The day of the choir outing dawned fine and warm and when I came downstairs I found Mum was already busy making sandwiches.

'I've made two lots,' she said. 'One lot is corned beef and the other is egg. I thought some of the others might be hungry.'

'I think they'll all bring their own food,' I said. It was just like Mum to think that they wouldn't bring enough food. Still, it meant that we could do some swapping.

'You'd better start your breakfast while I finish your lunch. It wouldn't do to have you still eating when Mr Norman arrives.'

I sat at the table and poured a bowlful of cornflakes, sprinkled on a spoonful of sugar and tipped on the milk. While I ate Mum added a couple of slices of cake and a couple of apples to the bag of food she was preparing and then put in a couple of bottles of Vimto.

'Have you got your bathing costume?' she asked. 'And a towel?'

I nodded, my mouth full of cereal.

'And I've got an extra jumper,' I said as soon as I'd swallowed.

'Buck up!'

'If you didn't keep talking to me I'd be finished!'

'We don't want them here with you still eating your breakfast.'

It was a close thing – Mr Norman arrived just as I was finishing my mug of tea. Mum loaded my food into one of her cloth shopping bags and I stuffed my towel and bathing costume on top. We were going down to Portsmouth in cars and from there we were catching the ferry across to the Isle of Wight. As soon as we arrived we were going by train to Sandown. It was a lot of travelling but going by car, boat and train promised to be good fun.

Mr Norman had a green Morris Minor and it was going to be a tight squeeze with three in the back. I was surprised to see PeeDee in the back with Chris and Bunny. Mr Norman said I should sit in the front. I waved to Mum as we drove off.

'I thought you were bringing your brother,' I said to Chris over my shoulder.

'Why would I want to bring that little pest?'

'I thought your Mum would make you.'

'I didn't tell her,' Chris said.

'You ain't disappointed, are you?' PeeDee asked.

I decided not to answer and turned back to watch where we were going. I felt my cheeks blushing as I realised that I was actually quite pleased PeeDee was coming with us. The day promised to be even more fun than usual.

It was touch and go as to whether the car would make it to the top of Portsdown Hill, but it did and so we didn't have to get out and push. From there it was all downhill and we arrived in plenty of time. While Mr Norman parked the car we stood by the harbour railings and watched the mud–larks. The tide was out and three boys were diving and scrambling around in the mud for pennies that people were throwing down to them. They were covered in what looked like thick chocolate and only their eyes stood out like two pale circles.

'I wouldn't mind having a go at that,' PeeDee said.

'How do they get clean?' Chris asked when Mr Norman came up.

'They swim out to sea and come up a bit further round where there's shingle and rocks,' he said. 'One of them found a gold sovereign last year,' he added. 'It must have been down there for years.'

The Vicar was the next to arrive with some of the younger kids and then one of the ladies from the choir arrived with the rest of the choristers and so our party was complete.

PeeDee hadn't been on a boat before so he was quite excited as we walked up the gangway on to the ferry.

'What happens if I'm sea–sick?' he asked.

'Lean over the side,' Bunny suggested.

'And make sure you're not facing into the wind!' Chris added.

'You won't be sick,' I said. 'It's fun and it doesn't take long. You'll feel the waves when we get outside the harbour, though. The boat usually rocks a bit until it gets going.'

We stayed up on the top and watched as they untied the ropes and got ready to go. The Vicar and the others were nowhere in sight and it really felt like the beginning of an adventure. I watched the look on PeeDee's face as the boat moved away from the dock. There was plenty to look at as we turned towards the harbour entrance and as soon as the ferry headed towards the open water we could feel the waves take hold of the boat. We walked as if we were drunk.

'My Dad walks like this most evenings,' PeeDee said as we made our way to the other side of the boat. It was strange the way the deck was under our feet one moment and then rolled away the next.

The rest of the journey was quite boring and fortunately it didn't take very long. We watched again as the ferry berthed at Ryde. I was thinking about how we would handle our raft so it was quite useful watching how it was done.

We caught the train from Ryde. PeeDee wanted to look at the steam engine but there wasn't time so we bundled into a compartment and as soon as the doors were shut the station master blew his whistle. We felt the train shudder as it began to move. The driver sounded the train whistle and we listened while the engine slowly got up speed. It didn't take long and soon we were moving quite quickly. PeeDee lowered the window and was looking out as we came to a tunnel. It was a bad move because the smoke billowed into the carriage and PeeDee's face was covered in black soot. We closed the window again and Bunny emptied his pockets – he'd got black jacks and ha'penny chews so we each made our choice.

We reached Sandown without any more mishaps although PeeDee's face was still covered in soot smuts. The beach looked fantastic and we made a bee–line for the waves.

The Vicar called us back and said he'd make a base up on the top of the beach. He'd hired a deck chair and he said we could leave our things with him for safe keeping while we went down into the sea. It didn't take the boys long to change – most of them already had their trunks on under their shorts – and they dashed off down to the sea. It took me a bit longer because I had to change under a towel and there was just enough wind to make it difficult.

When I got to the sea the boys were already splashing in and out.

'Come on in,' Chris called out. 'It's quite warm.'

I wasn't so sure – it looked pretty cold to me. PeeDee came

splashing out and flicked water at me.

'Scared Captain Nancy?' he taunted.

'Not at all,' I said. 'I'm just choosing my moment.'

He turned and dashed back in, jumping the ripple of waves at the edge of the sand. I took a deep breath and ran in after him. The water was freezing at first but I soon got used to it. Bunny had brought a football and we chucked it back and forth, up to our middles in the water.

'Is it dinner time yet?' Chris asked after a bit. 'I'm starving!'

We came out and went back up to the Vicar. The other adults had gone off somewhere and he was sitting alone, reading a book.

'Fed up all ready?' he asked.

'What's the time?' Chris asked.

The Vicar looked at his watch.

'Eleven forty–five,' he said. 'You could have lunch but then tea will be even further away. Why don't you play French cricket?'

'Haven't got a bat,' Chris said.

'But I have,' the Vicar said, putting his book in his bag and levering himself out of his deck chair.

We went down on to the sand and I got first bat. It was fun because we could hit the ball as hard as we liked without any fear of breaking anything. It wasn't long before I was out and the Vicar took over batting. He didn't bat like I did, protecting his legs but squared up like a proper batsman. This was going to be easy, I thought, but he was too good and hit the ball so hard that he had us running all over the beach. He even got PeeDee back into the sea chasing the ball after one of his mighty hits. I don't know how long we played but the other adults had come back when we finished so we all settled down and had our packed lunches together.

We spread a towel and put the food packets on it so that they didn't get too sandy. We might just as well not have bothered because by the time we'd shared out our sandwiches most of them had sand on them. PeeDee's were anchovy paste sandwiches and Chris had tomato and cucumber ones. Bunny had some sort of sliced meat in his and he didn't want to share so we left him to eat his own. I had cake and apples, Chris had fruit pies in boxes and PeeDee had jammy dodgers so we had quite a feast.

After we'd eaten as much as we could the Vicar said we ought not to go in the sea for at least half an hour so we dug a huge hole and buried PeeDee in it. He seemed to enjoy it so we dug him out and then he helped Chris bury me. I didn't find it as much fun as PeeDee and it took me ages to get the sand out of my costume – even after I'd been for a bathe it was still scratching my back.

Bunny suggested we look in the rock pools and so we all traipsed off to see if we could find anything. The tide had been out too long and there weren't many pools. Most of them had dried out.

'When we were down in Devon,' Bunny said, 'we found crabs and sea urchins, star fish and water shrimps. There were even anemones in one of them.'

We did find a few limpets on the back of some of the rocks and we collected razor shells. We washed them in the sea and left them in the shade by the Vicar.

'Don't be too long,' he said as we went down to the sea again. 'When you come back I'll treat you all to an ice cream.'

Well, it doesn't take a genius to realise that all of a sudden we changed our minds about going down to the sea again and so we went to the kiosk and all had ice–cream cornets, even Mr Norman! We took our ice creams on to the pier and walked its whole length. The afternoon went too quickly for us and soon it was time to get dressed and go for tea. The Vicar had booked set teas for us in one of the cafés just off the sea–front. We had more sandwiches and they'd done little jellies in waxed card party bowls and then they had topped them with a swirl of some sort of cream which was very sweet. There was tea in a huge brown enamel teapot or squash from a big jug. Most of us had tea because we were really thirsty – although squash cools you down it's not very good at quenching your thirst. Then we finished tea with all sorts of little cakes that they brought on a huge wooden baker's tray.

After tea there was just time to ride the dodgems in the funfair and then we had to rush to catch the train back to Ryde. This time PeeDee didn't stick his head out of the window every time we went into a tunnel. I think we were all too tired to do much so the four of us sat and chatted. When we got on the boat we looked over the rail as the Isle of Wight disappeared into the fading sunlight. It had been a real fun day and we were sad that it was ending.

Chris dozed off in the car on the way home and he was still asleep when Mr Norman stopped to let me out. He didn't even wake when I slammed the car door.

Chapter 28

There was another newspaper paragraph on Friday about the murder. They didn't tell me until after I got up on Saturday morning.

Theresa does it again!

Has 12 year old schoolgirl, Theresa Thomas, found the vital clue?

'We were in the woods,' she told us, *'and we found a couple of things that we thought might interest the police.'* Theresa and her friends handed their finds to the police who are actively following up new lines of enquiry.

Following the help they have already received from Mr Hurford, who had been walking his dog in the woods and who had remembered a van's number plate, the Guildford police informed us that a man is helping them with their enquiries. And now, with the new clues found by the children in the woods, the police tell us that they have been able to make connections between the recent murders and the Portsmouth bank robbery that took place earlier this month.

Inspector Johnson told us that they are confident that they will soon have a statement for the press.

It was getting boring. We never knew what the police were up to and we didn't think there was anything else we could do so we'd almost written it off. Anyway, we'd decided that we'd have the battle this afternoon and I was busy planning what we'd do. We'd chosen the afternoon so that we could do our errands in the morning.

'We don't want it messed up because one of us can't come,' Chris said.

I made a point of checking on the Misses March. They asked me if I'd ever heard anything more about the Prowler and I said that he didn't seem to be active at the moment.

'I expect it was all just some malicious rumour,' Miss Eileen said. 'Some person had a grudge and they wanted to get even so they started some gossip.'

'Don't be so silly,' Miss Barbara said. 'People wouldn't be so petty! And the police wouldn't have become involved if it had just been a rumour.'

'Some of my friends have actually seen him,' I said. 'And PeeDee's sister was actually chased by him.'

'Well, that doesn't sound like gossip!' Miss Barbara said rather tartly.

I ran an errand for them and they gave me a tube of Smarties for my troubles. I kept them for the afternoon's battle.

Dad was finishing off the lounge and so I kept out of the way. Mum had washed all the loose covers on the chairs and sofa earlier in the week and today she had the curtains out on the line drying in the sun. I went up to my room and sat at my desk in the window. I had been trying to come up with suitable pirate phrases. In the 'Swallows and Amazons' book Nancy has a whole range of favourite expressions but there wasn't much point in using those because no one would understand what I was on about, so I was trying to make up my own but I wasn't having much success. I was doodling in my notebook and suddenly I realised that I'd drawn a very ornate 'PD'. I looked at it in horror and then scribbled it out.

I was clean out of inspiration so I gave in and went outside, down to the shed. Dad's jar of brushes was on the little bench and there was a delicious smell of paint mixing with the smoke from Mr Looker's bonfire.

I felt strangely unexcited about the pirate battle. I don't know why, but all of a sudden it seemed curiously childish. Somehow I just couldn't recapture the enthusiasm I'd felt when I was planning the bank raid. I needed to do something to get me into the mood so I decided to scrounge a head scarf from Mum to try and make a pirate's hat. At first she wasn't too keen but in the end she relented and gave me an old red scarf which was ideal. She even showed me how to tie it.

'You look as if you're off to do the church spring cleaning,' Cath said. 'You can do my bedroom as well, if you want!'

I didn't even realise she was trying to be funny – that's how preoccupied I was. Finally the clock chimed two and I cycled up to the big pond. PeeDee was already there and was just sitting on the bank, looking at the two rafts. I dumped my bike, went over and sat next to him.

'The holidays are nearly over,' he said.

I didn't say anything. I thought he was going to go on but he stayed silent.

'School soon,' I said, trying to make conversation. 'But there's the church walk on Monday. That's usually good for a laugh.'

'Everything's changing,' he said, still in his pensive mood. 'It's not the same any more, is it?'

'What isn't?'

'Us. The gangs. We're not enemies any more. We're not two different gangs, not like we were at the start of the holidays.'

'Perhaps we've all grown up a bit,' I suggested. 'I mean, we can't stay kids for ever can we?'

'I don't want to grow up,' PeeDee said. 'I liked it as it was. Fighting and that.'

'Even grownups fight,' I said. 'Look at your Dad!'

'That's not the same. He's serious, but we were just mucking about.'

'We can still hang out together, and muck about.'

We fell silent. I think we were both busy with our thoughts. Now that PeeDee had said it, I realised that this was just what I'd been feeling, too. The others were arriving and the time for talking passed. PeeDee said my lot ought to have the big raft.

'Your Dad helped build it,' he said. 'It's only fair.'

'Why don't we all try them both out first,' I suggested. 'You never know they may both sink.'

The boys stripped off down to their swimming trunks and pushed the big raft out.

'Give me the rope,' I said. 'Then if it sinks we can pull it out again.'

'It's called a painter,' Oz said.

'That's a bit posh,' I said.

'You're not the only one who's read books,' Oz said.

The raft floated quite well although it was quite high in the water. Oz and Merlin scrambled up on to it and it settled better. I tied the painter back to its tree and we launched the other raft. It looked quite flimsy but it floated and was surprisingly stable. PeeDee and Beaky climbed up on to it and punted it out with a long branch they'd trimmed down.

It took us a while to work out how we were going to manoeuvre the rafts because they didn't steer at all. We tried using two planks like oars on ours but it was impossible to keep it going straight – all it seemed to want to do was to go in circles.

Merlin waded to the bank and got another plank. He tried to use it like a rudder and it helped but we still couldn't steer the raft. PeeDee's was no better and in the end we each had two of our members 'steering' by wading alongside the rafts. It was clear that we were not going to be able to 'sail' into battle so we abandoned that idea. Goat tried to tip us off our raft but it was too buoyant. The weather was fabulous so we ended up jumping off the rafts into the pond and then climbing back on. As we punted our way across the pond we nearly had a collision in the middle and so we changed the game into ramming each other.

Before long one of our oil drums came unlashed and we had to do running repairs. Everyone helped us manhandle the raft on to the bank and then Tod did his best to lash it back together again. After that we abandoned the idea of a pirate battle. By now we were all thoroughly soaked and so we towed PeeDee's raft out into the middle and took turns trying to stay on it while the rest rocked it.

The sun was beginning to move round behind the trees, and we guessed it was getting late so we hauled the rafts to the edge and sat drying off in the sun. The pirate battle hadn't worked out but sailing the rafts had been much better. Goat suggested that we should build a bigger one so that we could all get on it.

'We're supposed to be enemies,' Merlin reminded him.

'That's just it,' Beaky said. 'We ain't any more, are we? Not after Ten found the body and we took up detecting.'

His remark was greeted in silence. He'd said what we all felt but no one was going to be the first to agree with him. Finally PeeDee spoke.

'I don't see why we can't all be friends and still have competitions.' He paused and still no one spoke. 'I mean, we're all friends and it's been more fun doing things together.'

'You and me friends?' Merlin said as if the idea was totally preposterous.

'Rivals?' PeeDee suggested.

'We've got to think of the new estate,' Chris said. 'It won't be long before they come sticking their noses in. If we're one big gang we'd be stronger and could see 'em off more easily.'

'How about re–naming ourselves?' Oz suggested.

'How about *The Terrible Ten*?' Roller suggested.

'That's not fair on Ten,' Pud said. 'She's not terrible! Well, not too terrible!'

'No, stupid, there's ten of us,' Roller said.

'There're eleven of us,' I pointed out.

Roller counted up on his fingers.

'I forgot Tod,' he said.

'I've got it,' Beaky said, 'how about *The Three Ts*?'

'How about The Padnell Prowlers?' I suggested.

'Has anyone heard anything about him?' Tod asked. 'I mean, we still haven't solved that one yet.'

'I'm working on it,' PeeDee said.

'Got any leads?' Oz asked.

'Nothing firm,' PeeDee said, 'but I've got a hunch.'

'Ask Ten, she's supposed to have feminine intuition.'

PeeDee looked at Goat.

'We've talked about it,' he said.

Goat shrugged.

'It don't seem very important now, not after the other thing.'

I think we all felt that the dead body and the murder had been such a major event that everything else had paled into insignificance. Even the holiday was nearly worn out and we were almost ready to go back to school.

Chapter 29

The sun was already shining when I woke up on Bank Holiday Monday. I didn't stay in bed because we were all going on the church ramble and I knew that there'd be lots of things to be done. Mum was already up and was busy making sandwiches. She'd got three stacks of slices which she'd already spread with margarine and she was working through the first pile, spreading them with liver and bacon paste.

'You can put some cucumber in these and close them up,' she said.

I started slicing the cucumber as thinly as I could manage. Mum had a serrated knife which she always used just for slicing cucumber. She said it didn't slip like an ordinary knife.

As soon as we'd finished that pile Mum sliced some cheese from the block of cheddar and I spread pickle on them. The third pile was going to be egg.

'You can shell the eggs,' Mum said, busy cutting the cheese and pickle ones in half.

I cracked them on the side of the sink and began to peel them. Once you'd got the end bit off and made a start on the side, the rest of the shell usually came off in one big piece. I dropped the peeled ones into a basin ready for Mum to dice them up. She usually added Heinz salad cream to the eggs which helped to stick the mixture together. She added a shake or two of pepper and a good pinch of salt and I started spooning the egg mixture on to the bread while Mum spread it and closed them up.

Cath was moving about in the bathroom now and I guessed that she'd be down in a minute or two but Dad was not up yet. I think he was making the best of his chance for a lie in.

'Shall I go and wake him up?'

'I think we can give him another half an hour,' Mum said. 'He's up early every day so he deserves a little bit of luxury.'

Mum started tearing off some greaseproof paper to wrap the sandwiches and I got out the big basket that she was going to pack the food in. She'd already boiled the kettle and had poured hot water into the Thermos flasks to warm them up. I was going to have Vimto, and I guessed Cath would do the same, but it was nice to have a warm cup of tea if there was any left in the afternoon – it always seemed refreshing after we'd been playing French cricket.

We assembled outside the church and a motley crew we looked. The Vicar had a huge knapsack and most of the ladies had baskets of food. There were lots of little kids as well as older people. The ramble was not a serious walk – we didn't go fast so there was plenty of time for everyone to keep up. We set off at half past ten and made our way towards the woods.

'I hope you don't find any more dead bodies,' Mrs Looker said to me.

Mr Looker was far too busy with his dahlias to come, but Mrs Looker came for a good natter with Mrs Williams. Both of them were wearing the most enormous straw hats to keep the sun off. The Vicar led us into the woods. I think he knew where we played and chose a different route on purpose, carefully avoiding the dirt track, and where PeeDee and I had our dens. Chris had brought Sue, a girl who lived on the estate, and so PeeDee and I paired up with them and brought up the rear of the walkers. Mum and Dad were up the front talking with Mr and Mrs Martin. Cath had brought Deidre so she had someone to talk to as well. Pud was arguing with Tod but they seemed friendly enough – perhaps it was because their parents were just behind them.

We walked for just over an hour until we reached one of the grassy open spaces in the woods where we stopped for lunch and to give the older people a chance to rest. The Vicar had brought a Jokari set with him and we played for a bit. At first we tried being on opposite sides but the ball bounced so oddly that we kept missing it. Then the Vicar showed us how to stand on the same side and take alternate shots and it was much better. Bunny was clearly the best player and he beat us all.

Mum had spread a rug in the shade and we had our lunch. She'd done some things for a surprise and she asked the rest of the gang who didn't have parents to join us. She opened a package of sausages which she'd baked in the oven, and she'd got Hayward's Military pickle we could have with them. And then she'd baked jam tarts for afters. We all felt rather full up after lunch and nobody seemed too eager to make a move.

PeeDee started a game of French cricket and one by one the adults joined in. Mrs Looker surprised us all because she was a jolly good catcher and caught the Vicar out on his first go. After the cricket we were thirsty so we had a drink while the adults packed up their baskets. It had been a good day, nothing special but friendly and quiet. Then the Vicar produced some lists he'd typed out and set us younger ones off on a search for all the things he'd listed. Even Cath and Deidre joined in. Chris and Sue went off together so PeeDee and I paired up. The Vicar had been really mean and had put all sorts of tiny things on the lists. I mean, there were obvious things like an oak leaf and an acorn but there were things that we had to really search for.

The most difficult thing was a sloughed snake skin. The woods were notorious for grass snakes and adders and we often found the old skins of snakes, although this year I hadn't seen one at all. We spent a long time looking for a four-leaf clover as well. We were on our hands and knees, going through a patch of clover when it happened.

'Someone's watching us,' I whispered to PeeDee.

He looked up and gazed round. To all intents and purposes we were alone in a clearing, surrounded by trees. We could hear the adults talking in the distance and some of the younger children were making a noise a little way off.

'Are you sure?' he asked.

'No. Not exactly. But I've got this feeling that someone's watching us.'

'Not the dreaded feminine intuition?' PeeDee said, pulling a face.

I looked around. Perhaps PeeDee thought I was nervous.

'Perhaps it's the Prowler,' he said. 'Don't worry – he won't attack you while I'm here.'

'I wasn't worried about him,' I said. 'He's probably round your place, watching Sandy!'

Just then Chris and Sue came walking up. They looked mighty pleased with themselves.

'You got the lot?' PeeDee asked.

'Not yet,' Chris said.

'But we've been busy,' Sue said, rather coyly.
I noticed they were holding hands but I didn't say anything.
'Got to get on,' Chris said.
They walked on, trampling our patch of clover as they went.
'Clumsy oaf,' PeeDee muttered.
He looked a bit out of sorts. Chris was his best friend and I don't think PeeDee expected him to bring Sue on the ramble.
'Look!' I said.
PeeDee peered at where I was pointing. Where Chris and Sue had walked through our clover they'd crushed the over-long clover leaves and left footprints. On the edge of one of these there was a four-leaf clover. Now you don't see many of these at the best of times so this must have been our lucky day. We looked at it for a moment.
'It almost seems a shame to pick it,' I said.
PeeDee didn't say anything.
'Are you all right?' I asked him.
'It's odd,' he said.
'What? Finding a four-leaf clover?'
'No. Chris and Sue.'
'How d' you mean?'
'I didn't know they were going out. He didn't say.'
'She's nice. I like Sue.'
PeeDee seemed occupied.
'He didn't have to tell you,' I said. 'You're not his keeper.'
'But we tell each other everything. At least, we used to. Now he's got this secret.'
'Did you tell him about us going to the pictures?'
'Yes ... well, no. But everybody knew we were going. I didn't actually tell them what it was like.'
I was intrigued.
'What was it like?' I asked.
He blushed. Bright red! Again!
'It was ... it was kind of special,' he said. 'Nice.'
'Oh.'
'You must know that I like you, Ten.'
'And I like you, PeeDee. Even if you are my enemy!'
'Can't we stop being enemies? Can't we be friends?'

He reached out for my hand. I didn't stop him. My heart was beginning to thump against my ribs. I looked at him. He looked so uncomfortable that I nearly laughed. I would have done, too, if I hadn't felt the same. Something was going on. I didn't know what, but it was beginning to make me feel dizzy. Our eyes met and we looked at each other. I noticed the way his freckles fell down his cheeks, almost like tears. The sun was glinting on the gold of his eyebrows, lighting up his face. I'd never thought PeeDee was good-looking but at that moment, sitting in the middle of the woods in a clover patch, I suddenly saw a different PeeDee. He was no longer just one of the boys I played with, he looked older, more grown up, and I found him attractive. Pud and the others seemed so young and yet they were the same age as us.

I was confused and lowered my eyes. He was looking at me.

'Do you like me, Ten?'

'Yes,' I said, almost in a whisper.

'I never felt like this about anyone,' PeeDee said.

'Nor me.'

I only realised we were still holding hands when PeeDee let go of my hand.

'We'd better pick it and get on,' I said.

We reached for it at the same moment and our heads bumped. I held my breath, not daring to move. PeeDee froze, too. We stayed like that for what seemed ages and then, almost as if at some unseen and unheard signal, we turned and looked at each other. We were so close I could hear him breathing. Our eyes locked and the woods disappeared. For one moment I looked deep into his eyes. I'd never noticed before, but his eyes were a greenish hazel colour, flecked with brown. Then he leaned towards me and kissed me. On my lips!

If he'd have done that at the beginning of the holidays I'd have brought my knee up pretty smart but this was different. I liked it! We stood up and PeeDee gave me the four-leaf clover.

'You keep it,' he said.

'It'll be ours,' I said.

We were holding hands again and this time I leant forward and kissed PeeDee. He was so surprised! He didn't expect me to do it again. I think he thought I'd be embarrassed and not even want to talk about it, but I had proved him wrong. He put his hand round my shoulder and we stayed close together for a moment. We kissed again! It wasn't our first kiss but it was definitely our longest.

When we re-joined the others we didn't include our four-leaf clover. I think we both thought that it was our special good luck token. Anyway, Cath and Deidre won the competition because they'd got everything on the list except for the four-leaf clover. We didn't do badly but I didn't really care, it all seemed so trivial.

Chris and Sue, and PeeDee and I brought up the rear on the way back. I was holding PeeDee's hand and I noticed Chris and Sue were holding hands, too. It was a wonderful afternoon.

Chapter 30

The end of the school holidays came so quickly that none of us were really ready to go back to school. There were too many un-answered questions. We still didn't know what the outcome of the murder investigation was going to be and we had not solved the problem of the Padnell Prowler as we now called him. But going back to school wasn't something that we could avoid, no matter how much we wanted the holiday to go on.

Only Chris and I went to the grammar school, all the rest of our friends went to the local secondary school in the village.

The first day back was strange. For the last six weeks we had been doing more or less what we wanted and now, at eight o'clock on Wednesday morning, here we were, Chris and I, both in our school uniforms and waiting at the bus stop. We were no longer the youngest at the stop. Three new kids were waiting nervously at our bus stop. Their uniforms were so clean and new that they looked almost shiny. Our cases were battered and our blazers were what Mum called 'a little bit tired'. They'd seen better days but there was another year's wear and tear in them yet so we had to make do with them.

As soon as we were on the bus we separated – it wasn't the done thing for girls and boys to sit near each other. The boys held court raucously in the back of the bus and the girls occupied the front seats. I pitied the poor members of the public that morning because we seemed to be noisier than ever. Needless to say, one of the topics of conversation was the murder, and it wasn't long before I was called up to the back to tell the story.

And it didn't stop when we got to school. The whole murder thing was beginning to haunt me. It seemed as if everybody knew about it and it was the only thing they wanted to talk to me about. Suddenly I was the centre of attention and the Head even mentioned it in his first school assembly. Of course he went on about exam results and people who had gone to university but he also found time to say how proud the school should be that one of its members had been instrumental in helping the police in a serious murder enquiry!

By the time Friday came round I realised that I was missing PeeDee! I hadn't seen him since Tuesday but it seemed so much longer. I'd had homework to do in the evenings and there hadn't been time for anything else. School is like that, it takes over your whole life.

But this Friday was unlike any other Friday because it was the first meeting of The Friday Club. Normally, I would do all my homework on a Friday evening so that I had the whole weekend clear but tonight I wouldn't have time to finish it all. I started as soon as I got in from school and I didn't do badly – I only had French learning homework to do over the weekend.

The Friday Club was a new venture which one of the young couples at church was starting up. They said that Sunday school was probably too young for kids our age and so they were going to hold an evening session open to all the village kids of our age. I had persuaded PeeDee to come along. Since Chris was going, and Roller, he'd have someone to talk to. Swede was back and he'd be there with Bunny so there'd be a whole lot of us who knew each other.

I wasn't sure that PeeDee would show but he did. He and Chris called for me on their way so we all walked up the road together. Sue was waiting for Chris outside the church and she came in with us. I don't know how they'd done it, but Mr and Mrs Martin had found a table tennis table and had set it up at the back of the hall. They'd put a table out at the other end by the entrance to the kitchen and had made it like a refreshment bar. They had packets of crisps, biscuits, bottled drinks and squash for sale. Every member of the club was entitled to a packet of crisps and a drink if they showed their membership card – quite a good wheeze because we all joined!

At eight o'clock, Jim called us all to order and asked us to sit down in the ring of chairs he'd set up at the front. He told us that it was our club and we would have to elect our own committee to help run it.

'The club will be open to the whole village,' he said. 'The only concession we ask you to make is that we have a short time of Bible study together towards the end of the evening. It doesn't matter if you come from a different church, or even if you don't go to any church, your opinions will be just as important as any one else's for us all to consider.'

Then he let us do what we wanted but he told us that we'd have to nominate our committee by the end of the evening. He switched on the record player and put on the new Lonnie Donnegan single. PeeDee and I eventually got a turn at the table tennis but neither of us was much good. At first we found it almost impossible to keep the ball on the table but by the end of our turn we were managing short rallies.

Carol called us to order at nine o'clock and led us in our study session. She'd chosen the story of 'The Good Samaritan.' Most of us knew the story so it was quite a good discussion. PeeDee was surprised that Carol tried to persuade us that the Good Samaritan was in fact a busy-body, sticking his nose into everyone else's business. He suggested that even if it was true, what the Good Samaritan did was good. We closed this session with a short prayer and then Jim took over and talked about the committee.

Our contingent was well represented and they voted PeeDee and me on to the committee with three others. All together, the evening was good fun and PeeDee walked me home afterwards even though Chris cut off over the recreation ground.

PeeDee came round early on Saturday morning.

'Is he going to take you to the pictures again?' Cath asked.

'That's for kids,' I said. 'We've got better things to do!'

'D' you want to go round the green?' PeeDee asked.

'Better than staying here,' I said. 'Some people have such long noses!'

We didn't have anything in particular to do but I think we both wanted to be on our own. As soon as we'd turned out of the gate towards Padnell Avenue I felt PeeDee reach for my hand.

'I missed you, Ten,' he said.

I took a deep breath.

'And I missed you, too,' I said.

I think I was more embarrassed than I had ever been but now I'd said it there was no going back.

We had a visit from Inspector Johnson after tea on the second Thursday evening of term. Dad showed him into the lounge.

'I like the new wall paper,' the Inspector said.

I was impressed that he had remembered the old paper but I suppose that's what made him a good detective.

'I wanted to come and see you all,' he said as soon as we were all seated. 'There will be a major press release in the national newspapers tomorrow about the case that Theresa was involved in.'

He paused.

'There's absolutely nothing to worry about because we have solved this crime but I expect that you will have reporters making their way to your door for pictures and for interviews and I thought you should be forewarned.'

Mum took Dad's hand.

'It's not going to involve Tess is it?' she asked.

'It might do when the case eventually comes to trial, you see, it will be a murder trial. We are confident that we have all the culprits but it has led to a much bigger enquiry. We have discovered that the body here was one of the Portsmouth bank robbers and his accomplice was the other body found in Guildford. We were able to follow up the van registration that Mr Hurford remembered but we couldn't link its owner, Albert Pavey, to anything specific even though he was known to us.

When Theresa found the other clues in the woods we were able to obtain several sets of finger prints. We were able to match these to the van driver. He was facing a murder charge and he wasn't prepared to take the rap for that so he gave us information that led us to Harry Hargreaves. We had his finger prints, too, and other sets that we couldn't identify.

Even then that wasn't the end of it, though, because Harry Hargreaves shopped Mike Brewhorn, a notorious London gangster. Now, Mike is a serious villain. He's known as 'Mike the Menace' and the Met have been on his trail for a long time. They suspected him of master-minding a lot of crimes but they've never been able to pin him down. The finger prints that we found linked him into this case as well.'

He went on to explain how the police had fitted the case together. I was fascinated. It seems that the two men who robbed the bank in Portsmouth were hired by Harry Hargreaves on the orders of Mike Brewhorn. But the two robbers decided to keep back most of the money. They told Harry Hargreaves that they didn't get much and that the press report was wrong. Harry half believed them and reported what they had told him back to Mike Brewhorn.

Mike Brewhorn hadn't earned his nickname for nothing and he decided to pay them all a visit and he leant on one of the bank robbers, Alf Blouter, a little too hard. They dumped Alf's body in the woods at Guildford. The other robber, Steve Provest, was scared and he took them to the woods at the end of Padnell Road and half told Mike where they'd hidden the money. But Mike was a little too enthusiastic and went in search of the money in the den in the woods. He didn't find it, of course, and when he got back to the van Steve Provest, too, had died form the head wounds that Mike had administered with the help of the lever from the car jack in Albert Pavey's van.

Mike gave Harry Hargreaves one week to find the money and went back to London. Harry began to search the woods but kept coming up against us – although we never saw him. He started trying to warn us off by untying the rope and, when that didn't work he did over PeeDee's den. He made Albert Pavey scrawl the note so that it looked like kid's writing. They had a stroke of luck when they found the holly tree and the cash bags still inside.

He took the money up to Mike and, just to warn Harry to be more careful in the future, Mike worked him over, leaving him with a lot of bruises and a broken arm. The police checked the hospitals and found Harry had been treated up there. On a hunch they got a warrant to search Mike's house and found the money there.

Mike swore he didn't even know Harry Hargreaves but his finger prints were all over Albert's van, on the car jack lever and on the shed. The police matched blood from the car jack lever to Steve Provest. It was because of the evidence that we found, and the finger prints that were on it, that the case was solved.

'The Met are still making enquiries into some of Mike's other connections,' Inspector Johnson said. 'He used the same MO for his other operations and now we've cracked one, the Met reckon they can solve a string of other offences. The one thing you can be certain of is that Mike Brewhorn will not be out and about for a very long time. In all probability he will hang for the second murder if it's proved.'

Well, I expect you can quite understand that we were quite shocked at the whole story. Mum said it was very thoughtful of the Inspector to come and see us. It would certainly make the news easier to understand when it came out in the papers.

He chatted for a little while and then the Inspector left. We didn't know what to say for a while and just sat in the lounge.

'It's more complicated than an Agatha Christie book,' Mum said. 'It makes me shiver just to think about it all.'

'But it's all over now,' Dad said. 'And like the Inspector said, the woods are quite safe again.'

Mum said she thought we could all do with a good cup of tea and that brought us back to life again.

The next day, when the papers came out, it was the headline in most of them. I was mentioned, and PeeDee, and sure enough, reporters did come asking for interviews but, to my relief, Dad was quite firm – he let them take a photo and allowed a few questions and then he sent them away.

I quite expected it all to be over, so I was surprised just before Christmas when I received a letter inviting me, and all my family, to attend a 'brief ceremony' in the bank's head quarters in Portsmouth because I was to receive a reward for my part in the affair which led to the bank recovering its money from the robbery.

In fact, all the members of our two gangs had the same invitation.

Chapter 31

The ceremony was held in the board room of the bank's main branch in Southsea. We were all feeling nervous, Mum more so than any of us. We arrived a bit early but there was nothing we could do about that because we went down by coach. The bank suggested that we might find it easier if we all came together and they arranged for a coach to come and collect us and to bring us back again after it was all over. PeeDee's Dad was mightily impressed because the bank was paying for it as well!

Our parents insisted that we all wore our best clothes and they hung on to us in case we got them messed up. That meant that we had to sit in our 'family' groups on the way down in the coach. Pud and his parents were in the seats behind us and PeeDee and his family were in front of us. I could hear Merlin and Oz yelling to each other across the aisle down the front of the coach and every now and then I could hear Chris arguing with Tod – they were in the back of the coach – but we were all pretty quiet.

Mum nearly had a fit when we reached the bank. I think we all expected to be met by some old men in posh suits and we also guessed that the local paper would send a reporter, and perhaps a photographer, but we certainly didn't expect the mass of reporters that were waiting for us. We should have realised that if the Daily Mirror had already run bits of the story then it was only logical that they'd want to send a reporter for the end of it. But it wasn't just the Daily Mirror – I think every national paper had sent a team and they were lining the pavement two or three deep. The police had turned out to keep the crowds back and they were doing their best to keep the reporters out of our way.

The flash guns were going off even as the coach drew up and the police had their hands full keeping the reporters behind the line they made on the edge of the pavement.

'You'd better go first,' Dad said.

For a moment I thought he was joking but when I saw PeeDee's Dad keeping the rest of our gangs in their places I realised he was serious.

'Don't you think it should be a grownup?' I asked.

'First time I've ever known Ten to be chicken!' I heard PeeDee say rather too loudly.

Well, what else could I do?

'You'll have to come with me,' I told PeeDee, 'because you were with me when we found the clues.'

I was pleased to see that he suddenly looked bashful – perhaps he was not so brave, either. He looked very smart today and he was even wearing a tie! We went to the front of the coach and the driver came round and opened the door for us.

'You go first,' PeeDee whispered, 'and I'll follow you.'

As soon as the door opened the photographers went mad and I was nearly blinded by the flashlights. Someone started clapping and then someone cheered. I didn't know what to do and I stood there looking stupid. I think my mouth was open and I must have looked a right idiot. It must have looked just like a scene from The Bash Street Kids. I felt PeeDee give me a little shove so I closed my mouth and tried to look more positive. A man in a dark grey suit came forward and helped me down on to the pavement.

'It's so nice to see you, Theresa,' he said, shaking my hand.

I wondered how he knew my name. I guess he must have seen my picture in the paper.

'This is Peter,' I said. 'He was with me when we found the newspaper and the cash bag. It was his den they painted.'

The man shook PeeDee's hand as well and PeeDee blushed bright red with embarrassment. The rest of the gang were pushing down the steps and the man was being jostled by the crowds. He took a pace back and turned to the press and the crowd.

'Those of you who have official passes can make your way inside as soon as the youngsters and their parents have come in. There will be an opportunity for those of you want to speak with them after the ceremony. Now, if you'll stand back I'd like to show our guests in.'

The crowd eased back as if we were royalty and the man indicated that we should follow him. The bank was very grand and much bigger than the one in Waterlooville. He ushered us through towards one side where there was a wide staircase rising to the first floor. He led the way up and I followed him with PeeDee at my side. The rest of the gang followed and our parents brought up the rear.

The board room was huge and had very ornate decoration. The walls were panelled and there were pictures of past dignitaries on the walls in heavy gilt frames. Chairs had been set out in rows facing one end where there was a little platform and where a lot of people were already seated. When we came in they stood up. I recognised Inspector Johnson and Sergeant Marks. There was another policeman with them – he looked very distinguished.

The man who had met us showed us to the seats in the front which had been reserved for us and then indicated that our parents should sit immediately behind. The rest of the room was packed with people but I didn't have time to look at them. There were still three empty chairs in the centre of the little platform where the officials were sitting and I wondered who was going to sit there.

I didn't have long to wait because all of a sudden the room became quiet and everybody rose to their feet. We stood up, too, and I turned to see who was coming in. I could scarcely believe my eyes because there, in all his regalia, the Lord Mayor of Portsmouth was coming down the centre aisle. He came slowly to the platform and took the central seat.

Well, the ceremony was predictably boring. The chairman of the bank spoke first, welcoming the Mayor, the Chief Constable and the rest of us. He went on about how public spirited we had been and how, if it hadn't been for us, the bank robbers would never have been caught and the bank would never have recovered its money.

Then the Chief Constable spoke. He started off by telling us all how difficult police work was and how carefully every step had to be checked.

'But I am delighted that we have been able to arrange this ceremony,' he said 'because, even though we are still pursuing our enquiries, and despite the fact that the cases have not yet come to court, we are here because the bank's money has been recovered. And that is down to the sharp eyes and the quick wits of our young friends here.'

He pointed to us. And then he went on to explain how each part of the country had its own police force and how they had come together to work on this case. How what had started as a simple bank robbery in Portsmouth had grown into a murder investigation in the Waterlooville area. It had become even more complex when another murdered man was found in similar circumstances near Guildford.

It might have seemed as if they were not doing much, he said, but the police were quietly working through all the evidence that they had collected. All these enquiries were being rigorously pursued by each force but it was not until we found the missing clues that they were able to achieve their break–through. And what a triumph it had been with three forces working together to solve what had become a most complex case. Even as he spoke, he informed us, there were further enquiries being made in London itself.

'The fingers of crime reach far into our society,' he said, 'and without the help of the public the police would never be able to prise open their grasp. But more than that, when our youth are diligent in the pursuit of honesty, our country can rest assured that its future will be in good hands.'

Everybody clapped at that point. I think PeeDee had nodded off because he sat up with a start and looked around.

Then the Chief Constable turned towards me and fixed me in his stare. He looked so stern that for one dreadful moment I thought he was going to tell me off for interfering in police business! He paused and my heart began to thump. I thought I was going to be sick. Then he smiled.

'Most people who have the misfortune to discover the corpse of a murdered man take a long time to recover,' he said. 'But Theresa actually fell on top of a dead man. I can only guess what she must have felt. It is to her parents' credit that they have brought her up to be an intelligent and law abiding young girl. Her reporting of the body to her local policeman led us to realise that we were dealing with a crime of the most serious nature.'

He paused and everybody waited with baited breath for him to go on.

'She may have felt that we were too slow and heavy footed. Certainly she and her young friends knew the woods better than we did and the intelligent way in which they used this knowledge would be worthy of our best detectives. When she took it into her head to pursue her own investigation she was wise enough to preserve the crime scene and as a result we were able to acquire the essential evidence that enabled us to link together the various elements of this crime and arrive at a satisfactory solution.

It is not within our power to reward her or her young friends for their invaluable contribution in this case but it is our delight to award her with this scroll commending her public spirited help in the solving of this case.'

He turned to Inspector Johnson who handed him a scroll of paper, and then he turned back to me. I didn't know what to do and I just looked at him.

'If you'd like to come up,' he said, 'I'm sure the press will want some photographs.'

I stood up and as I did so the doors were opened and the newspaper camera men were allowed in. We had to pose for what seemed like ages while they took photos. First we had to turn one way and then the other so that they could all take pictures of our faces. My eyes began to hurt with the flashes and I could scarcely see to get back to my seat.

Then it was the chairman of the bank's turn to speak. The photographers squatted down on the floor so I guessed we were going to have to do it all again.

The chairman rambled on for a bit and I gave up trying to follow what he was on about and I started looking at the pictures on the walls. They all seemed to be of old men in suits with stiff collars, I guessed they were past chairmen. Then I felt PeeDee's elbow nudging me so I began to pay attention again. The chairman was still talking about the way in which banks had to be open to their customers and so, of course, they were also open to criminals.

'It was only luck that enabled the gang to escape our security system,' he said. 'But our safeguards, newly put in place, prevented them from making off with more money. I believe they thought that they would be able to take the money which comes in on Thursdays for payrolls.' He chuckled to himself. 'That money is always kept under the most stringent security so none of you need worry about that!'

I felt my concentration begin to wander again. Then it happened.

'But unlike the police,' the chairman said, 'we are able to reward these young people for their good work!'

My attention was riveted now. The mention of 'reward' seemed to have driven away all my boredom!

'In recognition of the valuable detection work these young people have done and as a token of our good will, the trustees of the bank have decided to award each of them the sum of £10. I hasten to tell you this has not been taken from the bank's funds – so your money is safe – but from our own resources.'

He then asked each of us to come up by name, shook our hands, and gave us a crisp, new £10 note. I think it was more money than PeeDee had ever seen. We were all smiling now! We were rich beyond our expectation. But the chairman hadn't finished.

'It is the custom of our bank to insure all the money on our premises. It gives me great pleasure to introduce you to Sir Ronald Taylor, the chairman of our insurance company.'

A gentleman who had been sitting at the end of the row stood up and came to stand beside the chairman of the bank.

'The circumstances of this theft have been unusual,' Sir Ronald said. 'Because of the skulduggery that went on between the various parties involved we were able to recover all the money from the premises where the police apprehended the master mind of this crime. In line with our normal practice we are able to offer a reward of ten percent of the sum stolen for its safe return. If Theresa Thomas would like to come up I have a cheque for her in recognition of the train of events her discovery of the body set off and for her subsequent part in the discovery of the clues which led to the successful outcome of this incident.'

I think the audience were as surprised as I was. There was an audible gasp when Sir Ronald mentioned the sum. I was numb. Ten percent of five thousand pounds! There is no other way to describe what I felt. Five hundred pounds was more money than I could imagine. I realised that the bank's chairman was speaking again.

'As a token of our goodwill,' he said, 'we have opened an account in her local branch where she may safely deposit her reward.'

The audience laughed at this and started to applaud. Once more I had to make my way to the platform and this time Sir Ronald handed me a cheque. The press photographers went a bit wild and I had my photo taken with Sir Ronald who pretended to hand me the cheque, first to one side and then to the other. Finally he let go and I returned to my place. I scarcely dared look at the cheque. When I did I saw it was made payable to me for the sum of £547.17.6d.

There were more photos and then a group picture. The press were still going mad. Later on Dad said it was the 'silly season' and there was nothing else to put in the newspapers but, all the same, it was great fun.

Sir Ronald also told us that Mr Hurford, who was unable to be present, would also receive a token reward for his part in helping the police to trace the van.

And then we all trooped downstairs where they had laid on a buffet for us before we went home. Not that I had much of a chance to eat because I was surrounded by reporters who asked the most stupid questions.

'What are you going to do with the money, Theresa?'

'Will you go out and buy lots of new clothes?'

'Are you going to celebrate tonight?'

At last Inspector Johnson came to my rescue.

'Why don't we let Theresa and her friends tell us their story,' he suggested, 'and then you can ask them questions.'

The reporters settled down and most of them took out their notebooks. Once more I told the story of how I had found the body, how the police took over. I said how good they were, particularly Constable Norris and Inspector Johnson – well, you never know, it might come in useful sometime. Then I told the bit about how things started happening in the woods – the rope and PeeDee's den – and how we all split up to search for clues. I turned to PeeDee and told him he had to say something.

He blushed a terrible colour and stammered. Then he seemed to settle down.

'Ten, sorry Theresa – we call her Ten because she lives at number ten – has been great. Pud said she only squeaked once when she fell on top of the body – I think I'd have run away! And it was her idea to look for clues. She's smarter than most boys I know and she's braver as well.'

This was getting embarrassing so I stopped him.

'PeeDee and I lead rival gangs,' I said. 'But we're all good friends.'

And as soon as I'd said it, I realised that it was true. We were rivals but we were also friends. We'd grown up together and we'd played together.

After we'd had our pictures taken again and answered questions from the reporters we all piled back into the coach. We'd had a good afternoon and now we were all sitting together. I think our parents had given up trying to keep us tidy and, anyway, we were on our way home.

But we discovered that we weren't going straight home. All our Mums and Dads had got together and had booked seats for us at the Theatre Royal to see David Nixon. And even better, when the theatre knew who we were, they offered to give us a tour back stage and a chance to meet Mr Nixon. And all that just because I fell off my bike!

Postscript

It was very late by the time we were all back in Cowplain. We were the last ones to get off the coach which dropped PeeDee and most of the others in Padnell Avenue before stopping at the corner for us to dismount.

What a holiday that had been! Standing and watching the coach make its way back to the main road it seemed a long time ago since we were playing in the woods and since the Vicar warned us that a man had been seen 'prowling about' after dark in the village. How excited we had been – a real mystery for us to solve, one right in the place where we lived and, moreover, we had all the time we needed to crack the case.

Thinking back, Miss Eileen was almost right when she said that the story about the Prowler was probably a rumour which had started out as gossip, and had been fed by people who only knew half the story and who didn't understand what they thought they had seen.

The honour of solving the mystery of the Prowler eventually fell to PeeDee. For once his hunch was right. The Prowler did have some connection with his sister although she knew nothing about it and it took him a while to find out all the details.

Sandy was a popular girl. She was pretty and she had the same ginger hair that ran in the family although in her case it was more blonde than ginger. She always had a ready smile and was petite – Merlin said she ought to be a film star. All the boys liked Sandy and wherever she was you could be sure there would be a crowd of boys. They queued up at the church dances to be her partner.

PeeDee had always said that he couldn't see what Sandy saw in Denis. He couldn't understand what made him such a good catch.

'I mean,' he told me, 'he's dead ugly!'

But Sandy had been going out with Denis for nearly six months so I guess she must have really liked him. Everything was fine until one of her friends told her that Denis was two-timing her with a girl from Clanfield. At first she wouldn't listen.

'I don't believe it,' PeeDee heard her telling his brother,

Malcolm. 'He wouldn't do that to me. He really loves me.'

'There's plenty more fish in the sea,' Malcolm said. 'Give him some of his own treatment!'

But although Sandy liked lots of boys she was loyal to Denis and she wasn't prepared to give him up without a struggle. Eventually her friends persuaded her to go out with different boys.

'After all,' they said, 'it doesn't mean that you don't love Denis, it just means that when he's not around you're not stuck indoors on your own.'

She saw some sense in that, particularly if it meant she could go out, so she started with Bunny's older brother, but that was never going to work because he was about to go and do his National Service. Next she turned her attention to a boy who worked in the office where she was a typist but after they'd been out a couple of times that lapsed, too. Love is blind, or so they say, and it seemed that Sandy really was in love with Denis because she didn't have the heart to go out with other boys.

However, Sandy's friends were determined that she shouldn't waste her time on Denis because they knew what he was really like. They started inviting likely boys to go out with them in the hope that Sandy would eventually fall for one of them. She was attracted to Keith who was a bit older than Sandy. He'd just finished his National Service and now he was back at home living with his parents. He had a good job in Portsmouth.

'He's ever so nice,' Rachel said. 'If I wasn't so set on Paul I'd take him like a shot.'

'He's a bit old,' Sandy said, 'but I like his hair!'

She went out once with him but she was still in love with Denis. Her friends almost gave up in despair but they had one more attempt at making her see sense. They found out that Denis was taking his new girlfriend to a dance in Horndean and they made up a party to go to the same dance. They took Sandy as well and when she saw Denis smooching with this other girl, Sandy went ballistic. PeeDee said he could hear her crying all night and when she went to work the next day her eyes were all puffy.

'If being in love and breaking up does that to you,' PeeDee told me, 'I'm not going to do it.'

But Sandy wasn't the girl to stay down for long. She came to her senses remarkably quickly because the very next weekend she brought Keith home to meet her parents. Her Mum and Dad were dead chuffed that she'd stopped crying and made him welcome. Later, when Sandy and Keith went out for a walk, PeeDee tagged along with them.

'I had a hunch,' he told me. 'Everything seemed to fit so I made myself a bit of a nuisance until Keith offered me two bob to make myself scarce.'

He grinned at the memory.

'Then I played my master-stroke. I told him that I had to keep an eye on Sandy because there was a dangerous prowler about.'

'What did he say to that?'

'He just laughed.'

'I told him that wasn't very nice.'

'Then he said the Prowler wouldn't hurt Sandy – not while he was with her.'

'He sounded pretty sure of himself,' I said.

'He was, but I repeated that someone had been seen following Sandy.'

PeeDee paused and took a deep breath. I guessed that he wanted to make himself the hero of the story so I tried to look suitably impressed.

'Then he told me everything. He said he was the Prowler!'

I tried to react as if I was surprised, but I'd already worked it out from what PeeDee had said earlier.

It seems that Keith had been watching out for Sandy all the time. He'd fallen for her in a big way but she hadn't seemed keen so he'd backed off. He liked her too much to come between Denis and her, even though he knew Denis was two-timing her, so he had decided to watch out for her – just in case. He had the feeling that Denis was going to dump her and he thought that she might need a shoulder to cry on when he did. At least he said that's why he followed her. That's what boys are like. They're funny like that. They think that they're the only ones who can put everything right even though they've caused the mess in the first place. For once I was glad that I was a girl!

The strange thing is that no one had made the connection between the Prowler and Keith. He still lives up the end of Padnell

- 215 -

Road and everyone says what a 'nice' boy he is – which, in fact, he is! It all seems so obvious now but thank goodness it wasn't back then. If it hadn't been for the reported sighting of the Prowler we'd never have started our detective work in the first place and we'd never have been ready to take on the murder case. Who knows, I might still think PeeDee was my enemy and we might never have had the chance to talk.

I could go on but I must stop now, I've got to get ready. PeeDee's taking me to the pictures tonight.

Acknowledgements

Although all the characters and events in this story are entirely figments of my imagination, I wanted to set it in a real place and at a definite time. Any resemblance to people or actual events is coincidental.

I grew up in Cowplain and my memories of the village during the 1950s were enough to enable me to start writing the story. However, as soon as I embarked upon the project I realised that my memory was inadequate and I started researching the important information that was essential if the story was going to work within its context.

At this point I discovered that there are relatively few recorded facts about life in the 1950s, let alone about life in Cowplain, and I began to widen my research base because by this time I knew that although the story would be a work of fiction, I wanted its setting to be as accurate as I could manage.

I met a few people when I visited the village and was put in touch with 'The Ratepayer' which subsequently ran an appeal for information for me, asking people with memories of the village as it was in 1958 to contact me. Several people replied.

A similar request to Radio Solent brought a live interview on the 'Julian Clegg Breakfast Show' which resulted in more contacts.

Celia Salter, the local reporter for The Portsmouth News contacted me and arranged a session at the Age Concern Borrow Centre in Cowplain where I met a number of people who were only too pleased to share their memories with me. Celia's subsequent article in The News produced more contacts and memories.

I would especially like to acknowledge the help my sister and her husband, Sue and John Gidney, have given me. When my memory has failed theirs has come to my rescue, when I lacked detail they have helped me to fill in the gaps. I am also indebted to Hugh Bland who has shared his memories of being a village policeman in the 1950s.

I offer my grateful thanks to all of these people whose recollections have been woven into my story – many of the incidents in this story owe something to actual memories and events. Listing names is a dangerous course of action but I feel that everyone who has helped should be remembered – if I have inadvertently missed out anyone, I offer my sincere apologies, please let me know and I will try to make amends in subsequent editions.

Amongst those who have helped me with their memories I would like to mention by name:
Derek Turner, Mark Collins, Graham Dash, Mick Davies, Eileen Gordon, Sonia and Jim Passingham, Jack Pyle, Ernest Smith, Derek Turner, Ken Urry, Phil Wheeler and Allan Yalden

I would also like to thank Amanda Mockler and her staff who made me so welcome at The Age Concern Borrow Centre in Cowplain.

Apart from her contributions to my knowledge of the village in 1958, I would like to thank Sonia Passingham for her illustrations which have added a new dimension to this story. In some uncanny way she seems to have visualised the characters and situations as if she was inside my head – perhaps our memories of the village are not so different, even after all this time.

The production of a book is a long process and I would like to thank my editor, Elizabeth Hauke, for tidying my text and correcting my errors. Her meticulous work and patience is much appreciated.

Some other books by Terry Wheeler

Eric the First (ISBN 978 184624 0218) *follows the life of a boy as he turns twelve into thirteen. Accident prone and misunderstood, he goes from one hilarious disaster to the next. With a sister who does everything in her power to make his life difficult and friends who are only too ready to lead him astray, Eric also contends with the possibility of a girlfriend, only to find that she has dated him just to fulfil a dare. But help comes when he least expects it and life suddenly takes a turn for the better – or does it? More humiliations follow.*

The book will appeal to girls and boys approaching their teens who want to find out what is in store for them, to teenagers who want to chart their progress, to parents who remember only to well what being a teenager was like and to grandparents who wish they could remember ...

Dear Mum and Dad (ISBN 978 184799 5193) *begins with a semi-biographical account of the years the author spent travelling the length and breadth of France, which he has drawn from letters he wrote to his parents. Eventually he and his wife moved to France and a series of chapters follow – descriptions of events or people he met and observed while living in Provence. Some are humorous, a few are serious and all are laced with the warmth and flavour of this colourful region of France.*

"I could smell the lavender on the breeze and it took me back to driving and camping in Provence," (Jill Earwaker)

Read more about Terry Wheeler's work on his website
www.terrywheeler.net